The
THIRD
MUSE

The
THIRD
MUSE

A NOVEL

DANA MICUCCI

NEW PARADIGM

MULTIMEDIA

New Paradigm Multimedia
New York • Los Angeles • Paris

First New Paradigm Multimedia Edition, 2014

Cover Image: © Museo Thyssen-Bornemisza, Madrid. Special thanks to the museum for permission to use the *Portrait of Giovanna Tornabuoni* on the cover.

Author photo: Stephen Sullivan
Cover design by Kathi Dunn, www.dunn-design.com
Interior design by Dorie McClelland, www.springbookdesign.com

Though aspects of this book are historically accurate, the characters and events are fictitious. Any similarity to actual persons, living or dead, is purely coincidental.

Passages in this book were quoted from *A Course in Miracles,* Foundation for Inner Peace, second edition, 1992 (In-2:2, W-p.II.293, T-26.IX.6:1, W-p.I.68), and *The Gospel of Thomas,* trans. Stevan Davies, Skylight Paths Publishing, 2002.

Library of Congress Cataloging-in-Publication Data
Micucci, Dana,
The third muse: a novel / by Dana Micucci.—1st ed.
    p.   cm.
ISBN-10: 069225112X
ISBN-13: 978-0692251126
I. Title.

In loving memory of Raymond Kennedy,
novelist, teacher, and dear friend

THE FIRST MUSE

Beauty

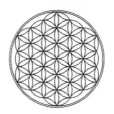

To all my sisters, in body and soul,

Though long in my grave, I still weep. For the blood on my family's hands cannot be erased. It has spilled throughout the ages and courses yet through your veins. According to plan, it is for you, dear women, to remake the dream. Reverse speed ahead; the way is clear. By the time you read this, you'll know what I mean. Remember, what is Real can never be threatened. I am you, and you are me.

Love and Only Love,

Giovanna

Chapter One

"Hold onto your seat, mademoiselle," Max said. "You're going to Paris!"

"What?" New York journalist Lena Leone brushed the dark curls from her face and held her breath, anxiously awaiting the news from her editor at the Balthazar bistro in SoHo. Turning toward Max, she inadvertently knocked over her wine glass. What was left of the red wine trickled onto the bar, and she quickly wiped it up with her napkin, which now appeared oddly bloodstained.

Max slung his blazer over a barstool and sat down beside her. Lena thought of him as a slightly younger version of Spencer Tracy, with his disheveled salt-and-pepper hair and kind, deep-set eyes and ruddy features. Max had never sent her abroad on an assignment; he was always so tight with the budget. And particularly now, with the magazine floundering, she could hardly believe his words.

"That's right." He beamed. "I loved your pitch. I want you to investigate the Ghirlandaio." He read from an email she had sent days ago: "One of the most valuable old master paintings in the world. A rare portrait of the young Florentine woman Giovanna Tornabuoni. Just sold for $48 million at Sotheby's London. Supposedly stolen several months ago, now hanging in the Louvre. Claude Weintraub, the Louvre curator, has been indicted for buying it."

Lena could barely contain her enthusiasm. Tingling shot up her back to the base of her skull. Her reflection in the mirror behind the bar revealed the refined, classic beauty of a 1940s screen star, to which she had often been compared. Slender and statuesque with innate elegance, she radiated a maturity beyond her twenty-eight years.

Max grasped her arm. "Interpol has begun an investigation based on an anonymous tip. It could be the art story of the year, Lena. Seeing as Tom is down with a broken hip, I want you to cover it." Tom was the senior editor and a top-notch writer. Lena felt only a little guilty for being happy about his hip.

"You're an excellent journalist."

"I don't know what to say, Max." Lena fidgeted in her seat, conscious of her racing pulse. "I'm thrilled, honored. It's a dream assignment!" This could be the opportunity she had long awaited, a chance to really shine.

Deep down, she knew she was capable of greatness, but she'd never completely trusted her instincts or given herself enough credit for her successes. Already an accomplished journalist, she had been on staff at the art magazine *Express* for six years now, having won an award for her incisive investigative reporting on the illegal trafficking of antiquities. A native New Yorker, she loved her work and the edgy, electric energy of the city, which conveniently complemented her own. She had a broad circle of friends, a few of whom enjoyed her closest confidence, and a brilliant, devoted boyfriend. Yet something was missing. There was a nagging emptiness ever since she abruptly lost her parents in a car accident on the Long Island Expressway when she was seven. Her subsequent soul-numbing shuttle from one foster home to another, and then finally to an orphanage, was now just a dimly suppressed memory.

Max leaned in closer. "Lena, we need this. The magazine needs this. Sales are down. Jobs are on the line, as you know. Can I count on you?"

"Of course. Yes, of course, Max. You have your journalist!" Her triumphal smile turned tentative. "I hope . . . I don't let you down."

"C'mon now, you *are* a workaholic. I practically have to throw you out of the office at the end of the day," Max joked. "Really, I don't know of any young journalist more ambitious than you are."

"I appreciate your faith in me," she said.

"You look great, by the way." He smiled warmly, nodding approval at Lena's silk blouse and leather mini-skirt, which showed off her long, sleek legs to maximal effect.

Lena had grown to accept Max's flirtatious compliments without judgment and was not attracted to him, charming and available as he was. Fourteen years her senior, he was more like a father figure. Max could be the harshest of critics. Initially, he had intimidated and annoyed her, having redlined so many of her stories over the years with his excessive editing notes. But she had to admit he had made her a better journalist. And she thrived on pleasing him as much as herself. Yet she was insecure and needed frequent reassurance.

Max lit up a cigarette and inhaled deeply. "I have to warn you, though. It could get dangerous. Are you absolutely sure?"

"Dangerous?"

"The art world has its share of criminals, and some will stop at nothing to protect themselves." He paused. "Anyway, the art crimes division of Interpol knows we're covering this. Here's their number." He handed her a slip of paper.

Lena flipped his words away with her hand and nodded with determination. "Yes, I'm sure."

Max produced a small box from his pocket and offered it to her. "A token of trust." She opened the box and saw a shiny silver Montblanc pen.

"Thank you," she said, touched by his thoughtfulness.

"We're on!" He slid a flight itinerary in front of her. "You have a week to pack."

"How long will I be there?" Lena's voice wavered, as she realized how much her day-to-day life was about to change. And how would Jud feel? They had been living together for almost three years, and he didn't like to be alone.

"We're on life support now." Max's expression turned serious. "Our publisher came through with a temporary infusion of capital. But it won't last long. I'll give you two months at the most, since it's an investigative piece."

What a fluke that she'd happened to sit down beside a stray copy of the French newspaper *Libération* on the subway last week. Her college French had served her well. She had picked up the newspaper and read about the scandal, then froze in recognition when she saw the small illustration of Giovanna Tornabuoni—the same painting she had first seen as a young girl on a school field trip to an exhibition at the Frick Museum. Entranced by Giovanna's otherworldly beauty, Lena remembered standing at length before the portrait, which had haunted her for some time afterward. She had even written a paper about the Renaissance painter Domenico Ghirlandaio for her college art history class, wishing to learn more about Giovanna. But those details were hazy now, and the same unanswered questions resurfaced: Why was she so taken by her, this Giovanna Tornabuoni? What secrets did she hold?

"Lena?" Max waved his hand in front of her.

"Sorry. It's just that I saw the portrait that I'm about to investigate in an exhibition a long time ago. I *love* her."

Max looked surprised. "Good, one step ahead. Oh, and I may need a few other stories from you, too, while you're over there."

"I could be your Paris correspondent?!"

"If we can get our numbers up, why not? Bartender," he called out, "two champagnes!"

By the time she left Balthazar, Lena's initial trepidation had diminished. Excited and eager to celebrate, she walked directly to the bank, withdrew $1,500 from her savings, and delighted in spending it throughout SoHo. She bought a black wool cape lined with velvet, a pair of suede boots, lacy lingerie, and an emerald silk scarf, all of which she decided to wear home. The boots were particularly expensive, but she rarely indulged herself. She'd be leaving for Paris in one week. Just one more week, thanks to Max's faith in her. This was her chance to help save the magazine and make a name for herself. At the thought, her insecurity resurfaced, and she grew nervous again. "No!" she said, shrugging it off. "I can do this!"

In the golden November sunlight, the streets surged with life. Lena passed by crowded boutiques, galleries, and cafés. A crisp breeze carried the scent of honey-roasted peanuts and fried food. Striding along Lower Broadway, she playfully adopted the posture of the Parisian model she had once seen on television sauntering across the vast Place de la Concorde, one long leg in front of the other, her head swinging from side to side. Paris! One week away! How she had always longed to go there. Swept up by the excitement, she tripped in her new boots and fell. An elderly gentleman kindly helped her up.

"Thank you, sir." She laughed, embarrassed, and brushed herself off.

Lena turned more than a few heads as she continued down Broadway, her new cape fluttering around her. Others had often remarked that she had a certain, undeniable presence, and she was well aware of it. She felt renewed, buoyant, as if she were crossing a threshold into a strange, new universe. I must risk all, she thought to herself as she had many times before, but without the same conviction. She reached into her purse and pulled out a tiny slip of paper that she had saved from a fortune cookie: "Soon you will reign over everything." What if it were true? What did it really mean? Fame? Fortune? Power?

A street violinist was playing a melancholy tune that sounded vaguely familiar. Feeling her festive mood dampen, she inquired about its origin. "Oh, it's very old," he answered.

On a whim, Lena darted into an antiques shop, where she found herself drawn to a glimmering gold chalice.

"A common fixture on the Renaissance table and in the church," the sales assistant said.

She could not take her eyes off the chalice, its beautifully molded grapes and garlands. She lifted it to her lips in what felt like a familiar gesture and paused with wonder.

"You can have it for two hundred!" The young man jolted her out of her trance. "Gold plate, of course."

Not knowing why, she impulsively purchased the chalice.

Outside the store, a crowd had gathered at the corner of Broadway and Grand, so she stopped to have a look. A man had been hit by a car. As he lay in an expanding pool of blood, a pedestrian tried to revive him. The now mangled white canvas the man had been carrying looked like a sinister abstract sculpture. Lena's buoyant mood dimmed as she hurried downtown, breathing in the crisp smell of the leaves crackling under her feet. Once home, she picked up the mail in the vestibule of her apartment building—a renovated, old red-brick warehouse on Laight Street in Tribeca.

One of the letters had a Paris postmark. Curious, she opened it and read: "Don't investigate the painting or else." No signature. Who could be threatening her? Jason. It must be Jason, her nemesis at *Express* who was recently laid off. He had always been envious of her success and the plum assignments Max gave her. Perhaps he had already pitched the story and Max had turned him down. He had probably asked a Paris contact to send this nasty, spooky note. What a silly prank. Or was it? Since she could not be sure, she dared not tell anyone, especially Max, who could take her off the assignment. Determined not to be thwarted, she stuffed the letter in her purse and pulled herself together.

She was barely inside the apartment when Jud rushed over, lifted her clear off her feet, and spun her around. "I missed you!"

"What? I'm only an hour later than usual."

"I know, I know. But I have some good news. I got the grant. I got it, Lena!"

He showed her a letter announcing that he would receive $20,000 from the National Endowment for the Humanities to complete his biography on the British writer D. H. Lawrence—a huge boost to his career as an English professor at Columbia University.

"Oh, Jud, I'm so happy for you!" She embraced him. But she was still anxious about the threat she had just received and couldn't stop thinking about it.

How could she tell Jud about her new assignment? Why intrude on his good news? After all, she'd decided to go without even consulting him, and he was so devoted to her. More than anything it was the way he spoke—the effortless refinement with which he chose each word, cultivated each sentence—that first attracted Lena when they met five years ago. On that June afternoon, she had come alone to Central Park to watch the Shakespeare Festival's performance of *Othello* with thousands of other New Yorkers who had packed picnic lunches for the long wait in line. She had spread her blanket on a patch of grass, and there was Jud sitting beside her, with crystalline blue eyes and a near perfect symmetry to his face. He had been sipping wine from a thermos. Noticing that she was alone, he offered her some. They talked for a long time and never did see all of *Othello* that night.

After they moved in together three years ago, they gradually threw themselves into their work and a comfortable routine. Of the two of them, however, it was Jud who doted more on Lena, creating for her a troubling paradox, for she both relished and resented his intense love, which sometimes felt suffocating.

"You're so beautiful, and you're mine," Jud whispered in her ear. He unbuttoned her blouse, then removed her boots and skirt. A familiar tingle worked its way up Lena's spine. In her eyes, Jud was the ultimate romantic, yet distinctly masculine. His sensitive nature perfectly complemented his sexy, athletic physique. She was aware that most women would find him hard to resist.

"That's somebody else's song," Lena teased, tussling his sandy hair. Her eyes settled on the slat-back oak chair and leather sofa in the living room and the copper mirror hanging above the fireplace. She would soon be leaving this cozy nest.

"Did anyone ever tell you that you have a certain power over people, and you know it?" Jud slowly slipped off her new lace lingerie. "Love this."

Lena's entire body quivered with pleasure, as he trailed his fingers down her back and along the inside of her thighs. She led him into the bedroom and lit two candles while he undressed. They made love tenderly, but for Lena it felt strained. The whole time she was thinking about how she'd tell him her news.

"What's bothering you?" Jud asked afterward. "You seemed distracted."

"There's something I have to tell you." She felt her heart pounding.

"Yeeesss?"

"You know how much I care about you." Her eyes moistened as a cascade of confusing emotions—guilt, anxiety, excitement, anticipation—surged through her.

"C'mon, Lena, what's going on?"

"I'm going to Paris!" she blurted.

"Paris."

"Max is sending me to Paris to get the scoop on a stolen Renaissance painting. Just sold for a huge amount." She waited hopefully for a supportive reply.

"Wow, that's great, honey. How long will you be gone?"

"Two months . . . maybe longer. Max may need some other stories." Lena folded her hands at her heart. "You'll visit!"

Jud's initial enthusiasm suddenly faded, and he fell silent.

"What's wrong?"

"You think it's okay, just taking off like that?" His tone was brusque.

Lena tensed. "Oh, Jud, can't you at least be happy for me?"

"You didn't even bother to discuss this with me!" From the nightstand, he lifted the Chinese cloisonné enamel vase they had bought together, turned it around in his hands, and carefully put it back.

"I thought you'd understand," Lena shot back, annoyed. "It's an incredible opportunity. And I'm not going to pass it up!" She spoke with such certainty there was clearly no dissuading her. "It's just for two months."

"But you said longer. Maybe longer."

"Well, maybe. Possibly."

"Men, they just come and go like actors in your production, Lena," Jud snapped. "There's a wall around your heart. The only thing you're in love with is your work!"

Lena turned away. She wanted to ask him to leave. But she was determined not to let anything ruin this magical day, her day. A single petal from the pink roses in the Chinese vase dislodged itself and floated gracefully onto the table.

"I've always loved you more than you've loved me." Jud's face looked drawn in the candlelight. His voice was filled with sadness. "You know your ambition can border on obsession."

Lena considered his words, recalling how Sister Ruth, the director at the Catholic orphanage all those years ago, rewarded her with affection whenever she aced a test, wrote the best story, or won a race. She could not deny that she was ambitious, competitive, too, though mostly with herself. And she had to admit that deep intimacy was difficult. Having lost her parents at such a young age, she had always felt so alone, consumed with a lingering doubt, as though she were always on the verge of losing something. Jud sat at the edge of the bed, his back to her.

"I do love you, Jud," she said with some regret. "But maybe you *are* able to love more deeply. I'm so afraid of failing that it sometimes overtakes me. So I keep pushing myself to succeed. Maybe I'd be different if I'd had the love and support of a real family, like you did." Her eyes filled with tears at what she had often felt but never revealed.

"So where does that leave us, Lena?" He turned, looking her square in the eyes.

What could she say? She remained silent, torn between her commitment to Jud and her need to break free. Was she doing the same thing with him that she had done with the other men she had dated? Those relationships had not lasted long. Was she subconsciously pushing Jud away? No, she decided, it was different this time. Her career was really about to take off.

"A wise man once said, 'The way in and the way out is through the heart,'" Jud continued. "I learned that when Lindsey died eight years ago, and my heart cracked wide open. Loving you is enough for me. All there is, really."

"I'm sorry about your sister, Jud." Lena stroked his arm. "I know how close you were, and it wasn't fair that she died so young from leukemia. But I don't see what that has to do with us." She shot him a puzzled look. "Or why you have to keep quoting people all the time to support your case"

He closed his eyes and shook his head. "You don't get it."

The telephone rang. Relieved by the interruption, Lena raced into the living room to answer it. "Sure, Max, yes . . . that's fine. I understand . . . Bye."

"What was that about?" Jud asked, as she crawled back into bed.

"Max forgot to tell me he doesn't want me to interview Marv Steinert, the old master paintings dealer. Thinks he's a crook who supposedly smuggled paintings out of Mexico years ago." Lena crinkled her brow, pondering her options. "I'm going to call Steinert anyway. I have a hunch he could be helpful."

Jud glared at her with a mix of suspicion and concern. "I'm not sure you know what you're getting yourself into. He's sending you on a wild goose chase, and you'll be getting mixed up with shady characters. It's dangerous!"

Lena pressed her lips together hard. That's just what Max had said. And what about the letter? Was she being naïve? Maybe she should rethink this whole thing. No, that was not an option.

"Oh, Jud," cooed Lena. "Maybe it's time for a break."

"I thought we were good together."

"We are, but . . ."

"But what?"

Agitated, she struggled for an explanation. "I need a breather. I guess I'm feeling . . . stuck."

"With *me*? Fine, I'll leave!" Before Lena could respond, Jud had jumped out of bed and yanked on his clothes.

"Wait, where are you going?!" she yelled as he stomped out of the bedroom.

"Grand," he muttered, referring to the neighborhood hotel where they often met friends for drinks. The door slammed behind him.

Lena sunk beneath the sheets, weighed down by a hollow pit in her stomach. She resented Jud for making her choose between him and her work, yet she was certain that she had made the right decision. Her apartment was dark except for the faint glimmer of the candles, whose wax had dropped and hardened into milky circles on the nightstand. She blew out the flames and tried to fall asleep, completely spent from the day's emotional twists and turns.

The following morning, Lena awoke alone. There was Jud's watch lying on the nightstand. Their fight came flooding back. She supposed he had spent the night at the hotel. She began dialing his number on her cell phone, then stopped. Why stir things up again?

After a quick breakfast, she headed out with a heavy heart to the New York Public Library. The library's massive, old-world reading room was one of her favorite Manhattan spaces, with its beautifully painted domed ceilings and long mahogany tables with brass lamps. Once there, she searched on a computer for books about the Italian Renaissance and Ghirlandaio, wrote down their call numbers, and anxiously waited for a clerk to find them. Finally, with a stack of books in hand, she found a seat and began researching the history of the Giovanna Tornabuoni portrait.

Despite recurring thoughts of her fight with Jud, the more she read, the more intrigued she became by her subject. Before long, she was completely immersed in Renaissance Florence and the power struggles between its wealthy families. Again, she could not take her eyes off a photo of the painting—the young, ethereal Giovanna in profile with opalescent skin and an attractive, otherworldly countenance, her blonde hair knotted at the back and plaited in ringlets at her ears. Wearing an ornately patterned Renaissance dress and a diaphanous mantle, she radiated an inner beauty and serenity that captivated Lena, as she had that day long ago at the Frick Museum exhibition. She appeared so human, so real, as though Lena might catch a glimpse of her at any moment, gliding between the book stacks. Ghirlandaio had painted Giovanna in 1488.

Turning a page, Lena lapsed into a reverie as she fixated on a photograph of the famous Santa Maria Novella church in Florence, with its unusual green, white, and pink marble façade. The sights and sounds of her immediate surroundings vanished as she was pulled into the cool, dim Tornabuoni Chapel inside the church.

Chapter Two

In the Tornabuoni Chapel of Santa Maria Novella church, the twenty-year-old Giovanna Tornabuoni, a woman of striking grace and elegance, and her husband, Lorenzo, ten years her senior, stood admiring new frescoes in which Giovanna had been depicted by the popular local painter Domenico Ghirlandaio. Lorenzo, who emanated an aura of reserved self-assurance, was a prominent merchant and art collector from one of Florence's wealthiest families. Nearby, in equally rapt admiration, was Lorenzo de' Medici, arts patron, de facto ruler of Renaissance Florence, and cousin to Giovanna's husband.

"You could not be more beautiful," Medici said, kissing Giovanna's hand. "And your husband could not be more fortunate." Giovanna blushed. She did not accept compliments easily, humble as she was.

"My dear wife and I have noticed that you seem unusually quiet today," Lorenzo replied. "Not your usual good-spirited self." Giovanna nodded in agreement.

The tall, dark-haired Medici hesitated. "I believe my life is in danger . . . again," he lowered his voice. "Saturn seems to have impressed the seal of melancholy on me from the beginning, as my childhood tutor Ficino once said of himself."

Giovanna gasped, covering her mouth with her hand. Lorenzo's expression turned grave as he pulled Medici closer. "Cousin, we will do anything we can."

"I have many enemies, as you know," interrupted Medici, whose family had created a powerful banking empire. "The Pazzi, they would still have me dead."

Possessed of an innate dignity and magnetic charm, Medici looked every bit the statesman, impeccably dressed in polished black leather boots, close-fitting knit pantaloons, a regal red wool tunic embroidered all over in gold with the family's coat of arms, and a black felt hat, from which protruded a large white ostrich feather. Lorenzo, who was fair and blue-eyed, was dressed much the same, but for his considerably less adorned tunic.

Giovanna lowered her head in shame. Through her mother, she was a member of the aristocratic Pazzi family, who resented Medici's power. Her father's family, the Albizzi, also had a longstanding rivalry with the all-powerful Medici clan.

"I'm sorry," she said softly. "This animosity between our families has caused me great pain. But I have no part in it, Lorenzo, as you know. I would give anything for peaceful relations."

"My dear Giovanna, you are a model of goodness," Medici tried to comfort her. "I hold nothing against you. You can always count on my friendship and affection." He closed his eyes briefly. "But with your cousin, Francesco de' Pazzi, a leader in what our townspeople call the Pazzi Conspiracy, I had no choice. I had to execute him for murdering my brother and attempting to assassinate me."

Giovanna instantly raised her hand in truce. "Though my family has been disgraced, we are all as one. It is only our belief in separation that makes it real."

Medici appeared baffled. Giovanna's sparkling brown eyes radiated forgiveness. Her expression was serene. She did not indulge in judgments or hatred; her heart was pure and filled only with love. And for this, she was both admired and misunderstood. Her husband, a man of great integrity whose family had established the most thriving spice trade in Italy, lovingly grasped his wife's hand. "Some say she is not of this earth." Turning to Medici, he offered his unequivocal support. "We are in this together, and we *will* prevail."

Giovanna stood contently by his side, stroking the bejeweled crucifix dangling from her neck. "Love will see us through," she said confidently. "Love breeds magic but needs faith."

"I hope you're right." Medici's face brightened, and he embraced the Tornabuonis in turn. "Your support is most appreciated, my friends."

As the three walked silently out of the church, Medici became disturbed by a raven circling overhead in the bright mid-summer sky. "An ominous sign," he winced. "Symbol of death."

"And rebirth," Giovanna quickly added. "Perhaps we should not take it so literally. Nevertheless I will pray for you, Lorenzo. I see the priest has just arrived for Mass."

Giovanna kissed her husband goodbye and waved the men off before slipping back inside the church, its dim recesses fragrant with frankincense. Late afternoon sunbeams filtered through the exquisite stained glass windows, casting rainbow stencils on the Doric columns and mosaic stone floors. She found a place in one of the rear pews, where she prayed and sang the hymns with her usual devotion, then proceeded gracefully to the altar to receive communion, aware of the gazes of her fellow churchgoers.

Though Giovanna typically shunned attention, she could not deny that she was a known figure in town, given her own aristocratic heritage and affiliation with the Medici. Some people even bowed in her presence. She often dispelled any projections of superiority by casually chatting with strangers on the streets. A regular at Sunday Mass, Giovanna also enjoyed attending weekly services whenever her schedule permitted. Her main activities were philanthropic ones. She had established a Platonic Academy for Children, where the spiritual philosophies of Plato, Marsilio Ficino, and other great thinkers were taught. And she read to prisoners at the

Bargello these same philosophies as well as works of Renaissance literature, another passion.

After the priest placed the communion host in her mouth, conferring a symbolic union with the body of Christ, he held out a gold chalice filled with red wine, representing the blood of Christ. Giovanna grasped the chalice with both hands and slowly swallowed the wine, feeling that she had blissfully merged with the Christ Consciousness. It was a sacred, empowering ritual. She murmured a prayer as she walked solemnly back down the aisle to her seat, her hands folded at her heart, a defining gesture that was as natural to her as the gentle smile that always hovered on her lips, instantly warming those in her presence. On her way out of church, she lit two votive candles. "For Medici," she whispered to herself. "And one for my Lorenzo."

Chapter Three

A loud sound pulled Lena back to the here and now. A young woman sitting beside her inched her chair in, its legs scraping against the floor. Lena glanced at her watch. Nearly thirty minutes had passed, though she could not account for them. How strange. She looked around the library. She must have dozed off. After jotting down some notes, she got up to leave. Lena liked nothing better than to walk the city streets after a hard day's work; the cacophony of sights, sounds, and smells cleared her mind.

Making her way down Fifth Avenue, she noticed for the first time a discount clothing store called New Renaissance. Such an odd name, given that the clothes on display in the window were clearly contemporary. Her thoughts drifted back to Giovanna, who emanated a curious, mysterious power. Who, really, was this woman?

Lena headed for Beth Israel Medical Center at Union Square, where, Hannah, her best friend, worked as an obstetrician. Lena had invited her to dinner at Jacques 1534 in Nolita. Hannah was waiting outside, dressed in casual slacks and a V-neck sweater, noticeably fit and suntanned from her frequent jogs in Central Park. They greeted each other with a warm embrace and chatted happily as they strolled downtown. There was such a fluid ease and playful familiarity between them. Hannah had short-bobbed russet hair, translucent green eyes, and a slight southern accent from her youth in Alabama. They had been college roommates at Columbia and had been inseparable ever since, sharing everything with the unshakeable trust and respect that defines the rarest of friendships.

"I can't believe you waited so long to tell me!" Hannah scolded after she heard about Lena's assignment. "Congratulations! You so deserve this."

Lena's faced clouded.

"What's wrong?" Hannah asked, concerned.

"It's Jud."

"How did he take the news?"

"Not well." Lena fought back tears. "He's been so good to me, but after all this time, I'm still afraid to get too close. Maybe I need a break. I'm not sure the relationship will last." She folded her hands in a prayer-like gesture at her heart.

"Maybe, maybe not. You may just find yourself missing him." Hannah observed her friend with curiosity. "You do that a lot with your hands, like you're in church or something."

Lena pulled her hands down. "Funny, you know I'm not religious." When they reached Lafayette Street, she stopped in her tracks. "Look!" She pointed to a storefront, grinning with surprise.

"Yeah, so what? It's just a pharmacy," Hannah said.

"But it's the Santa Maria Novella pharmacy! I never noticed it before. Let's go in." Lena hurriedly crossed the street.

The cavernous space had soaring copper ceilings and shiny gilt and mirrored shelves displaying an array of expensive products. In her typical investigative manner, Lena cornered a salesgirl and peppered her with questions. She learned this was a branch of the luxurious Florentine pharmacy named after the famous church.

"I have just been reading about this church and its connection to the woman in the painting!" Lena turned to Hannah, tickled by the coincidence.

"Wow, now why don't you try to manifest a husband for me!" Hannah joked.

Before leaving, they sampled some of the essential oils on display. Lena was drawn to the rose oil, called Essence of Magdalene. She dabbed some on her wrists, inhaling the beautiful sweet scent, and spontaneously purchased a small bottle to take with her to Paris.

Back outside, Lena stopped to admire the pretty votive candles burning in the window display. She thought of the candles in her bedroom last night and remembered her disturbing confrontation with Jud. The women turned the corner onto Prince Street, buzzing, as usual, with crowds frequenting trendy shops and restaurants.

"C'mon, Lena, it's time to celebrate!" The upbeat lilt in Hannah's voice instantly cheered Lena, as they walked arm in arm into the restaurant.

Later that evening, when Lena returned home, she was relieved to find Jud at his desk correcting papers.

"How was your night at the hotel?" she said gently.

He continued reading, ignoring her.

"Jud!"

"I don't have to report to you." He gazed at her indifferently.

"Okay, I won't bother you again." She felt her face heating up with anger and hurt.

They passed the rest of the night in silence. Jud slept on the living room sofa, while Lena spent another night alone in their bed.

Over the next few days, they carried on their routines with the same strained detachment and minimal communication. Neither had the courage to sever the relationship, nor did they feel like reconciling. It was as if they had each made a secret pact to endure this uncomfortable ambiguity until Lena left the country, after which she felt they might gradually and less painfully slip away from each other. She suspected Jud anticipated the same. Despite this emotional turmoil, Lena was preoccupied with her assignment. She'd soon be on a flight to Paris.

On her last day in New York, Lena took a taxi across town for her appointment with the art dealer Marv Steinert, ignoring Max's warning. She pressed a buzzer at his townhouse on East 77th Street, then proceeded through a heavy oak door. The short, frail Steinert greeted her with an elitist air and led her into his living room. Lena guessed him to be in his late sixties. She complimented the beautiful pedestal table that stood at the room's center, inlaid with dazzling multi-colored stones in the Italian pietra dure style.

"I thought you were here to discuss your assignment," Steinert interrupted, adjusting the navy blue ascot peeking out of his neatly pressed white shirt.

"Yes, Mr. Steinert." Experienced in dealing with the sometimes curt, self-inflated attitudes of the New York art world, Lena remained calm and focused. "I was hoping you might have some information about the Ghirlandaio."

"Ah . . . the lovely Florentine woman. One of the many thousands of old masters I've sold over the last four decades."

"The portrait just sold at Sotheby's London for $48 million, as I'm sure you know." Lena said in a firm professional tone. "Purchased by the Louvre Museum. There's speculation that it had been stolen several months ago. And the career of one of the Louvre's top curators is in jeopardy. As I mentioned on the phone, *Express* wants to be the first to expose the scandal."

"So why don't you talk to the curator?"

"He's on my list." Lena quickly scanned the living room again, the Regency armchairs, gilt torchères, and rows of bookshelves, many of them bulging with faded accordion folders likely containing records of the deals that had made Steinert one of the wealthiest men in Manhattan.

There was a crusty heaviness about him that saddened Lena and seemed to have transferred to his surroundings. His townhouse felt lonely and oppressive. It was dark and musty and curtained off from the life outside by heavy olive green portières. All the canvases of anemic counts and countesses staring down at her made her uncomfortable. Lena thought about how she could transform this space, brighten it up and throw a big party like the one she imagined for her first book, perhaps based on this very assignment. But those details could wait. She wrote down some observations, dubious of Steinert's intentions.

Waving an index card and pressing back a few strands of silvery hair at his temples, Steinert proclaimed: "Christie's London, 1985, 350,000 pounds. Showed up at auction in Geneva three years later. I bought it for 840,000 Swiss francs."

"Are you sure that painting was the Ghirlandaio? Who bought it from you and when?" Lena was relieved to be making progress.

"Please don't question my integrity, young lady. I could never mistake the smooth curve of her high forehead, her glowing countenance, the knot of hair at the back of her head. A woman of such grace and dignity that is rare today. It is, without a doubt, your Ghirlandaio."

"And the buyer? Do you have any contact information?"

"A fellow from Munich. Baron Eric von Heisendorf. I sold it to him seven years ago. He's amassed one of the finest art collections in the world." Steinert walked over to a desk, wrote down the Baron's email address, and handed it to her.

"I wonder what happened to the painting from that time until it wound up at Sotheby's." Lena thought out loud. "The consignor was reported as anonymous."

"You obviously read the article in *Libération*. I'm impressed."

"You've been so helpful, Mr. Steinert." Lena decided that it was in her best interest not to push further. And feeling claustrophobic, as she sometimes did, she needed fresh air.

"If you use any of this information, I expect to be quoted in full!"

"Certainly." Lena was distracted by the bright colors in a painting hanging above the marble fireplace. "How beautiful."

"You have excellent taste. And what is beauty?" Steinert mused in a professorial tone.

Lena pondered his question. It was, after all, what she did every day, write about beauty.

"I'll tell you what it is," he declared. "It is order. It is structure. It is harmony and wholeness. Infinite rapture. Eternal bliss."

"Well said." Lena shook her head in agreement.

Steinert pointed to the painting Lena had just noticed. "That beach scene is by the turn-of-the- century Spanish painter Joaquín Sorolla. One of the Spanish Impressionists I discovered before his work became all the rage. I never get any credit."

Lena thanked Steinert for his time and started toward the door. The large canary perched in a cage in the hallway began to screech and flutter its wings violently.

"Remember, 'taste is the feminine of genius,' as da Vinci said. Now, there was someone with taste!" Steinert shouted from his doorstep, as Lena walked back into the late afternoon sunlight, satisfied with her interview. The droning horns from the cars stalled along Madison Avenue assaulted her senses. She was glad she would be leaving tomorrow.

Back home, she sent brief emails to the Baron and the Louvre curator requesting interviews and did some additional research online about the old masters' market. Then she anxiously reviewed all the lists she had written to herself. Jud had often teased her about this compulsive habit. She picked up the phone and listened to her voicemail. One message was from Jud saying that he would be working late on his research. His tone was businesslike. Disappointed, she had expected him to be with her on her last night. Then again, she had not given him a reason to believe that they had a future together. Lena wandered from room to room, unsure of what to do next. The apartment already felt empty, as though anticipating her absence.

She walked into the office they both shared. Between two tall bookcases, a framed movie poster of Ingmar Bergman's *The Seventh Seal* hung at a slant. A peace lily stood wilting on the windowsill, surrounded by Jud's first-place trophies from the triathlons he ran to raise funds for leukemia research. His desktop was covered with interlocking coffee cup stains and crumpled sheets of paper—drafts of a goodbye letter to her that he apparently could not finish writing:

> Lena, these last years have been the best of my life, mostly because of you. Maybe it wasn't meant to . . .

On his desk, too, was a photograph of the two of them embracing on the steps of the Metropolitan Museum and an empty bottle of her perfume, L'Air du Temps, which he used as a paperweight, the frosted glass dove on its cap poised to take flight.

Losing him was almost too much to bear. And yet she had to move forward, accepting that possibility. Lena opened her desk drawer and pulled out a beautiful love poem that Jud had once written for her birthday. Reading it now again, she blinked back tears. What if the situation were reversed? How would she handle it? She wasn't sure. Yet she was able to tap into the deep pain of his loss and felt something of the same—abandonment, betrayal, disappointment. Would it all be worth it? In the blink of an eye, her life had changed. The uncertainty made her stomach churn. She'd stepped off a cliff and was dangling mid-air. Jud was loyal, kind, and had always been there for her. Was she making the worst mistake of her life? She took a deep breath. It was only a matter of time before she would either crash or fly.

When Lena awoke the next morning, she walked into the living room and saw Jud had already left for class. On the kitchen table was a brief note:

Goodbye, Lena, and good luck. Remember what Tolstoy said: "Your chief task in life is the care of your soul, and you can improve it only with love."

Again, her heart sank, and tears filled her eyes. He had apparently already let her go. She quickly wrote a note to him:

Thank you for everything, Jud. Thank you for loving me. Thank you for being you. I'll miss you very much. Love, Lena

Would he be here when she returned? How would she feel if he was? But there was no time to dwell on their fractured relationship. Hannah would be picking her up to take her to the airport in just a few hours. Lena set about packing with her usual single-minded focus, growing more excited by the moment. At the last minute, she threw into her luggage a meditation CD that Jud had given her months ago. She had not yet listened to it, thinking it such a waste of time to sit in silence when there were so many things to accomplish. The horn beeped outside.

"Traveling light, I see," Hannah joked, helping her with four large suitcases.

Lena laughed heartily, her new cape, black palazzo pants and tunic, and emerald green scarf forming a dramatic silhouette against Hannah's white Mustang. Hannah's surgical scrub shirt was stained with perspiration from her morning jog. Lena admired her friend's perpetually healthy glow, which made her look at any moment as if she had just returned from a cruise. As they sped off, she reviewed her packing list for the third time to make sure she hadn't forgotten anything. Just in case, she checked her shoulder bag again for her passport, notebooks, and the folder with information about the painting that she had researched online and in the library. All systems go. She drew a deep breath and tried to relax.

"I haven't seen you in that color before. Emerald. It suits you." Hannah said.

"Thanks, it's new."

"You look tired. How did you leave things with Jud?"

Lena's faced stiffened. "We've barely communicated. I'm not sure where things stand. And with the pressure of the assignment, it's all so draining."

"Don't worry. I'm sure Paris will lift your spirits."

Lena thought about how Hannah was so good at taking care of others that she often forgot about herself.

"You know, I think you and Max would really hit it off," Lena said. "He needs someone generous and nurturing like you. He's smart and caring, and he'd pay lots of attention to you. I'm surprised it never occurred to me."

"Oh, I don't know."

"I'm serious. I thought you wanted a husband."

"I do," Hannah reconsidered. "What does he look like? How old is he?"

"Think Spencer Tracy at forty-two."

"Good visual."

"Then I'll give him your number?"

Hannah mulled over the option.

"Hannah?!" Lena grew impatient. When she saw an opportunity, she moved on it quickly. She realized that her bold, direct manner sometimes made Hannah uncomfortable. Though she attributed her friend's more reserved nature to her southern upbringing, it bothered Lena that Hannah didn't always have the guts to go after what she wanted. She had even sailed into medical school without much effort, brainy as she was. Whenever Lena wanted something, she imagined herself climbing a tree and picking one pear after another with considerable focus and precision. Pears were her favorite fruit, so sweet and satisfying. There were always more than enough on the trees. Hannah didn't think that way.

"Pear, Hannah. Remember my pear tree?"

"I know, I know. Okay, give him my number. Thanks." Hannah reached for Lena's hand.

"Great. Done!" Lena opened the window for some fresh air. The red lights seemed to be lasting an eternity.

Just then, a sobering news announcement interrupted the R & B music on the radio: "More arrests today on Wall Street. Two top bank executives confess to fraud and extortion.

"More good news," Hannah moaned. "Anyway, what do *you* really want, now?" She turned to Lena.

"I want to be a great writer, of course. I want to be recognized. First, a great article. Maybe the Pulitzer for it. Then a book. And more. I want to inspire people." Lena's voice rose with passion. She paused to reflect further. "I want to risk everything. I want to disturb the universe." She would not have made such a grandiose statement to anyone else. But it was the truth, her truth. And she knew Hannah would understand without judging her.

"And love? What about love?"

Lena brushed the curls from her face. "Of course, I want it all." She thought about Jud again and wondered whether she was making a big mistake. The threatening letter she had received the other day had warned her not to proceed. She grew suddenly apprehensive. What if . . . ? Whether it was Jason's doing or not, there was no turning back now. She trembled slightly at this realization.

Hannah smiled. "I'm sure you'll have it all, Lena. You know how to make things happen."

"What would I do without you?" Lena had immense respect for her friend, who had seen her through so many tribulations, and she would miss her dearly. She watched the sun sink behind the skyline, her heart racing with anticipation.

THE SECOND MUSE
Truth

Chapter Four

Lena walked excitedly across the Pont des Arts to the Louvre Museum, admiring the majestic gold-grey Beaux-Arts buildings with wrought-iron trim and the pale lindens and leafy plane trees fringing the quais in brilliant yellow and orange autumnal hues. Everywhere she looked she was saturated with beauty, her senses heightened as never before. It was almost too much to contain.

She had taken just a few days to move into her tiny apartment that Max had procured in a modern five-floor building in Montparnasse. In addition to the living room, with its twin bed-cum-sofa, drop-leaf writing table, and a tall window overlooking a courtyard garden, the apartment had an efficiency kitchen and a newly remodeled bathroom. It was extremely spare but clean and functional. A few objects that she had brought from New York—framed photos of her and Jud at the Bethesda Fountain in Central Park and of her and Hannah at a party, and the gold chalice she had just purchased at the SoHo antiques store—made her feel more at home. She had already roamed the city to get her bearings. There were so many mysterious old streets to explore, ancient churches and monuments, hidden squares, and gorgeously manicured parks that it would be easy to get distracted from her real mission.

"Focus, focus," she repeated to herself, as she found her way to the great glass pyramid at the entrance to the sprawling museum—a seventeenth-century palace that once housed the French royalty. Bypassing the long lines of tourists, she went straight to the media desk, showed her press pass to one of the attendants, and asked for directions to the Italian Renaissance gallery where the *Portrait of Giovanna Tornabuoni* was hanging. It seemed to take forever, darting through the Louvre's wide corridors, lined with life-size classical sculptures of gods and emperors, until Lena finally reached her destination. There she was! Lena paused for a long time in front of the portrait, protected by a red velvet rope. It was small and intimate, unlike many of the monumental paintings in the museum. And Giovanna was even more vibrant and beautiful than in the photographs she had seen. It was, indeed, the same Giovanna that had so entranced Lena as a girl.

Having timed her visit just prior to closing, she was happy to have Giovanna all to herself, for the crowds had thinned considerably. Lena could not take her eyes off her. It was all there—the flat knotted bun of blondish hair with wavy strands at her ears, the serene profile and high forehead sloping into a wistful gaze, the sheer gold mantle hanging delicately over her long-sleeved bodice in a red-and-gold latticework pattern. Her skin had the glow of porcelain, and there was a hint of melancholy in her distant gaze. Ghirlandaio also seemed to have expressed her inner beauty, for she emanated an aura of refinement and virtue.

Giovanna's belly protruded slightly. The corner of a bookcase framed her head and slender neck. Her hands, clasped together on her lap, appeared to be holding something that Lena couldn't quite make out. In the bookcase were a string of red beads and what looked like a prayer book. A cryptic Latin inscription on a small sheet of parchment hung behind Giovanna. Lena anxiously copied the words into her notebook, intending to have them translated. She wanted to touch Giovanna, but instantly stepped back as a dapper elderly man approached her. He stood silently admiring the portrait.

"Such a pity she died in childbirth," he said in English with a heavy French accent. He must have assumed she was American.

Lena had not discovered this information in her research. "How do you know that?"

"Museum catalogue." He studied Lena with curiosity. "You seem taken with her."

"I sense a connection. I can't explain it." She smiled briefly, as he tipped his hat goodbye.

Overcome with sadness, Lena tried to imagine what Giovanna had been thinking as she posed for the painting just before she died. Suddenly realizing that the press office would soon be closing, she hurried back out of the gallery, past the legendary *Mona Lisa*, smirking from behind bullet-proof glass, and numerous renderings of the Virgin Mary with plump cherubs by other Italian masters like Veronese, Titian, and Raphael. By the time she reached the press office, the receptionist was about to leave.

"I need to talk to the European paintings curator," Lena said breathlessly. "Is he still here?"

The young woman eyed her with suspicion. "I'm sorry," she said, applying her lipstick. "You have to send a written request by email."

"I've already done that. I'd like to speak to the communications director. Who's your boss?" Lena planted herself in an armchair. She was not about to leave until she made an inroad.

"We're closing." The receptionist frowned. "You'll have to go now."

"Then I'll just wait for your boss to come out." Lena peered into the back office where she heard someone shuffling papers.

In a huff, the receptionist picked up the phone. Within seconds, a tall, stylish woman appeared and introduced herself as the communications director. Explaining her assignment, Lena handed her a press card, upon which the director greeted her graciously.

"I understand your urgency, mademoiselle." She guided Lena toward the door out of earshot from the receptionist. "I wish I could help you. But because Monsieur Weintraub has just been indicted for buying the painting in question," she lowered her voice, "which many believe to be stolen, he is not permitted to talk to the media. I hope you understand."

Surprised and disappointed, Lena scrutinized the woman, considering her options. Unfortunately, she had none. What a setback. "I see." She crinkled her forehead with frustration. "Please let me know should the situation change."

"Of course. We will not be removing the painting unless the charges can be proven. Naturally, we stand behind our curator."

"Thank you very much." Lena shook her hand and rushed back down the hallway toward Giovanna, glancing at her watch. She would have just enough time to take one last look.

Standing before the *Portrait of Giovanna Tornabuoni* again, Lena's disappointment gradually faded as her resolve strengthened. Transfixed by the portrait, she drifted deeply into thought, as if trying to access a buried memory.

Chapter Five

A noticeably pregnant Giovanna strode into the high-ceilinged reception room of the imposing Palazzo Tornabuoni—one of the most sumptuous palaces in Florence—carrying a colorful majolica pitcher and two pewter mugs. The early morning sunlight streaming through the high, arched windows cast a golden hue on the black-and-white checkered ceiling, polished marble terrazzo floors, and the long Persian-carpeted table, where Lorenzo was engaged in vigorous conversation with the famous Florentine painter Domenico Ghirlandaio. Smiling peacefully, Giovanna placed the mugs on the table and filled them with fresh apricot juice.

"Why not leave that to your maidservant?" Lorenzo addressed his wife. "You should be resting in your condition."

"Please, Lorenzo, I'm perfectly capable," Giovanna said, winking at Ghirlandaio. "You look very well, dear Domenico. We were just admiring your beautiful frescoes in the church the other day."

"Many thanks, signora." Ghirlandaio instantly rose from his seat and bowed respectfully. His deep-set hazel eyes radiated intensity, which had a hypnotic hold on others. He was a whole head shorter than Lorenzo, stocky with a slightly crooked, aquiline nose and large, paint-stained hands.

"No need for such formalities, Domenico. We are friends."

"Blessings upon this new, radiant life!" Ghirlandaio gently touched Giovanna's belly.

She was hoping for a girl this time, having given birth the year prior to her son, Giovannino, who was sleeping peacefully in her private chamber.

"We are most pleased." Lorenzo beamed, sipping his juice. "So, will you accept my offer?"

Ghirlandaio pondered the question, stroking his stubbly chin. He, too, had much to celebrate, for he could barely keep up with the commissions for portraits and frescoes that inundated his busy studio. When it came to portraying the daily life of Florence and its inhabitants he had no equal.

"Four hundred florins!" Ghirlandaio said finally. "And if it should give satisfaction one hundred more." He patiently awaited Lorenzo's response.

"You drive a hard bargain, my friend, but you deserve it, no doubt. It's a deal." Lorenzo raised his mug, turning to his wife, who appeared perplexed.

"What is this all about?" she inquired.

"My dear, I've just commissioned a painting from Domenico. A portrait of you carrying our child." He reached for her hands. "I wanted to surprise you at the first sitting. But it is impossible to keep a secret from you."

"Oh, Lorenzo!" Giovanna embraced her husband passionately. "I love you so, now and forever."

Ghirlandaio watched the two with tender admiration. "I must be going now, lovebirds," he chuckled. "Much to do back at the studio."

Exchanging warm-hearted goodbyes, Giovanna and Ghirlandaio agreed to meet for her first portrait session the following week.

In anxious anticipation, Giovanna, with the help of her young maidservant, Francesca, spent extra time preparing herself the morning of Ghirlandaio's next visit. She wore one of her finest embroidered silk dresses and a few carefully selected pieces of jewelry—her gold wedding ring, a gold brooch, and a string of red glass beads. They spent the most time on her hair, twisting, curling, and combing it to perfection, so that not even a single strand was misplaced. Though she always looked elegant, Giovanna was not typically one to fuss over her appearance. But this day was special, as her time as an expectant young mother with this child would soon be over. Giovanna relished each moment and was thrilled to be able to preserve for posterity the particularly joyous state in which she now found herself.

Lorenzo had already left for his trading office nearby on the banks of the Arno River, when Ghirlandaio arrived promptly at the Palazzo Tornabuoni with his painting supplies and a bouquet of pink roses.

"These reminded me of you." He presented the bouquet, surveying Giovanna like a proud father. At nearly twenty years her senior, he could easily have assumed that role.

"Oh, Domenico! You are so kind. They remind me of the Magdalene. How appropriate that today is her feast day."

Francesca disappeared into the kitchen with the roses, while Giovanna led Ghirlandaio into the study, which she had deemed to be the most suitable place for her sitting. *A Virgin and Child* portrait by Ghirlandaio, Filippino Lippi's *Annunciation*, and paintings of saints, biblical scenes, and Florentine cityscapes by the finest local artists hung from the lavender walls. The portraits of Mary Magdalene and Saint Francis of Assisi, Giovanna's patron saints, were her favorites. A marble sculpture of Jesus with outstretched arms stood on the elaborately carved ebony desk.

Before long, Giovanna was seated on a stool before a tall bookcase, feeling slightly nervous about being scrutinized so closely. Ghirlandaio removed all but one book, her personal diary-prayer book, from the bookshelf behind her. He affixed a piece of ink-scrawled parchment on it, and advised Giovanna to remove her red beads and gold brooch and put on the other necklace that she had brought with her—a simple three-pearl pendant.

"Ah, yes!" He arranged the brooch and beaded necklace on the bookshelf. "This will add color and depth to the composition. Now, we can begin." With great concentration, he set up his easel, opened his paintbox, and began mixing the oil and tempera pigments on his palette.

Giovanna tried not to flinch as Ghirlandaio made the first stokes on his canvas. He usually began his sessions with a joke or two to help his subjects loosen up. And the pious Giovanna was no exception.

"So one monk said to another, 'What do you think is closer to us, Greece or the moon?' The other thought for a minute and then replied, 'Well, can you see Greece?'" Giovanna's giggles were barely audible above Ghirlandaio's deep belly laugh. "I love that one." He stopped to catch his breath and steady his paintbrush.

"You're one of a kind, Domenico."

"As are you," he replied. "Seriously, I have some news for you, beautiful lady. My friends, the Strozzi, would like to send their child to your academy. I've told them you teach the works of Plato and Ficino there. I myself should know more about them."

"How wonderful. I'll be so pleased to talk with the Strozzi." She folded her hands at her heart with joy. "Remember, Domenico. As a master artist, you are already much like these great philosophers. Their sole mission was to express the truth."

Ghirlandaio bowed humbly. "And there is talk on the streets of your success instructing the prisoners at the Bargello." He stepped back from the canvas to inspect his progress. "You are a woman of great moral power, unlike many of our fellow Florentines."

"I am no different than any other." Giovanna blushed. "We have entered a new Golden Age, and there is much to celebrate."

"You are aware of the outrage against Medici and his supreme power." Ghirlandaio instinctively lowered his voice. "It is growing daily."

"Yes, but I do not focus on that which divides us." Giovanna was tiring of having to sit up so straight. She fidgeted in her seat, moving her head from side to side to relax her neck.

"Your own family is a formidable force. The Pazzi will not be silenced. You must be careful, given your husband's connection to Medici."

"I was very much against the Pazzi Conspiracy, as you know," Giovanna declared. "Violence has never solved anything. And I do not wish to take sides."

"My dear Giovanna, I admire your convictions." He paused to mix a deep vermillion color on his palette. "Even so, you must be careful. And pardon me for saying, but I do not believe it is safe for you to spend so much time with the prisoners."

Giovanna remained undaunted. "You sound like my Lorenzo. You need not worry. I have no fear. Our mission in this world is to repair ourselves, to restore the divine sparks. And we cannot do that without also repairing others." Her voice was soft and melodious.

Ghirlandaio peered at her intently, clearly at a loss for words. Then, switching brushes, he applied the final flourishes to his canvas. "Magnifico! I have captured just enough of your fair form to complete the final work in my studio."

"I know you will make me into a better version of myself. Thank you!" Giovanna said upon viewing the canvas. She excitedly embraced him, then walked over to an agate bowl filled with dark green Fiorentina pears and offered them to him. "You must be hungry by now."

"You are most kind." Ghirlandaio gratefully selected one and began packing up his supplies.

"From the Medici gardens." Giovanna bit into one of the pears with obvious relish. "My favorite fruit!"

"I have often seen you wandering through the gardens when I go to visit Medici."

"Surrounded by such earthly beauty, I can more easily access the Divine essence flowing in and through all." She smiled serenely. "I have the same feeling when I look at your beautiful paintings. It is only by contemplating beauty that we can ascend to its Source."

Just then, Francesca appeared with little Giovannino, who had been crying for his mother, and she handed him to Giovanna who cuddled him tenderly, instantly comforting him.

Ghirlandaio gazed wistfully at mother and child. "I remember you yourself at that age, when I visited your family at the Albizzi Villa, so pure and radiant you were even then. Your father had given me one of my first commissions as a young artist. Sad that he is no longer with us, such a generous soul."

"I miss him every day," Giovanna said, placing her hand on her heart. "He left this world much too early. Of all the children, I was closest to him. I think my older brothers always resented our connection." She looked away, as though captured by a memory. "This has caused me pain, yet I have never stopped loving them."

"Your brothers now run your father's successful gold mining business and control most of the broker's shops on the Ponte Vecchio," Ghirlandaio reminded her. "I should think they have nothing to complain about!"

"All this emphasis in our time on wealth and power has gone too far, Domenico," she lamented, a trace of guilt in her voice. "Though I realize I have been a fortunate beneficiary, I believe I would still be happy without all this . . . fuss." Giovanna swept her arm around the room in reference to her lavish lifestyle, then gently kissed her son's forehead.

"Yes, yes you would be," said Ghirlandaio, who had been lost in contemplation. "You know, I had thought to allow the young Michelangelo, one of my workshop assistants, to finish your portrait. But I will do myself the honor instead. The frescoes at Santa Maria Novella will have to wait."

"Excellent. I can't wait to see the final portrait! Now, I must go to the prisoners," Giovanna said with resolve.

Visibly taken aback by her defiance of his warning, Ghirlandaio nevertheless politely kissed her hand. "Until next time."

Giovanna noticed him admiring her beautiful crown-shaped gold wedding ring with the letters *G* and *L* engraved above the Tornabuoni family crest. She placed her hand on her belly, delighted to feel the stirrings of new life within her. With a mix of slight awe and deep gratitude, she believed that her life could not be more perfect.

After seeing Ghirlandaio off, she walked the sleeping Giovannino back to his cradle in her bed chamber. Then she quickly removed her pearl necklace, replacing it with a simple silver pendant embossed with an image of Mary Magdalene, changed into a long black skirt and white blouse with an emerald sash, and hurried to the Bargello for her afternoon reading appointment.

Giovanna entered the imposing stone fortress through a heavily armored rear door. The prison guard greeted her with a familiar smile and led her down a dim corridor to the cell of Antonio Renato. A portly, middle-aged man with a ruddy face and bulgy, dark eyes, he was serving time for a string of robberies and two murders. One of Giovanna's neighbors had died while defending himself against Antonio, who had broken into his home late one night.

Antonio stood silently beside his rough-hewn platform bed. The cell was dark and suffocating, with plaster-chipped walls, a wooden stool, and a single candlestick perched on a shelf, beside which lay a tattered image of Jesus in his ascension, surrounded by a halo of light. Giovanna had given Antonio the picture when she first started visiting him over a year ago and had taught him how to meditate with it. Though she valued her time with all the prisoners, she had developed a particular fondness for Antonio, who, despite his transgressions, had shown himself to possess a gentle, sensitive soul that yearned for forgiveness. He always treated Giovanna with the highest respect and often wept as she read aloud passages from the Bible and great works of literature.

"Dear Antonio," she said, extending her hand to him. "I hope you've been at peace since our last meeting."

"Signora," he bowed awkwardly. He had once told Giovanna that he was often overcome with anxiety for several days before her visits due to what he called her "special powers from heaven."

She turned to the prison guard. "Thank you. I will need about an hour, as usual." He nodded and promptly locked the iron-barred gate behind him. Giovanna's thoughts drifted briefly to Lorenzo, who was uncomfortable with what he called the "imminent danger" of her spending time alone with the prisoners in their cells. She was aware that she was taking a risk, particularly given her aristocratic background. But she harbored little fear and always trusted in a higher guiding force, which she simply called Spirit, to take care of her. And she found that the more she trusted, the more joy and peace she felt inside, which naturally rippled outward toward others.

"It is good to see you again, signora." Antonio nervously paced the cell, rubbing his palms together. "I have been in such a state!"

Giovanna sat down on the stool, concerned, and lifted a volume of Plato's *Phaedrus* from her leather satchel. "What's going on, Antonio?"

"One of the prisoners. He doesn't want you coming here anymore. He is very angry and is trying to turn the others against you."

"But I don't understand."

"I don't know what I would do if you stopped coming to see me," Antonio pleaded, kneeling beside her. "You are the only light in the darkness."

"I am honored, Antonio, but please don't worship me." She placed her hand on his forehead. "The same light burns within your own soul. Believe it, and you will feel it."

With these words and this gesture, Antonio's entire body loosened and relaxed, and the tension in his face instantly disappeared.

This often happened when Giovanna tried to comfort others. Antonio, who had reported feeling alternating sensations of heat and chills in her presence, was a frequent beneficiary of her healing gifts and had grown dependent upon her.

"When you have made yourself one with Spirit you will no longer need me," Giovanna said lovingly. "'As above, so below,' the ancient sage Hermes Trismegistus said. That is what I'm trying to teach you."

"But don't you care that this prisoner is betraying you?" Antonio's voice trembled. "He talked of your relation to the Medici and said you are a traitor to your own family. He said the Pazzi will release all the prisoners when Medici himself falls." He hesitated. "They are planning again to get rid of him."

"Who is this man, and how does he know?" Giovanna pressed, distressed by the accusation against her family.

"He . . . I can't say his name. He will kill me. He knows many people on the outside."

Giovanna's pulse raced, and she began to feel claustrophobic in the cramped cell. She quickly took a deep breath and returned to her center. "Well, I can tell you my family is *not* involved. We have healed the wounds of the past. All we can do now is feel compassion for this prisoner who is spreading such rumors."

"But, signora . . ."

Giovanna gently touched his shoulder. "Place your attention on the light, and you will not be disturbed by the dark forces. They are not real anyway. Only love is real."

"As you say, then." Antonio sat at the edge of his bed, closed his eyes and began whispering a prayer as Giovanna read from the *Phaedrus*:

"'I have known the temptations of pleasure, positions of extraordinary splendor, extravagant terms . . . courage and endurance, courage and wisdom, come into existence and pass away. . . . We must start all over again.'"

Chapter Six

"Closing time!"

Lena snapped out of her trance to see a security guard walking through the gallery making his announcement. She mulled over the unexpected stream of information that she had just received about Giovanna, as though she were back in Renaissance Florence observing her life. It was such a strange and unsettling sensation, one that Giovanna's image seemed to have triggered, like before at the library. She had never experienced such a thing. Was her extremely active imagination working overtime? Were these some weird psychic dreams? True visions of the past? She jotted what she could remember in her notebook. Thoughts of her pressing deadline made her anxious. She glanced again at the portrait before leaving.

Lena passed through three galleries of French paintings on her way out of the museum, pausing to admire Delacroix's *Death of Sardanapolis*, with its turbulent swirls of pink, gold, and red, and then the towering stone statue *Winged Victory* at the top of the stairs. In the ground-floor gift shop, she bought a museum catalogue and several postcards of Giovanna before ascending the staircase to the exit, topped with a massive, glass pyramid. Outside, the late afternoon sunlight flickered across a pool of water, where the pyramid multiplied itself toward infinity. Lena dipped her hand in the cool water. Curiously, she smelled a sweet, rose scent, reminding her of Giovanna's bouquet of roses in the vision she'd just had. She checked to see if there were flowers nearby. No, the Tuileries Gardens were all the way at the other end of the courtyard. How odd. Why did she buy the essential rose oil at the pharmacy in New York? Essence of Magdalene. It was still in her luggage; she had almost forgotten about it.

Her thoughts drifted to Jud, their familiar routine, and how she missed him already. But Paris, not New York, was her city now, and all the newness was so refreshing. Feeling inspired, she emailed Hannah from her cell phone:

Hi, miss you. You'd love it here! So beautiful and the ghosts of so many famous writers. My flat is small, but great garden view. I feel light & breezy, not claustrophobic like back home. Hope you're not working too hard! Love, L.

She thought about writing to Jud. But their relationship was so ambiguous. How would he respond? She emailed him anyway:

Hope you're making progress on the biography. Enjoying Paris. Work going well. You would like the hotel here on R. des Beaux Arts where Oscar Wilde died. He once said, "The two greatest tragedies in the world are living your dream and never having lived your dream." Makes me sad, L.

Then she called Max and left a voice mail:

"Lena, checking in. I just saw in the French press that the heiress Madame de Trouville consigned the painting to Sotheby's, a new lead. I'll track her down. I'm meeting Baron Eric von Heisendorf at an auction soon. He supposedly once owned the painting. By the way, my friend Hannah is an incredible woman, a doctor, beautiful and single, Upper East Side. Why not call her? 2125550437. Au Revoir!"

Suddenly, a young man approached out of the crowd of tourists and handed her a flyer. It was an advertisement for a book about past lives. The author would be speaking the following week at the legendary Left Bank bookstore Shakespeare and Company.

"Très intéressant!" the youth said, brushing a tuft of dark hair from his eyes while removing his plaid beret. He then switched seamlessly to English, his obvious first language. "One appearance only!"

Thank you." Lena studied the flyer, skeptical yet intrigued.

"Hey, can I paint your portrait? You're beautiful." He retrieved some sketches from his backpack and showed them to her.

She smiled, mildly flattered. "I really appreciate it, but, no thanks, not now."

Over the next few days, hoping to uncover more information about the painting's provenance, Lena poured through stacks of old auction catalogues and art magazines at the American Library, where she could thankfully read in English. In a Sotheby's catalogue, she saw Marv Steinert's and Baron Eric von Heisendorf's names listed as former owners of the Ghirlandaio; old news. Unfortunately, she did not find anything further. One day, frustrated by her lack of progress, she began reading a museum catalogue on a Ghirlandaio exhibition that had toured Europe several years ago. She gasped in disbelief. A description of the *Portrait of Giovanna Tornabuoni* and its subject stated that while few records existed about Giovanna's day-to-day life, it was known that she was a devout Florentine whose patron saints were Mary Magdalene and Saint Francis of Assisi. Exactly what Lena had seen in one of her visions of Giovanna! There were paintings of the saints in Giovanna's study. And the description of her palazzo—the marble terrazzo floors and black-and-white checkered ceiling—was also how Lena had seen it. How could she have known all this? Lena felt faint, and her head was spinning. She left the library in a heightened, agitated state.

In an effort to relax, she walked along the broad, leafy Quai

Anatole France overlooking the Seine and its barges, and browsed the many green bookstalls bulging with old French detective novels and expensive watercolor renderings of the city. But it was hard to concentrate. She couldn't stop thinking about Giovanna.

After a brief lunch at a café on the quai, she cut back along the narrow Rue Bonaparte weaving between art galleries and shops displaying frames and fabrics. Lena had read there were two lesser known paintings by Ghirlandaio in the Luxembourg Museum, housed in the former palace of Marie de' Medici. While it was not essential to her story, she wanted to learn as much as possible about the artist. Max had always complimented her on her thorough research. He appreciated her overwhelming curiosity and perfectionist tendencies. These qualities, combined with her passion and dedication, led her to be an expert on the subjects she wrote about.

Lena found her way through the small museum to the two Ghirlandaio paintings, a Florentine cityscape and a portrait of an old friar, neither of which had the exquisitely transcendent quality of the *Portrait of Giovanna Tornabuoni*. She studied the paintings awhile, absorbing Ghirlandaio's masterful execution, while taking notes with the new Montblanc pen Max had given her.

Afterward, she strolled through the nearby Luxembourg Gardens, filled with its usual afternoon crowd of students, tourists, and young mothers with babies. She admired the mothers and how much they allowed themselves to be needed. So strong and capable; not one of them looked tired or disgusted, just peaceful. They probably didn't even wish to be anywhere else. Sometimes Lena got so carried away with all the other things she could be doing that she was unable to be in the now.

Dragging a chair through the gravel, she found a spot close to a bed of hyacinth and scarlet sage and settled down to watch the sun set behind the chestnut trees. Urns of orange, yellow, and crimson mums encircled the garden like a jeweled necklace. She tried to halt her darting thoughts, but they kept rushing back again. She watched a dove soar, pliant as a glider, and a leaf spin aimlessly above the boat pond before finally falling to rest. Looking hard, she practiced becoming the dove and the leaf for a moment, in the same way she felt she had merged with Giovanna while gazing at her portrait in the Louvre. Suddenly, a diminutive old man appeared from behind a tree.

"Ah, ma jeune fille!" he cried, jolting Lena out of her solitude. "I must sit. I'm tired of walking." He pulled up a chair beside her.

Bewildered, she offered a brief smile. "How far did you walk?" They spoke in French.

"All the way from the Champs de Mars."

"That's very far."

"I'm only seventy-five! My wife, she died back in Algeria. I'm alone now. I walk a lot."

Lena felt his loneliness. She concentrated on his face, which was long and dark and creased into weathered ridges. "And your children?"

"No children." He nodded with resignation and leaned forward on his walking stick to kiss her hand. "A man and a woman together, beautiful, yes?"

"Yes," she agreed softly.

"Thank you, ma chérie, you have been very kind with me. Please," he hesitated, his eyes clouding with tears, "be careful! You are kind and beautiful. People will want things from you."

Lena pulled her cape up around her neck, disturbed by the old man's words.

"Just one more kiss, please, if you don't mind, ma jeune fille." He kissed her on each cheek, his whiskers needling her skin, before he retreated behind the chestnut trees.

Contemplating this strange encounter, Lena started back toward her apartment along the Avenue de l'Observatoire, lined with life-size, marble sculptures of Roman men and women, the sun setting on her back, a heavy light.

She cooked herself a dinner of fresh green beans and russet potatoes sautéed in butter. Then she lay down on her sofa, exhausted. As she closed her eyes, she was flooded by a collage of images of Jud reading at the Hungarian pastry shop, Hannah at her stainless steel sinks, Max hovering anxiously over his computer, lovely Giovanna and her terrible fate, and the old Algerian man and his unsettling warning. She missed New York but was content to be alone with her own heart, surging with grand ambitions and a quick and aching tenderness. "Anything is possible," she said to herself, "anything at all." She remembered what she had read once about sacrifice: "The boundless resolve, no longer limitable in any direction, to achieve one's purest inner possibility." And as she fell asleep, she already felt herself on the verge of awakening.

Chapter Seven

Days later, Lena stood at the back of a crowded saleroom at the Hôtel Drouot auction house, shifting between bobbing heads for a clear view of the action up front. The auctioneer gestured toward an exceptionally beautiful palissandre and ivory desk by Émile-Jacques Ruhlmann, the noted Art Deco designer.

"Sept million!" the auctioneer shouted. "Sept million cinq cent mille. Huit million!" An international gathering of twentieth-century decorative arts dealers and collectors sporadically coughed, craned their necks in search of a familiar face, and waved their hands at the auctioneer. There were eleven different salerooms, some smaller than others, occupying two floors at the Drouot complex, which resembled a large concrete warehouse. Its shoddy interior, with exposed construction work and metal folding chairs, could hardly compare to the elegant New York auction houses.

Brushing her curls away from her face, still sparkling with traces of the afternoon rain, Lena scanned the auction floor for Baron Eric von Heisendorf, whom she hoped to recognize from a photo she had seen in an article on the world's top collectors. One of the wealthiest men in Germany, the Baron was a valued guest at international auctions and museum fundraisers. She soon spotted a balding, rotund man in the front row, wearing a monocle and waving a tiny German flag, a peculiar bidding habit for which the Baron was known. She was excited to interview him.

"Neuf million!" the auctioneer barked. A Japanese man bowed, and the crowd gasped with anticipation. The Baron stridently waved his flag at the next increment. Several rows behind the Baron, Lena noticed an attractive, ebullient French man, who was yelling "encore" after each bid. When the bidding escalated to ten million Euros, he jumped onto his chair—an extreme gesture that intrigued Lena. Standing with his hands on his hips, he nodded at the auctioneer.

"Dix million!" the auctioneer bellowed, smashing his gavel onto the podium and flinging his arm toward the highest bidder. "Voilà, c'est fini! Monsieur, à gauche. Dix million. J'adjuge!" The French man punched his fist into the air, affirming his victory, then climbed down from his perch and casually lit a cigarette.

"Merde!" someone yelled. Lena suspected it was the Baron, who glowered, shaking his head. She quickly carved her way through the crowd to speak to him.

"You are correct, miss, I am he." Baron Eric von Heisendorf rose to his feet after Lena introduced herself. He eyed her suspiciously through his thick monocle, still distracted by his defeat.

"Sorry about the desk," Lena attempted to console him.

"That's Henri for you. Little snake!"

"Henri?"

"Dealer here in Paris. He'll do anything for attention," he groaned.

Not wishing to waste time, Lena cut to the chase. "Baron, I'd be so grateful if you can tell me who bought that wonderful Ghirlandaio from you. I'm sure you had no idea then that it would become the most expensive old master painting in the world."

The Baron scowled, nervously tugging at his gray-flecked beard. Lena was just tall enough to see over his shiny, bald crown. He leaned backward as he talked as if to offset the downward pull of his inflated belly.

"A shame what's happening to Claude Weintraub at the Louvre." He puckered his fleshy lips. "It's unthinkable that one of the most respected curators in the world could be indicted for buying that painting. Just a rotting pile of hearsay!" He let out a booming laugh. "Anyway, miss—"

"Lena."

"Yes, how lovely, as in Magdalena. You know, the other Mary. I have a beautiful portrait of her in my collection."

"You were saying?" Lena was struck by his reference to Mary Magdalene and, again, by the saint's connection with Giovanna.

"Though I detest scandals of any sort, I find it hard to withhold information from such an attractive woman as yourself." He inched closer, making her uncomfortable. Lena had on one of her sexiest dresses, a burnt-orange jersey wrap-around with a plunging neckline. "But be careful, Miss Lena, you may be getting in over your head."

"My editor sent me here for a reason."

"Why don't we discuss this over a drink tonight at the Hôtel de Crillon, where I'm staying. On the Place de la Concorde." The Baron adjusted his monocle. "You know, where Louis XVI and Marie Antoinette went to the guillotine."

"I'm sorry, but I'm busy tonight." Lena studied the Baron's eyes. They were grayish blue, cool, and flat, like a matte finish on porcelain.

Frustrated that she had pried nothing from the Baron, she continued her questioning. "I wonder if you know Madame de Trouville, the French heiress who consigned the portrait to Sotheby's? According to the French press, she allegedly bought it from a Florence dealer, who has since disappeared. I don't suppose you know him, too?"

"I must say, I feel like I'm on a quiz show." The Baron raised his eyebrows in a stern arc, pointing across the saleroom to an elegant middle-aged woman wearing a wide-brimmed red hat. "There she is. As for that dealer, I know of no such person."

Just as Lena caught sight of Madame de Trouville, the woman dashed out of the saleroom with a male companion. "Damn, she's gone," Lena mumbled.

"What was that, dear?" The Baron inched closer again.

"Who bought the Ghirlandaio from *you*, Baron?!" Lena's tone was authoritative.

Just then, the French man who had won the Ruhlmann desk interrupted them, beaming with self-satisfaction. He shook the Baron's hand, noticeably taken with Lena. "You're always the under-bidder," he teased.

"You scoundrel! I knew you were aggressive, Henri, but that trick topped everything." He turned to Lena. "I'd like to introduce you to miss . . . miss . . ."

"Lena," she prompted, sizing up Henri in a long, lingering glance.

"As in Magdalena," the Baron added.

"Henri Lemien, enchanted to meet you." Henri's dark eyes met Lena's with laser-beam intensity.

His smile was electric, and he was even more handsome up close, with smooth olive-toned skin, classic Mediterranean features, and thick, wavy black hair. Lena noticed his shirt collar and cuffs were neatly ironed. His suit, made of the finest wool, hung grace-fully from his compact body.

"A pleasure." Lena shook back her curls and smiled confidently.

"Had we met sooner you may have distracted me from bidding," he said, laughing.

"Miss Lena works for a magazine in New York, covering the sup-posed stolen Ghirlandaio," the Baron said. "I was just about to tell her that I sold it to that eccentric old boy from Houston, Jonathan Fisher Gilbert. Inherited his family's oil business. Worth billions." He stared pensively into the distance. "Biggest mistake I ever made, letting go of that cursed portrait."

"Billions?" Lena repeated, scribbling in her notebook. "Where is he? I have to talk to him right away!"

"I see you don't let any grass grow under your feet, Miss Lena," the Baron said. "I like that. Aggressive. Yes, I rather like that in a woman."

Henri lifted a blue-and-gold enameled Fabergé cigarette case from his vest pocket and offered it to Lena. She declined. All the cigarette smoke in the room had made her eyes burn. He lit up a cigarette and puffed leisurely, carefully waving the smoke away from Lena toward the Baron.

"Disgusting habit, smoking." The Baron frowned at Henri. "Wouldn't you agree, Miss Lena? So how long are you in Paris?"

"Not sure. So getting back to . . ." Lena tried to contain her impatience.

"I don't think Gilbert would be much help to you," Henri interrupted. "Very reclusive, hardly even speaks."

"So you know him?"

Henri gazed at her intently, drawing the cigarette to his mouth in long, lazy sweeps. "No, only what I've read in the papers."

"Well you name it, he collects it," the Baron said. "Art Deco, Vienna Secession, rare books, old masters, netsuke. When he's not holed up in that old château in the Loire Valley, he flits between his apartment in New York and Schloss Rugenwald near Salzburg."

Lena jotted down more notes. "What else, gentlemen?"

"Haven't heard anything about him in years," Henri offered.

The Baron reflected for a moment, rocking back and forth on his heels like a bowling pin. "When I think of Gilbert I think of compulsion. Now, there's a difference between compulsion and collecting, right, Henri?"

"They're the same thing. A person collects because he must. He has no choice, like with alcohol or sex. Some people never have enough. In fact, nothing is really enough, when you think about it." Henri held Lena's eyes as he spoke, ignoring the Baron.

"I've often thought that." Lena glanced at her watch. She was anxious to speak to Henri privately. The Baron was getting in the way.

Two men in gray overalls began removing the last pieces of furniture that had failed to sell. Lena watched as they lifted an end table, with wrought-iron legs in arrow and star shapes, by the mid-twentieth-century French designer Gilbert Poillerat. It was as if the arrows alone directed the movement of the table, which appeared light enough to float. She thought of herself as an arrow, sailing swiftly to its goal.

"I must admit I have a soft spot for the old masters, too," the Baron said. "Fortunately, I have the means to buy them, built my timber company from scratch." He winked at Lena, who was aware he was trying to impress her.

"And why did you sell the Ghirlandaio?"

"I advised him to get rid of it because it's a fake," Henri said. "Old Gilbert must not have had such a discerning eye, after all. He thought it was a masterpiece."

Lena's eyes grew wide with disbelief. She had not expected this complication to her line of questioning. "But how could a museum spend $48 million on a fake?!"

"I sent several letters to Claude Weintraub at the Louvre. Obviously, he paid no attention to my warnings."

"I shouldn't have listened to you either," the Baron said dismissively. "I should have held onto that painting and sold it to the Louvre myself! Fake or no fake."

"So you're an expert on old masters, Henri?" Lena asked, noting the pleasant woodsy scent of his aftershave.

"Among other things." He grinned broadly. "Sell them at my Left Bank gallery along with museum-quality twentieth-century furnishings." He turned toward the cashier's window in the hallway. "If you'll excuse me for a minute, almost forgot to pay for the Ruhlmann desk!" With that, he dashed off. Lena watched through the doorway as a small group of people gathered around him.

Clearly unimpressed, the Baron began flipping through his auction catalogue. "Merde," he grunted, making notations beside certain objects that he had failed to purchase.

"Odd that you and Henri are both experts in such widely different fields," Lena mused.

"The twentieth century can't compare to the old masters in my opinion!" the Baron proclaimed. "It's just an enjoyable divergence for me."

Henri returned shortly, whistling and carrying a newspaper under his arm. He lifted a long-stemmed pink rose out of the folded newspaper and offered it to Lena. "For you."

"Where did this come from?" Lena said, flattered, sniffing the rose. "Thank you."

"There was a big arrangement in the stockroom when I went back to see the desk. I asked one of the boys for his newspaper and just popped this in."

"Has no smell whatsoever!" The Baron inhaled with effort.

"Well, I have to get down to the Loire Valley to see Gilbert as quickly as possible. Max is going to love this." Lena slung her cape over her shoulders and slid her notebook back into her purse, casually letting her arm brush against Henri's. "Would either of you happen to have his address?"

"Max?" Henri asked.

"My boss in New York."

"Let me show you out of this place, Lena, I really should be going, too." He reached for her hand.

"But Miss Lena and I were just about to take some champagne— Dom Pérignon, of course—at the Crillon, weren't we, dear?" the Baron said. "I'll tell you more about Gilbert there."

"Actually . . ." Lena cleared her throat.

"How depressing," Henri said. "Really, Baron, that place is full of tourists."

"I happen to be in their black file, Miss Lena. We'd be given special treatment." He removed his monocle as if to emphasize his sincerity.

"Nonsense." Henri laughed, silencing the Baron, who appeared outraged.

"The thing is, gentlemen . . ." Lena stepped forward so that she was standing between the two men. "I need directions to Gilbert's castle." She folded her hands hopefully at her heart.

"I can get that for you in a flash," the Baron insisted.

"That's in my files," Henri countered.

Lena paused, conscious that she was now an object of desire, waiting to be snatched up by the highest bidder. Only this time, she would be the one deciding.

"Let's go, Henri. I'll be in touch, Baron." Lena shook the Baron's clammy hand and thanked him for the information. Henri smiled wryly at the Baron, downcast and stroking his beard, and they hurried out of the saleroom together.

It was still gray and drizzling outside, so they headed to the nearest café. Henri graciously pulled out a chair for Lena at a streetside table under a red and gold awning. Lena fluffed up her hair and quickly applied a fresh coat of lipstick.

"I see you don't mind being quiet even when you're with someone," Henri said, breaking the silence. "You're not afraid to be alone. I mean, you seem very self-sufficient, resourceful." He gazed at her with bemused curiosity. "You always get what you want, don't you?"

"I like to think so. But how do you know that? We just met."

"I just know," he laughed as a waiter approached to take their order.

"Well, there are a lot of things you don't know about me . . . yet." She playfully challenged him. "Guess you'll have to find out."

"Espresso for me, and for the lady?" Henri turned to the waiter.

"Tea with honey." Lena became suddenly distracted by a man walking toward them on the sidewalk across the street. He looked vaguely familiar. It was Marv Steinert! Lena waved him over.

"Mr. Steinert, so nice to see you." She stood up to greet him. "What are you doing here?!"

"Hello there." He appeared equally surprised to see her. "I came for the old masters auction tomorrow."

"Marvin," Henri nodded.

Steinert nodded back, stone-faced. He stood at a distance from their table, holding an umbrella.

"You two know each other?" Lena asked, stunned.

"We met ten years ago in New York," Steinert explained, a trace of animosity in his voice. "When he bought a Vermeer I had put up for auction. He sold it five days later at twice the price."

Lena thought he looked misplaced here, outside the confines of his oppressively dark living room. His face was ashen white, paler than she remembered it. His voice sounded scratchy and frail. The sun peeked through the clouds, casting a soft light on the wet street stones. A single ray illuminated Steinert like a spotlight.

"Why don't you join us?" Lena pulled over another chair from the marble-topped table nearby.

"Thank you, but I have another engagement. I really must be going." He offered a tepid smile, avoiding Henri's eyes.

"Have a nice stay, Marvin," Henri said curtly.

"Funny, I'd have expected you to keep better company, dear," Steinert quipped as he marched off.

"Wait!" Lena shouted. "Where are you staying? I'll call you."

"L'Hôtel on the Left Bank," Steinert called.

Lena made a note on her napkin and slid it into her purse. She grew anxious, not sure what to make of his comment about Henri.

"I don't trust that man." Henri answered her thoughts. "You're better off not getting mixed up with him."

The harried waiter finally delivered their drinks. Lena was happy to warm herself with the tea. "Why? I don't understand what's going on between you."

"If you had checked him out, you would know he was once indicted for smuggling a Sorolla out of Mexico."

Lena recalled the colorful Spanish Impressionist painting that had captivated her at Steinert's townhouse in New York. She felt apprehensive. Though she barely knew Steinert, it was her nature to look for the best in others. "But in New York he's so respected. Besides, I already confirmed his reputation with some other art dealers."

But Max had also warned her about Steinert. Confused, she decided to call Steinert anyway and ask him to come to the Louvre to confirm the authenticity of the *Portrait of Giovanna Tornabuoni*. Even if his past was tarnished, she respected both his knowledge and his taste.

"Ah, but there is always that which transpires beyond that which appears," counseled Henri. "Don't be so trusting." He sipped his espresso with gusto. "This gentleman's business, as they say, is full of crooks. I mean, look at the American dealer who went to jail for stealing all those Tiffany windows from cemetery churches. Horrible!"

He placed his hand protectively over hers. Lena quickened to his touch as a wave of warmth coursed through her. A white terrier ran up from the sidewalk and plopped himself at Lena's feet. She lovingly petted his wet fur, wondering where his owner was. Animals always tugged at her heart. She'd never had a pet of her own. Henri withdrew a small leather appointment book from inside his suit jacket and paged through it with intense concentration. Each page was thickly covered with ink.

"You're obviously very busy." Lena yawned. The rain had made her sleepy.

"I travel a lot appraising collections and looking for art to sell. I hate to waste even one minute." He casually stroked her hand. "If I do, I feel disgusted, like when I've held a beautiful woman in my arms and realize afterward I'd been thinking the whole time about the record price for a Daum vase."

"I agree. Carpe diem, as they say. Seize the day!" Lena threw up her hands, inadvertently knocking over her tea cup. "Oh, no! How clumsy." She dabbed the tea off her dress with a napkin.

"You're funny, Lena of New York." Henri laughed heartily then grew serious, beset with a sudden realization. "I'm late for an appointment!" He hurriedly placed a few bills on the table and grabbed his trench coat. "How about we meet for lunch Friday? One o'clock at Les Deux Magots on the Left Bank."

"What about Gilbert's address?!" Charmed by Henri's formidable presence, this key piece of information had temporarily slipped Lena's mind.

"Have to search my files. I'll give it to you when I see you."

"But I haven't said, yes!" Lena coyly protested.

"You don't have to." He nipped her goodbye on both cheeks. "I know you'll be there!"

She giggled as she watched Henri dash down the street, jumping gingerly around the puddles and waving to her. Finishing her tea, she tingled with anticipation of their next visit.

The next several days, Lena researched Giovanna's background with a disciplined schedule of visits to the Bibliothèque nationale de France, whose turn-of-the-century grandeur reminded her a bit of the New York Public Library. Thankfully, her language skills were improving, so translating from French was less of a struggle.

One morning, sitting cross-legged in one of the library's long aisles, immersed in a dusty tome about the Renaissance, she noticed a husky man dressed in black who kept weaving in and out of the stacks around her. She paid no attention until she had the unsettling sensation that she was being watched. She kept looking up from her book, trying to catch a glimpse of his face. But the shadowy figure just as quickly disappeared from her view. Was her imagination working overtime? She tried to relax. Startled by something brushing against her back, she whirled around. But no one was there. That's when she remembered the letter: *Don't investigate the painting or else.* What if it wasn't a prank? Vigilant, she continued reading about Giovanna's family, archrivals of the Medici. Each word and sentence came alive with great immediacy, and, despite her agitation, she soon found herself mysteriously transported though time and space, experiencing events that extended far beyond her research.

Chapter Eight

Ablaze with candlelight from massive iron torches and hung with
stunning, intricately woven tapestries, the cavernous, vaulted dining room of the Palazzo Tornabuoni was filled with laughter and
merriment. Giovanna had invited a group of their closest friends
to a sumptuous banquet to celebrate Lorenzo's thirtieth birthday.
The long oak table was replete with meats, fruits, and cheeses;
they were served in beautiful silver and gold bowls complete with
the tazze Giovanna used only for the most special occasions. Gold
candelabras and a royal blue, hand-woven silk tablecloth added to
the formal ambience, while Tuscan wine from the Medici vineyards
flowed freely.

"To Lorenzo, my cousin and best friend, for his generosity, loyalty,
and trustworthiness!" Medici shouted, raising his goblet toward the
young nobleman.

Other guests followed suit, calling out Lorenzo's noteworthy
qualities. He bowed to each of them in turn, raising his hand as if
to signal he did not deserve such praise. Then, with characteristic
playfulness, he said, "Is that all?!"

"Don't let this go to your head, Lorenzo. I see the wine already
has," Giovanna teased, holding up an empty bottle.

The two sat side by side at the center of the table, their hands
lovingly intertwined. Every so often, Giovanna whispered in his ear,
to his obvious delight.

Suddenly, the front door swung open. Giovanna's roguish older brother, Salvatore, burst into the room half-drunk with two women clutching his arms. Medici quickly slipped away from the table and out the back door.

Lorenzo's former gaiety instantly faded. "I don't believe you were invited!" he snapped, rising from his seat to confront his estranged brother-in-law. He had not been able to forgive him for supporting the assassination plot against Medici several years ago. A hush fell over the room.

"Is this not my sister's home, too?" Salvatore challenged him. He had a severe, forbidding look, with sharp, angular features and a closely shaven head, and was taller and more muscular than the other men.

Giovanna rushed over to her brother and embraced him. His women stepped back. They were not of a refined nature like the Tornabuonis' other guests but were ladies of the streets with whom Salvatore frequently kept company.

"You are always welcome here, brother." Giovanna led him by the hand to the table. "I barely see my family now that I'm married," she lamented. "But love knows neither time nor space."

With a loving glance from Giovanna, Lorenzo reluctantly softened and continued drinking his wine. She then whispered to her husband to remember the praise he had just received for his admirable character, whereupon he kissed her hand. Their friends soon began conversing again among themselves.

"Medici has gone!" a guest suddenly observed. Lorenzo eyed Salvatore accusingly.

Remembering what the prisoner Antonio had confided to her, Giovanna grew suddenly anxious and wondered if her family were, indeed, behind the new plot on Medici's life. Up until now, she had banished this dark thought from her mind. She decided to have a word with Salvatore at an appropriate moment, having already alerted Medici in a letter the day she heard the news, just in case. But she did not want her husband to know, given his tense relations with her family.

"I'm not surprised Medici's gone," said another guest, an archbishop and longtime friend of Giovanna's family. "He still has blood on his hands for the execution of Francesco de' Pazzi, leader of the Pazzi Conspiracy, as we all know. You, dear Giovanna," he turned to her, "have admirably forgiven him, though I know you still mourn the loss of your cousin. But how could Medici face your brother, having not yet confessed this great sin nor received penance?"

Salvatore nodded solemnly in agreement, as each of his women kissed him in turn on the cheek.

"Let's have a game of dice!" Giovanna said, wishing to divert attention from her brother and the rising tension. She hastily moved several items on the table to clear space.

Within minutes, the merriment resumed. The men tried to outdo each other throwing dice. With considerable passion, Salvatore joined in and wound up winning, much to Lorenzo's dismay. Giovanna wandered gracefully around the room, refilling her guests' goblets with wine as another game of dice began, accompanied by shouts and laughter. The women cheered on their men for a brief time, then formed small groups of their own, chatting about their children and homes and the latest news from mutual friends.

Giovanna observed the festivities with obvious satisfaction, pleased to see that her brother was enjoying himself. She caught his eye and motioned for him to meet her in a far corner of the dining room. He reluctantly excused himself from the game.

"What is it sister?"

"I heard some disturbing news." Giovanna nervously cleared her throat. "At the Bargello, where I go to read to the prisoners, as you know . . ."

"Yes, tell me!"

"One of the prisoners said our family is conspiring against Medici again."

Salvatore became noticeably agitated. "I wish that were so, but that would be foolish. Medici's forces greatly outnumber ours."

"Then why would he fabricate such a thing?" she asked, distressed.

"As I've told you, you're wasting your time with those outcasts." He scanned the room as if he were looking for someone. "They are deluded. Rest your mind, dear sister. The power-crazed Lorenzo de' Medici will bring upon his own ruin."

"So be it!" Giovanna waved her hand as if to dispel any mistrust between them.

Just then, the portly archbishop, gentle of speech and dignified in bearing, approached them. He and Salvatore shook hands with familiarity and moved away to speak privately. Observing their interaction, Giovanna clasped her hands at her heart. She was thrilled her brother had found acceptance among the clergy and wanted to tell Lorenzo, but he was preoccupied with the other guests. She watched the two men from a distance with curiosity. The archbishop handed Salvatore a small leather pouch. Giovanna suspected that perhaps it was a rosary or a relic, or some other religious token, signifying an absolution of his wayward habits. Salvatore kissed the bishop's ring and then, summoning his women, sauntered unsteadily to the door, further inebriated by the additional wine he had consumed.

"Salvatore, wait! Where are you going? Don't leave us so quickly!" Giovanna started after her brother.

Lorenzo pulled her back. "Let him go now. He's drunk and will only cause more problems here."

"But . . . " Giovanna fell silent as her brother left, saddened that he had not bothered to say goodbye.

"Come, dear wife, and be joyous!" Lorenzo urged. The archbishop concurred with a broad, toothy smile.

Chapter Nine

The famous café Les Deux Magots on the Left Bank, where Picasso and Hemingway once drank absinthe, was bustling at lunchtime with businessmen in suits, starry-eyed couples, tourists, and solitary souls immersed in books and newspapers. Lena sat across from Henri in a red leather booth against a smoky mirrored wall, laughing and finishing the last delectable bites of her trout almandine, as he pulled out a thick wad of cash to pay the waiter for their lunch. She felt particularly alluring in her black miniskirt and sheer, low-cut magenta blouse.

"Very funny!" She leaned forward, laughing at his joke, her breasts noticeably grazing the table. "Do you realize, Mr. Lemien, that you have successfully distracted me during this entire lunch from the real reason for our meeting?"

"Have I?" Henri rested his leg against hers, sending a tingling sensation up her spine. "And what was that again?" He met her eyes with electric intensity. There was something mysteriously exciting about him, and Lena relished his attention. He looked casually elegant in his cream-colored cashmere V-neck, which accentuated the contours of his well-toned chest.

"You were going to give me the contact info for the collector Jonathan Fisher Gilbert." She playfully stared him down.

"I know. I've been avoiding telling you that I can't find it." He grimaced. "Sorry, I looked through all my files."

"Now what," Lena sighed, extremely displeased.

"You're the sleuth. I'm sure you'll get it somehow."

"I'm sure I will." She dropped her formerly flirtatious tone.

"Getting back to the painting, Henri."

"All the uproar has gone overboard. It's a fake, as I said at the auction. Maybe that's your story."

"How can you be so sure?" She was becoming increasingly anxious about this potential twist to her investigation and where it might lead.

"I inspected the painting myself, and I cannot say without a doubt that the brushstrokes are Ghirlandaio's," Henri said with authority. It was obvious that he did not enjoy being questioned.

"But no one else has raised the issue, Henri, not even the Louvre!"

"It only takes one good eye. There are a lot of self-professed experts out there who fall far short."

"I don't know." Lena shook her head adamantly. "That portrait is so bewitching. Giovanna seems so real, whether Ghirlandaio painted it or not. I can't get her out of my mind."

"I admit the forger did a good job!" Henri gulped down the last of his Sancerre and checked the messages on his cell phone. "Have to get back to the gallery, though I can hardly wait to see you again."

"I'm serious, Henri," Lena said as they left the café. "It's like I can actually see into her life, the events that took place. The other night, I saw her posing for the painting in her palazzo. She had on a beautiful pearl pendant. Her skin was so fair and glowing. She sat upright on a stool, her eyes fixed on a portrait of Mary Magdalene, her patron saint." Lena stopped to catch her breath, growing more excited by the flow of images again.

"I could see the slight bulge in her stomach; she was pregnant. And there was Ghirlandaio's face, like a close-up in a photograph. His long nose and stubbly chin. Then, like a film that keeps fast-forwarding, other scenes flashed in front of me. I saw a birthday party and an unwelcome guest. I felt like a voyeur." Lena continued to recount the details of her startling visions as they strolled down Boulevard Saint-Germain.

"You've been so focused on this article you're probably just dreaming," Henri said, smiling.

"No, it's more than that." She grew pensive.

"Hey, I have an idea. Why don't we stop by my apartment for a few minutes. I forgot about some old files there, which may have Gilbert's address. That way, we'll be sure."

"What a line, Henri. You just substituted an address for the proverbial etchings!"

"Oh, I'm not going to take advantage of you." He winked mischievously. "C'mon, it's just around the corner on Rue de Fleurus. But we have to make it quick."

Buoyed by the prospect of making further headway on her story, Lena agreed. Henri gripped her hand firmly as they picked up their pace.

His apartment was decorated sparely, which made it appear much larger than its actual size. It was filled with exquisite Art Deco furnishings and objects. Lena loved the sleek, sharp geometry of the living room, softened by milk-toned walls and calf-skin sofas low to the ground, the golden hues of fruitwood tables, and wrought-iron and alabaster wall sconces in large saucer shapes.

"Voilà, ma maison!" Henri beamed, stretching his arms out wide.

Though she barely knew him, Lena sensed they were very much alike—passionate, ambitious, adventurous, and probably rather stubborn and impatient, too. It's that recognition of sameness, she thought, that attracts people to each other. That's where the intrigue comes from, the sameness, not the differences.

"What about Gilbert's address?" Lena gently prodded.

"Be right back!" Henri dashed into his office, while she made herself comfortable on one of the sofas.

Henri soon returned with a sheepish expression. "No luck. Sorry, but I wanted to be sure."

Once again, Lena's spirits sagged, though she should have expected as much given her recent hurdles. "Thanks anyway," she said glumly. She walked over to admire an ivory and silver espresso service on a glass cart, the unusual oviform vessels signed G. Jensen.

"I like to surround myself with beautiful things." Henri took her in his arms, instantly melting her disappointment. "There's a certain romance to objects, running your hand along their surfaces, holding them. It's the same with architecture. That's why people come to cities like Paris. They like to touch old structures and monuments, let history seep through them. Gives them a sense of place in the world."

"I can see that." Lena gracefully broke away and peeked through the drapes of the living room window overlooking the Luxembourg Gardens. She imagined Henri walking up behind her, unbuttoning her blouse and touching her breasts. She would then slowly draw the drapes, arching her back to the feel of Henri's hands on her from behind.

"Have to get back to work now." Henri slung his blazer over his shoulder. "But first let me show you . . ." He led her into a long, narrow gallery with a large skylight and pale violet walls hung with old masters, specifically seventeenth-century vanity paintings. There were still lives and portraits by Jan Davidsz. de Heem, Pieter Claesz, Francisco de Zubarán, and others. Seashells, lemon peels, fluted glasses, classical busts, candles, mirrors, strands of pearls, and human skulls cluttered the canvases, suggesting the ultimate futility of all human endeavors.

"Vanity of vanities; all is vanity!" Henri exclaimed. "I don't know who said that, but it stayed with me."

"Savonarola, the Dominican preacher who ridiculed the vanities of Renaissance Florence." Lena had a talent for remembering trivia, and it served her well in her work.

"I'm impressed."

Walking up closer to survey the paintings, she suddenly slipped on the parquet floor. Henri rushed to catch her, and they both began laughing. She tingled all over as they kissed spontaneously. Afterward, she felt a touch of remorse, remembering her first kiss with Jud. But it had not been as passionate. Then the challenges of her work resurfaced, and she grew anxious. Between Henri and Giovanna, Lena felt her life beginning to change irrevocably.

That night, she had a dream in which she was reading a book illustrated with pages of brilliantly colored butterflies and inscribed with the words "Document Everything" in huge letters. Upon waking, she carefully recorded the dream along with the unsettling waking visions she kept having about Giovanna. Although she realized such personal information would not be appropriate for her article, it seemed extremely important nevertheless. Two weeks had already passed, and time felt elastic. It was as if she were on a high-speed train headed to an unknown destination, unable or unwilling to get off. One thing was certain; there was no time to waste. Max's recent phone message only turned up the heat:

"Lena, what's going on over there?! I just heard *Advance* is onto this story, too. And you know how I detest being scooped by a competitor. Get back to me soon with some news!"

Lena left messages for Steinert and the Baron, and again for the heiress Madame de Trouville, whom she had glimpsed at the auction and who was proving to be particularly elusive. She was eager to question Steinert further about the painting's authenticity and wondered whether he had already left for New York. The other old masters dealers and curators whom she had already contacted refused to comment while Interpol was conducting its own investigation, which frustrated her immensely. She was blocked again when she called the Interpol headquarters in Lyon, France, and was told that it was too early to share information with the press.

Strained by the mounting pressure and in need of reassurance, she called Hannah.

"Hi, Hannah, great to hear your voice. Yes, I'm okay. Only things are getting confusing."

"What do you mean?"

"I can't seem to make any progress with the article, and yet it feels like Giovanna—the woman in the painting—is with me all the time. I know it sounds crazy, but there's something so familiar about her. Like I've known her all along. I keep seeing and hearing her."

There was a brief silence. "How strange," Hannah said.

"Maybe it's the stress of my deadline and being so far away. Have I gone off the deep end? I'm worried."

"Don't worry, you *will* get this story, and it *will* be great. And about this Giovanna. Your imagination is one of your greatest gifts. But sometimes it takes over and throws you off track. Just a little reminder. I know you'll be fine; you're always fine."

"Thanks. How are you? Has Max called?"

"Haven't heard from him. I'm training for my next marathon, delivering lots of babies, the usual."

"I'll remind him, then."

"Leeeeeena."

"Just leave it to me.

"Okay," Hannah acquiesced. "Have to see a patient, now. Love you."

Cheered by her brief talk with Hannah, Lena sent Max an email:

Working around the clock, trying to nail down interviews. As you know, I'm committed to uncovering the truth about the painting. Will keep you posted. Don't forget to call my friend Hannah. I think you two would really hit it off. L.

One morning, while sorting through pages of research in her apartment, Lena came across the flyer from the young painter at the Louvre advertising the book event at Shakespeare and

Company, which was taking place that very afternoon. Needing a break from her work, she arrived just in time and found a seat in the front row on the second floor of the cramped bookstore, a Left Bank literary landmark across the river from Notre Dame Cathedral. The small room, with its narrow aisles of dusty, bulging shelves, was filled to capacity. The featured author, Bill Bradley, a boyish-looking, Harvard-educated psychiatrist, presented his recent book *Many Lives, Many Miracles*. Personable and soft-spoken, he described regression therapy—a practice that connects people with their past-life experiences to help them become more fulfilled—and read from the interviews he had conducted with patients.

"During her regression, Catherine said: 'I see the army surrounding the castle. My sister and I are watching the others in our community march down the mountain. We can hear their screams. They are being stabbed and tortured. I grab her hand, and we run for our lives down a rocky pathway. I keep turning around, thinking someone is always behind me, ready to kill me.'"

"In her current lifetime, Catherine has a lot of fear," Bradley continued. "She often feels she is being followed. When she retrieved this past-life memory her fears diminished."

Lena listened intently. Though skeptical of Bradley's work, she could not help thinking about her connection to Giovanna and her haunting visions of her life. When Bradley finished and said he would be happy to answer questions from the audience, Lena was the first to respond.

"How do we know for sure that past lives really exist?"

"Well, I have just given testimonies from eight different patients, and there are many more in the book."

"But we all have imaginations, some more active than others." Lena enjoyed challenging him. She had been one of the top members of her high-school debate team. "You haven't shown any scientific proof, and you *are* a medical doctor." She smiled politely so as not to appear too confrontational.

"Imagination is more important than knowledge, Einstein said." Bradley exuded an air of confidence that might have deterred someone less strong-willed than Lena.

"I agree that imagination is important, but there is a fine line between imagination and delusion," Lena said.

"Yeah, she's right!" A young man called out.

The French woman seated beside Lena turned to her with a frown. "But what about the profound healings these patients had?!"

"And what about placebo experiments where sick patients have healed themselves with the power of their thoughts?" she countered.

"I would like to point out that I'm not the first person to conduct research in this field," said Bradley, attempting to tone down the heated discussion. "I'm not trying to convert anyone. I'm merely presenting new possibilities."

Deciding that she had grilled the doctor enough, Lena remained silent as he fielded other questions. She admired his passion for his work. After the talk, she introduced herself.

"I didn't mean to put you on the spot. It's my nature to ask a lot of questions. I'm a journalist."

"Obviously a very intelligent one," he said with a good-natured laugh. "Don't worry, I expect to be challenged. This kind of thing is far-fetched for most people." He lifted a book from a stack on the table and autographed it. "Take this as a gift from me. I'd be curious to hear what you think."

"Thank you, Dr. Bradley, how kind of you." Lena accepted the book graciously. "Though I have to admit I'm still skeptical."

"And here's my card, in case you ever want to write an article." He hesitated, as though he had been too bold in his assumption. "Well, you never know."

Lena read the card with surprise. "You have offices in both Paris and New York, where I'm from."

"The two best cities in the world!" He thanked her for coming as someone else vied for his autograph and attention.

Just then, the French woman who had challenged Lena during the question-and-answer session approached her.

"You think you know everything, but you don't!" She scurried downstairs before Lena could respond.

The comment stung, for Lena could not bear deliberate unkindness. Feeling rather depleted, she walked home along Boulevard Saint-Michel, back behind the Panthéon and down the lively, pedestrian Rue Mouffetard, lined with quaint restaurants, cafés, crêperies, and numerous market stands of fresh produce, fish, meats, and cheeses. She enjoyed being swept up in the flow of activity, enticed by the aroma of freshly baked bread from the patisseries and the upbeat bohemian mood. But she could not stop thinking about Giovanna and Bill Bradley's research. She sat down on a curb near the Place de la Contrescarpe and began reading his book.

"Many of my clients were able to heal past-life traumas by reconnecting with those lives through regression therapy," Bradley wrote. "Traumas ranged from physical incidents, such as drowning, suffocation, torture, and being burned at the stake to emotional issues like betrayal, abandonment, grief, and feelings of lack and limitation. Clients were also able to reconnect to positive aspects of past lives so that they were able to experience and embody those thoughts and feelings again."

Lena wondered what would happen if she had a regression. Would it be effective? What part of herself might she heal? She didn't know what to make of it all.

"Mademoiselle!" a loud voice broke her concentration.

She looked up from her book. It was an eager vendor waving her over to his stand, reminding her that she was hungry and needed groceries. She selected a plump eggplant, a bunch of carrots, three heads of broccoli, and a few apples, which he quickly bagged, weighed, and priced.

"Wait!" She reached for a ripe green pear, searching for an extra coin in her purse. "I'll take this, too."

"Très belle!" The brawny vendor smiled appreciatively, refusing payment for the pear. "Un cadeau pour vous, mademoiselle!" Noticeably struck by Lena, he kissed the tips of his fingers as she bit ravenously into the pear.

Lena considered how she had been showered with gifts on this particular day and took that as a good omen. Approaching Les Gobelins métro station, she noticed a decal on a car window. It was an intriguing symbol of interlocking circles forming what looked like numerous small flowers joined together in a large hexagonal shape, something she had never seen before. She wondered what it might mean. Back home, she reviewed her notes and called Steinert again at his hotel room, ignoring Henri's warning about his criminal past. Fortunately, he agreed to meet her at the Louvre to discuss the Ghirlandaio.

Late the following afternoon, Lena watched with great curiosity as Steinert closely inspected Giovanna's portrait, extending and retracting a large magnifying glass in slow, discreet motions.

"Excellent condition," he said. "And painted with such delicacy. One of the finest surviving examples of the female portrait."

Lena scrutinized the painting. "Is that a prayer book on the shelf?"

"Yes, a Book of Hours is a prayer book that was read every day during the hours devoted to prayer and meditation," Steinert explained. "In Quattrocento Florence, most Books of Hours were richly illustrated to manifest their owners' spirituality. Religious iconography was important in the life of Florentine merchants. The chambers of their mansions contained religious artworks that expressed the family's piousness while invoking protection for the family."

"I can almost feel Giovanna's goodness." Lena instinctively folded her hands at her heart.

"Who told you this was a fake?" Steinert asked, lowering his voice.

"Henri. He advised Baron von Heisendorf to sell it."

Steinert brushed off her comment with a wave of his hand. "I've been in this business a hell of a lot longer than Lemien, and I don't see any evidence that it's a fake. It's the same painting we spoke about in New York, the one I sold to von Heisendorf seven years ago. Do you think I'd jeopardize my reputation?"

"So, who am I supposed to believe?" Lena's pulse raced. She quickly reviewed the known details of the painting's provenance. It had gone from Steinert to the Baron and then to the collector Jonathan Fisher Gilbert. What had happened to it between Gilbert's possession and its recent consignment at auction by the French heiress Madame Genevieve de Trouville, whom she had yet to interview, was still a mystery. Was Steinert, the Baron, or Gilbert— or all three of them—involved in the alleged theft?

"Believe me," Steinert grumbled. "Case closed. Now, would you like to join me for some hot chocolate at Angelina's just down the Rue de Rivoli? Best you'll ever find, more like hot fudge."

Lena was so nervous and annoyed—not knowing whether to trust Steinert or Henri—that she inadvertently agreed. The old-world café hummed with high-pitched conversations and the clink of spoons against porcelain. They made their way through a large group of American tourists huddled around the pastry case to a small round table. On it someone had left a copy of the daily newspaper *Libération*, where Lena had first read about the scandal she was now investigating. The low-hanging smoke made her eyes tear. Steinert offered his handkerchief. His fingers were long and smooth as candle wax. The whole little man seemed to Lena to be coated with a fragile waxen glaze capable of melting at any moment.

Steinert was right about the hot chocolate, and Lena savored every thick, velvety drop. He did most of the talking, telling her how he had started out as a painter on Manhattan's Lower East Side, how he had known Mark Rothko and Robert Motherwell, describing his early days as an art dealer. His eyes, like those of a frightened raccoon, darted swiftly about the café as he spoke. Lena wasn't sure yet how much she liked him. But since he had so far been useful to her, she was careful to nurture their relationship. She rubbed her throbbing temples. Her reflection in the café window revealed a brief, closed-lip smile and distant eyes.

"I've been meaning to ask you," she said cautiously. "There have been some rumors . . . that you smuggled a Sorolla out of Mexico. Is that true? Please, I have to know I can trust you."

"I assure you it was a set-up." He scowled, biting into a flaky brioche. "Some lousy jealous dealer wanted my business there. I was and still am completely innocent." He pounded his fist on the table with long-buried rage.

"I'm sorry that happened to you." Though she couldn't be sure, Lena felt he was telling the truth.

The compassion in her voice instantly relaxed him, and he gazed at her almost longingly for some moments. She nervously looked away, finishing her hot chocolate.

"Excuse me. It's just that you remind me so much of my daughter. The way she used to be. That determined look, so vibrant and full of hope. There's a fire inside you. And it makes me . . . well, it cheers me up."

"Where's your daughter now?"

"England. Don't see her much. She never forgave me for divorcing her mother," he paused, slightly embarrassed. "You don't need to hear all this."

"I don't mind at all."

"Heavens." Steinert tapped his watch, "I have an appointment with a collector on Rue Saint-Honoré. What do you say we stay in touch? If you have any more questions, you know where to reach me in New York." He paid the cashier, and they proceeded toward the métro at Place de la Concorde.

"But you can start again . . . with your daughter. Someone just has to make the first move." Lena searched for words to comfort him.

"I'm afraid it's too late. Funny how something seems so much more beautiful once you've lost it."

Lena's thoughts drifted to Jud, his goodness, his loyalty and depth. She could not deny that she missed him and felt a pang of sadness, even regret. Steinert's confession softened his sharp edges, and Lena appreciated his vulnerability.

"Listen, I know someone at Interpol who could be helpful to you." He reached into his pocket and pressed a crinkled piece of paper into her palm. Scrawled on it was the name and phone number of one Mssr. Crespin.

"Thank you very much." Lena hesitated. "Oh, and I forgot to ask. The other day, when I saw you on the street. You and Henri were not exactly pleased to see each other."

Steinert's expression dimmed. "I have reason to believe that one of Lemien's friends was behind the set-up I mentioned. I've seen them together at La Rotonde café. I would be careful."

He shook her hand goodbye, then headed toward Rue Saint-Honoré. Lena stood motionless, shaken by his accusation. With some difficulty, she scrawled a few notes with her Montblanc pen; her hand was trembling. Then she called the Baron again on her cell, leaving another message for him. Descending into the Concorde métro station, she took one last look at the Eiffel Tower, poking its sleek, iron tip into the clouds, and she tried to calm down. It was much too early to make any assumptions.

Chapter Ten

Leaning back against a cold stone wall underneath the Pont Saint-Louis, her legs wrapped around Henri, Lena took him as far as possible inside her, riding him like a wild stallion.

"Do you like that?" he whispered.

Overwhelmed with pleasure, Lena could not respond. This was not how she had anticipated first making love to Henri. They had been out to dinner on Île Saint-Louis and then for a romantic walk along the Seine on this full-moon night, eventually winding up at the base of the bridge. For the first time, she was letting go. She had not been able to surrender to Jud like this. He was more complicated. This was pure lust. And why not indulge herself? She was a free woman again.

As Lena and Henri saw more of each other, Steinert's accusation about Henri's friend felt less threatening. She simply regarded it as a petty vendetta of a bitter, aging man. Henri took her to the finest restaurants in Paris—La Tour d'Argent, Lapérouse, and Maxim's. Sometimes she awoke to find a wrapped box from him on her doorstep—flowers, a bottle of champagne, a book of French poetry, petits fours with pink icing. On several occasions, with a trace of guilt, Lena started writing emails to Jud, but she didn't send them. She felt so drawn to the worldly, thrilling Henri she felt no need to revisit her past or seek out other friends. Even so, she did not allow her new romance to detract from her assignment. Its encroaching deadline, now just a month away, continued to weigh heavily on her. She remembered from previous assignments how long it could take to gather information and conduct interviews at the mercy of other people's schedules. Fortunately, Henri was supportive of her work, as he was extremely busy himself. When he was not at the gallery or appraising local collections, he was traveling to Geneva and London for auctions and meetings with clients.

"I don't understand," she complained one night in bed at Henri's apartment. "The Interpol contact that Steinert gave me won't release any information about the stolen painting. I've called so many times. I thought a personal connection would have helped!"

Henri cradled her in his arms, gently stroking her hair. "Maybe you're being too aggressive. This is France. Feminine charms go a long way, as you know."

Lena pulled away, offended. Up until now, she had not mentioned anything about her meeting with Steinert, but it felt like the right time. "Steinert said your friend set him up."

"That's ridiculous. He'll say anything to vindicate himself. He just can't let it go." The phone suddenly rang in Henri's office, and he jumped out of bed to answer it.

"What?! I don't care. You have the cash. Just do what it takes!" Henri slammed down the phone. Lena could hear everything from the bedroom and wondered what was going on.

He returned, agitated, and began making love to her again, more intensely than ever. Lena focused only on the waves of pleasure cascading through her body as all else faded from her consciousness.

"You're going to wear me out!" he said afterward, fondling her breasts.

"Henri, what was that phone call about earlier?"

"My assistant, Yves," he grumbled. "He's trying to buy a Raphael drawing for me at an auction in Rome. Apparently, the bidding war has heated up. He doesn't have the stomach for it. Should have gone myself."

"I see." Lena felt uneasy about the call, though she couldn't say why. Perhaps because it was the first time she had seen him so angry.

"But I'm much more interested in you right now." He kissed her on the lips, and then down along her neck, as they fell back onto the sheets again in a passionate embrace.

That week Lena completed her telephone interviews with curators at the Metropolitan Museum of Art in New York City, the J. Paul Getty Museum in Los Angeles, and the Uffizi Gallery in Florence, all of whom educated her about Ghirlandaio and other Quattrocento Renaissance painters. Her articles always included fascinating, in-depth art historical information, which her readers had come to appreciate, as evidenced by the letters *Express* received praising her efforts. She had never considered herself a mere reporter. The biggest coup was finally getting through to Madame de Trouville, who reluctantly agreed to meet her upon returning from a trip, with the hope that Lena would "once and for all stop calling her." Her brusque, superior tone already set the stage for what Lena knew would be a challenging interview.

Satisfied that she was making progress with her work, Lena nevertheless felt unexplainably on edge as she and Henri walked hand-in-hand along the chic Rue du Faubourg Saint-Honoré to a weekend cocktail reception at the American Ambassador's residence. They had been invited to a special black-tie fundraising event for the American Center in Paris. Henri was in his tuxedo, and Lena was in a sleek red-beaded dress.

But for the sharp wind rustling the lindens with a metallic, wintry smell, it was an unusually mild evening for December. They arrived at the elegant eighteenth-century mansion to find the garrulous ambassador from Texas greeting each guest at the end of a long entrance hallway. His wife stood silently at his side, with her frosted blonde bouffant. The mansion was like a Chinese toy—boxes within boxes. One massive room opened into another, but they all looked the same. Dark Savonnerie tapestries hung from ceiling to floor. Marble-topped consoles with elaborate bronze work held Ming porcelain vases, while pyramid-shaped crystal chandeliers cast a saffron glow on the ambassador's meandering guests. The banquet room was framed with heavy powder-blue curtains and ornate Louis XV gilt-paneled walls.

Several young waiters wove through the crowd, refilling champagne flutes. On the long hors d'oeuvres table, surrounding an ice sculpture of the Statue of Liberty, were tiny cucumber and salmon sandwiches, apricot and quince tarts, silver tureens of caviar, trays of foie gras garnished with endive, and an assortment of cheeses and fruits. Henri dipped a toast point into the caviar and held it up to Lena's mouth. He waved to a group of people, informing Lena that the short man with the ponytail and black sunglasses was the well-known contemporary art dealer Yves Sanson. The younger women with him were two of his artists, whose names Henri couldn't remember.

"That ponytail is just a prop," Henri said derisively. "Gets him lots of television interviews." He led Lena through the rooms, introducing her to friends and colleagues, who made quite a fuss over her. Despite her underlying anxiety, she was her typical ebullient self, conversing and laughing with ease, even inserting a few French phrases when she felt comfortable. And she enjoyed all the attention.

"Well, well. Look who's here!" Henri and Lena turned to find Baron von Heisendorf walking toward them, his arm securely clenched around the waist of a beautiful young woman.

"Baron." Henri shook his hand, and Lena forced a smile. She was still annoyed that he hadn't returned her phone calls.

"May I introduce my lovely friend Blondine." The Baron winked at Henri as he pecked Blondine on the cheek.

Blondine blushed, brushing a strand of shiny black hair away from her heavily made-up face. She was slender and fit, with sparkling blue eyes and perfectly manicured long fingernails. Lena suspected she spent a good part of each day tending to her beauty needs, though she could not have been more than twenty-five or so.

"Enchantée," Henri and Lena said in unison.

"I believe I saw you at the Louvre the other day, Miss Lena, with that hateful old bastard." The Baron glared at her through his monocle.

"You mean Marv Steinert?" Lena replied, disturbed by the Baron's remark.

"If you prefer to mention his name, yes."

"Mr. Steinert is a very kind man. What do you have against him?"

"He's a cheap good-for-nothing!" The Baron shoved a quince tart into his mouth, unaware he had showered himself with crumbs.

"Oh, Ducky, you should try to be a little more considerate." Blondine caressed the Baron's arm. "Now, why don't we get you a bit of that foie gras, too."

"Baron, I've been trying to reach you," Lena said.

"Yes, well, I have been . . ." The Baron became distracted and lifted his champagne flute toward a guest across the room. "Why there's my collector friend Charlie, haven't seen him in years! If you'll excuse me." He bowed politely and scurried away. Blondine followed him, waving goodbye to Lena and Henri.

"What is it about Steinert anyway?" Lena mused out loud.

"He owes von Heisendorf money," Henri said. "I sold one of the Baron's old masters to Steinert two years ago, and he never paid his last installment."

Lena made a few notations in her notebook and slipped it back into her purse. She wondered if there was something other than the money that the Baron had against Steinert.

"One minute, I'll be right back." Henri left her at the hors d'oeuvres table to join two couples at the doorway. Lena recognized their faces from the auction at Drouot. Henri helped the women slip out of their coats and called over one of the champagne boys.

Clients, Lena thought, noting his eagerness to please. She couldn't remember ever seeing Henri really angry, except for the phone call he had received that night in his apartment. It was as if his darker emotions were only revealed occasionally. For the first time, she had the unsettling impression that perhaps he was not the man she thought he was. And she wondered why he had been traveling so excessively on business recently. But she realized she was racing ahead of herself. She was still getting to know him.

As Lena scanned the banquet room, she felt oddly dissociated from it. She didn't really belong here. No one, not even Henri, really knew her. Just then, the ambassador instructed his guests to move into an adjoining room for Christmas carols by the Yale Gospel Choir. The carols—"Silent Night," "Deck the Halls"—made Lena happy, like she belonged again. She glanced at the other seated guests to affirm her upbeat mood. But they were all so serious. She was the only one smiling at the singers. Henri looked like he was a thousand miles away, arms folded at his chest. She suspected it was because of the clients he had spoken to earlier. He obviously hadn't made a sale.

The choir was just beginning its second refrain of "The First Noel" when loud voices broke out in the banquet room. A few heads turned, but the singers continued, undaunted. Then the other voices grew louder until the song was barely audible. Some visitors started moving into the banquet room, and others followed in small waves. Lena cut through the crowd to find that the shouts were coming from the Baron and Marv Steinert, poised like a bull and a fragile toreador at the center of the room. Steinert, who was still wearing his overcoat, had obviously just arrived. Lena thought he'd left for New York days ago.

"I want it now!" the Baron yelled.

"Don't have it yet, I said!" Steinert shouted back.

"Damn you. You've owed me for two years!"

"You old buffoon. You don't need it. You have enough money to wallpaper every room in this place!"

The Baron lifted his pant leg and reached for a gun that was strapped to his ankle. Within seconds, Henri pushed his way through the crowd and, grabbing the Baron's wrist, deflected the shot upward into one of the massive chandeliers. There were shrill screams as shards of crystal rained down. The Baron gasped for breath and collapsed on the floor. Blondine fell down beside him, sobbing. Distressed and not knowing what to do, Lena wiped the Baron's brow with a stray napkin, as the ambassador nervously called for an ambulance. Another man and two women lay bleeding from the shattered chandeliers. Lena rushed over to comfort one of the women who was crying. Trays of food were overturned. Bits and pieces of tarts and caviar were scattered about the floor. The torch had been spliced off the Statue of Liberty ice sculpture, now melting into an indefinable blob. Lena watched as the waiters swept the shards of glass into several piles.

"Has the Baron been ill?" Lena asked Blondine.

"He's old, what do you expect," she muttered through tears.

Wanting to be of further assistance, Lena instinctively began searching the Baron's jacket for medical information, anything, that might revive him, while Henri ushered the remaining panic-stricken guests out of the mansion. She retrieved a folded piece of paper from one of the Baron's pockets. It was a list of auction prices next to names of paintings by Ghirlandaio.

Tucked inside of it was a photograph of Giovanna Tornabuoni, whose albescent face shone like a pearl. Lena glanced around, wondering whether anyone had seen her and her discovery. Suspecting foul play, she placed the list and photo back in the Baron's pocket and anxiously scribbled some notes.

Blondine was too shell-shocked to notice anything. When the paramedics finally arrived to treat the Baron and the others, Lena walked briskly to the grand foyer to look for Henri, who stood talking heatedly to Steinert at the massive mahogany doors as the last of the guests departed.

"Henri!" She called, running to him.

"Gotta go! Business emergency! I'll call you."

"Wait!" Lena shouted.

He blew her a kiss and disappeared into the darkness with Steinert.

Lena was furious. Why would he leave so abruptly? Still shaken, she approached the ambassador and his wife, who, despite the chaos, were trying to stay calm.

"I'm so sorry about all this," she said.

"So are we," the ambassador replied stiffly. His wife offered a nervous smile.

"I'm a journalist investigating the alleged stolen *Portrait of Giovanna Tornabuoni* hanging at the Louvre," Lena continued. "Here's my business card. Please let me know if you hear anything about it."

"Yes, of course." The ambassador politely accepted the card and shook her hand. "Thank you for coming."

Lena pulled her cape close around her neck as she crossed the stone courtyard outside. Her breath made smoke trails in the icy air. At the rear end of the courtyard near an iron gate, one of the ambassador's attendants had built a bonfire. The crashing chandelier had toppled the Christmas tree in the banquet room and severed some of its branches. The attendant threw one pine branch after another into the fire, each time causing an explosive blast of flames. Lena stopped to watch the burning heap, nauseated by the charred pine scent.

When she arrived back at her apartment, there was a message from Henri on the answering machine:

"Sorry to have left, but Steinert was desperate and needed my help. I have to go to Geneva again to appraise an estate collection. I'll call you soon."

Lena was still fuming. Given Henri's and Steinert's apparent dislike for each other, this didn't add up. Why so many business trips? Then again, she was guilty of the same workaholic tendencies, as Jud had pointed out many times. Even if it was just lust, was Henri really the right partner for her? He would have some explaining to do. She listened to another phone message, relieved to hear Hannah's voice.

"Hi, Lena, it's me. I don't know how to tell you this or even *if* I should be telling you this, but I would feel terrible hiding something from you. Okay, Jud is seeing someone else. I saw them walking together in Central Park, holding hands. I'm sorry if this causes you pain. I thought you should know. Call me if you want to talk. Love you."

Though she knew her relationship with Jud was over, Lena was surprised and hurt by this news. Then again, she was sleeping with Henri. Why was she jealous? Did she really still love Jud? The full import of her leaving him weighed heavily now. Jud's love for her had been the one constant in her life. And now it was gone for good. Frustrated and uncertain of how to proceed, she sat down at her computer, glancing now and then at the postcard of Giovanna lying on her desk. The faraway expression in the young woman's eyes filled her with an inexplicable sadness. Too exhausted to call Hannah back, she sent her an email.

Hannah, you were right to tell me. Hard to take, even though I've met someone myself. Don't be mad I didn't tell you sooner, wanted to be sure about him. Henri is French, fun, and handsome. I don't care if you tell Jud. It's obviously over between us. Wish you were here. Love, L.

The following morning, the telephone rang.

"Lena, any news?!" demanded Max. "I can feel *Advance* breathing down our necks. And, now, I've had to lay off staff." His voice was strained.

"Don't worry, Max, we'll get the exclusive," she reassured him, brushing the sleep from her eyes. "I have some leads and will soon be interviewing Madame de Trouville, the heiress who cashed in on the painting. Sorry about the layoffs. I know how much we need this story. You can count on me."

"Hope so," he said flatly and hung up.

Lena spent the rest of the day on edge, trying to uncover more information about the Baron and Steinert online. But she did not turn up anything useful to her investigation. That evening, still disturbed by Jud's new girlfriend, the events at the ambassador's party, and the mounting pressure of her assignment, in need of an escape, she attended a concert at Notre Dame Cathedral. The breathtaking ambience, infused with incense and lit with numerous flickering votive candles, instantly soothed her nerves. She took a seat in one of the front row chairs, close to where the string quartet had assembled, and waited eagerly for the concert to begin as people continued to file into the cathedral.

The beautiful stained-glass windows depicting garlands of roses captured her attention. Lena had read about the rose windows and their reference to Mary Magdalene and Divine Mother, Our Lady, after whom Notre Dame was named. She saw them also as a symbol of the divine feminine aspect of every woman. She closed her eyes, lifted her hands to her heart, and spontaneously began reciting "The Hail Mary" prayer. Though she had prayed as a child at the Catholic orphanage, she had long distanced herself from that religion, which had felt much too confining. How odd that this prayer would now resurface.

The room hushed, and the musicians began playing a score that sounded strangely familiar to Lena, even though she was not versed in classical music. She read the program; it was a composition by Joaquin Desprez, c. 1445–1521, from the Renaissance period. So moving were the notes that Lena felt an overwhelming surge of emotion and burst into tears. She could not bear to stay. As quietly as she could, she rose from her seat and tiptoed to the exit.

"Are you all right?" asked a kindly priest.

"Thank you, Father, I'm okay," her voice quivered. "I don't know why, but this music has made me extremely sad."

Outside, a sliver of new moon was barely visible through the charcoal clouds. Gone were the masses of tourists. Turning toward the river, Lena noticed two figures hurrying away from the church. It was Steinert! He was with someone who looked familiar. Was that the elusive man she'd felt observing her in the library stacks the other day? She dared not call after Steinert. Instead, she watched suspiciously as the two men headed toward the Pont Saint-Michel, enveloped by mist. Suddenly, a startling image of a great fire appeared to her, much like the pyre she had seen in the Ambassador's courtyard, only larger and more fierce and destructive.

Unsteady and short of breath, she took off in the opposite direction. She stopped behind the church and grabbed onto a tree for support. So many thoughts cluttered her mind she could barely make sense of them. Again, it felt like she was watching a film she had already seen. Her body was limp and weak. She had never felt so depleted. When she arrived back home, she undressed and climbed right into bed. Though her body wanted to sleep, she lay awake, her mind still racing. Who was that man with Steinert? What to make of her unexpected outburst at the church, her unnerving connection to Giovanna? She lifted a book from her nightstand about Renaissance Florence and began reading:

> Lorenzo de' Medici surrounded himself with the greatest minds of his time, often holding salons at his extravagant palazzo. He commissioned so many artistic masterpieces that Florence rose to become the cultural epicenter of Europe . . .

Within minutes, Lena dropped the book. It was as if she had plugged into some sort of universal hard drive that nearly blew her circuits.

Chapter Eleven

Giovanna sat silently in one of the rear pews at Santa Maria Novella church, her head bowed in prayer. She had stopped here briefly on her way to Medici's evening salon, where many of Florence's great artists, writers, and thinkers gathered to share inspiration and lively conversation. The Tornabuonis were frequent guests, for Medici valued their cultural sophistication and especially admired Giovanna's metaphysical wisdom. Lorenzo happened to be working late, so Giovanna decided to attend on her own. She enjoyed the camaraderie and heightened energies of the salons, and, in the interest of her Platonic Academy, thought it important to stay informed about the city's cultural affairs.

Only this evening, she was not her usual ebullient self. Ever since Lorenzo's birthday celebration, she could not erase the thought that Medici was in danger, even though her brother, Salvatore, had dismissed the prisoner's accusation that her family was again plotting to murder him. All she could do was pray that Medici be kept safe and protected and that her brothers steer clear of any wrongdoing. "Lord Jesus Christ, have mercy on them," she repeated under her breath. She was not typically given to worries and anxieties, preferring to dwell as much as possible in the present moment, wherein she felt most peaceful. Through constant daily prayer and meditation, she was often able to release unsettling thoughts about the past and future, so that her equanimity was rarely disturbed. And yet, to her dismay, she now found herself besieged with those very thoughts. She often envisioned a bright violet flame surrounding her and blazing up through her entire body, burning away all discordant energies. She did this again now, as she continued praying, "Lord Jesus Christ, have mercy on me." When she felt she had finally dissolved this unwelcome inner turmoil, she smiled peacefully and left the church feeling that all would be well.

Giovanna walked briskly to Medici's palazzo on Piazza San Lorenzo, carrying a fruit cake packed in a marbled-painted gift box and anticipating the theme of this evening's conversation, typically chosen by Medici to stir a lively debate. She delighted in the bustling early evening activity of the streets, the townspeople gathering at the open food market on the piazza and all the horses and carriages traversing the cobblestones. Brunelleschi's newly completed red-tiled Duomo hovered over the city with watchful majesty. And there was the Bargello tower, where she had been reading to the prisoners again just days ago. Antonio had been unusually silent and had not revealed anything more about the alleged conspiracy against Lorenzo de' Medici. She noticed a tall, elegant man hurriedly leaving the prison. It was her eldest brother, Stefano, from whom she had been estranged since her marriage. He had not forgiven her for marrying into the rival Medici clan. Giovanna stiffened. What was he doing there? Was he involved in the plot to kill Medici? Her heart raced, and her palms were moist with sweat. She was now more certain that her disquieting premonitions were accurate. Whatever was happening behind the scenes was not of the light, and she felt a grave responsibility to do everything in her power to stop it. But how?

She arrived at the Medici palazzo to find many of the regulars— including Sandro Botticelli, Marsilio Ficino, Andrea del Verrocchio, Leonardo da Vinci, her friend Domenico Ghirlandaio, and the young Michelangelo Buonarroti—drinking wine, laughing, and engaging in passionate conversations around Medici's dining room table, at the head of which he sat like a satisfied prince surveying his kingdom. Silver trays bearing a variety of cheeses and breads, garnished with pears and grapes, were passed among the guests, illuminated by the glow from wall torches. On the dining cloth, printed in gold was a large symbol of multiple overlapping circles arranged in a flower-like pattern forming a hexagon. Giovanna was familiar with the ancient sacred geometry of the Flower of Life, said to hold the secrets of the universe. She felt instantly enlivened by the heady ambience, pulsing with fresh, new ideas and perspectives on classical antiquity and humanist theory in the spirit of secular freedom that Medici had intentionally cultivated.

"It is the individual in his divinity *and* humanity who will change the world," the philosopher Marsilio Ficino pronounced. "We are not powerless as the church might have us think." Slight of build with delicate, almost feminine features, he raised his fist in the air.

"Our forebears the Greeks have much to teach us . . ." the imposing, long-bearded Leonardo da Vinci chimed in.

Medici looked typically fashionable in his high-collared gold and red embroidered tunic, as he listened with great interest to his talented friends, injecting his own scholarly opinions into the mix. His charismatic nature drew many to him, particularly the artists he patronized with generous commissions for both public works and his own residences in the city and countryside.

"My dear Giovanna, thank you for coming." He rose to his feet and greeted her warmly, gratefully accepting her gift cake. "We always benefit from your transcendent presence! Where's my devoted cousin Tornabuoni tonight?"

"He's working late. I did not want to miss out." She was still unnerved by her brother's unexpected appearance moments earlier. "Lorenzo," she whispered, leaning closer. "I assume you are taking precautions, having received my note."

"Yes, yes, of course," he reassured her. "All is well. I am protected by many loyal workers and townsmen who remember my favors. Please don't worry. You have more important things to concern yourself with." He grasped her hand, nodding at her distended belly with a broad smile.

Giovanna thought it best not to mention her brother Stefano visiting the prison, as she did not want to further implicate her family on an assumption alone.

"Okay, but please be careful, Lorenzo."

He winked at her, then raised his hand to make an announcement, whereupon the banter subsided. "My friends, I have something special to share with you tonight!"

Medici walked across the room to a large easel bearing a draped canvas. He flung away the sheet with dramatic flourish to reveal a shimmering new painting.

"Behold the magnificent *Birth of Venus*, my latest commission from our talented friend here!" He extended his arm toward the handsome, young Botticelli, who stood beside him. "It will now grace my home."

Gasps were heard as everyone crowded around the painting of the sensual goddess Venus rising in naked exuberance on a clam shell from a primordial sea. There was a hushed silence until da Vinci, possessed of child-like wonder, was moved to speak.

"Such a daring celebration of erotic desire has, to my knowledge, never been expressed in art, let alone with such unapologetic bravado," he declared. "The nude as Spirit ascending. Bravo, Botticelli! Bravo!"

The others joined in with rousing congratulations, which the young painter humbly and gratefully received, beaming at his proud patron and friend Lorenzo de' Medici.

The painting held special meaning for Giovanna, who was captivated by its raw physical beauty. She could identify with the fecundity of life that it celebrated. For her, the sacred and the sensual were intimately intertwined, and she did not believe in denying one at the expense of the other, though she rarely spoke of this to her equally pious friends and acquaintances.

"Thank you for your willingness to explore the new and the dangerous, Sandro Botticelli." Giovanna spoke up, to the surprise of the others, as she was the only woman present. Women were not encouraged to voice their opinions in public, but Giovanna projected an aura of such strength and self-assurance that her daring assertion was not questioned.

"Excellent!" Medici proclaimed.

"And thank you, Lorenzo, for all you've done for Florence." She addressed him with respect and affection, glancing lovingly at each of those present. "Our culture has exploded from your support of these great artists. We have da Vinci's glittering *Magi*, Michelangelo's exquisite marbles."

"Ghiberti's gold doors!" Botticelli continued.

"Brunelleschi's radical Duomo!" Ghirlandaio added. The others called out more masterpieces.

"This would be the perfect time to begin our debate tonight," Medici announced enthusiastically, as everyone returned to their seats at the table. "Plato said we are each primarily guided and motivated by one of three ideals—the true, the good, or the beautiful. What do you think, my friends?" He regarded his guests with curiosity, while gulping wine from a ruby-encrusted gold goblet.

"That is not so difficult, seeing as though we are mostly artists here," Ghirlandaio pointed out with a hearty laugh. "We were the children in school who were staring out the window at the clouds and flowers and trees, deaf to the teacher's words."

Medici reflected for a moment and shook his head in agreement. "To the beautiful, then! The good and the true shall serve only beauty."

"I disagree," the philosopher Ficino countered. "Truth is paramount, our inner compass."

"I believe the beautiful and the true are in service to the good, which in its highest expression is only love," Giovanna said.

The men observed her with a quiet reverence. "I will not argue with a woman's wisdom," Medici conceded. "Let us toast our dear Giovanna and her three muses—beauty, truth, and love. May they guide us through this divine comedy and tragedy we call life."

Giovanna smiled bashfully, as the men saluted her. "And bring us into harmony with the Absolute," she completed his sentence.

"You exemplify all three, cousin," Medici said, turning to her. "But how do we ever know their full measure until we take action?" The question was clearly rhetorical, and perhaps directed at himself, though Giovanna carefully weighed his words.

"Yes, and we must be willing to suffer the consequences of our ideals." She began to feel unsettled again as regretful, sad thoughts of the longstanding rift between their families resurfaced. Still not convinced that Medici would remain unharmed, she decided to confront her family with her suspicions, at the risk of estranging herself for good.

Later that night in bed, Giovanna awoke abruptly to a loud outburst from her husband, who was thrashing about. She shook him awake, wrapping her arms around him.

"Dear husband, what dream troubles you?" She lit each of the four candles in the tall gilt candelabra at their bedside. In their elongated shadows on the wall, husband and wife were barely distinguishable from each other, as they were both clad in sheer linen dressing gowns.

Lorenzo sat up, disoriented, rubbing his eyes. "I saw my ships being confiscated and my trade license revoked. It was terrible, my love. I lost everything!"

"It is just your own inner shadow making itself known." Giovanna tried to comfort him. "You have inherited the most successful spice trade in Florence. We are well fed and happy, and our new child," she placed her hand on her belly, "will soon be with us. Let us not dwell on fears and shadows."

"There is something I have not yet confided to you, dear Giovanna." Lorenzo paused, his head hanging low.

"What is it?" She grew uneasy.

"I have been receiving letters from the Minchelli enterprise, my competitor. They have accused me of monopolizing the trade routes to the Near East and are threatening to take me to the courts." His voice was strained and barely audible. "I didn't want to burden you."

Shocked by this unexpected news, Giovanna embraced him. "We will defend ourselves as necessary. My faith in you is complete."

"Forgive me." He held her tightly. "Please, forgive me."

"Lorenzo, you are a reflection of the Absolute, whole and innocent." She remained unperturbed, her eyes glistening like still ponds in the candlelight. "All has been forgiven and released. That applies to Minchelli, too."

"Them, too?! No, that cannot be!" Lorenzo fell back with anger.

"How many times do I have to remind you, dear husband. You are Minchelli, Minchelli is you. If we are all One, then there cannot be anyone else out there!" She became frustrated when Lorenzo either denied or did not understand certain metaphysical truths, which were so naturally apparent to her.

"Lorenzo, there is something I must tell you, too." Her face instantly clouded over with anxiety.

He reached for her hand.

"It's about Medici," she hesitated. "One of the prisoners said my family is planning another attempt on his life." A single tear trailed down her cheek.

Lorenzo sat motionless, alarmed by this news. "You should have told me sooner, Giovanna!"

"Salvatore has denied it, yet I have seen Stefano at the prison.

Oh, Lorenzo, my heart is tormented. I no longer know who to believe."

"Rumor or not, we must warn Medici. He was right in his suspicions!"

"I already have." Giovanna was relieved to have shed the burden of her secret. "I didn't want to alienate you further from my family. I'm sorry."

"Dear wife, once and for all, I beg you to stop going to the Bargello!" He collapsed onto his pillow, exhausted. "Perhaps the prisoners themselves are behind this . . . please . . ." His voice trailed off as he drifted to sleep.

Giovanna kissed his forehead and blew out the candles. She slept fitfully the rest of the night. The following morning, after Lorenzo had left for work, she summoned her horseman to take her to her brother Stefano's palazzo on the far side of town. Though she had not visited him in years, she was determined to protect Medici. But no one was at home, so she reluctantly headed back for her appointment with the Strozzi family at her Platonic Academy for Children. This school was a smaller version of the original Platonic Academy founded by Medici's grandfather, Cosimo, at the Villa Careggi just outside Florence. The Strozzi had brought their thirteen-year-old daughter, Regina, whose gentle nature was much like Giovanna's own and with whom she developed an instant rapport. Giovanna did not take long to make a decision, for the child's answers to her questions proved that she had a sufficient knowledge of philosophy, astrology, sacred geometry, and alchemy— the principal subjects taught at the academy. Her mother and father, both from aristocratic families like Giovanna's, were delighted that Regina would be admitted to the next cycle of classes. It was unusual for girls to apply to the academy, which saddened Giovanna, who believed that men and women were intellectual and spiritual equals, even though most would never entertain such a notion.

"Congratulations, Regina," Giovanna said, noting that the girl looked suddenly overwhelmed. "But why do you now appear unhappy?"

"I'm afraid I won't be able to keep up with such a heavy workload." She nervously played with her hair. "I studied very hard for this interview, because they," she glanced meekly at her parents, "pushed me. But I can't do this. I'm sure the other students are far superior." She stood up and turned to leave. Giovanna rushed over to her and led her by the hand back to her seat.

"This is a golden opportunity," she pointed out. "You have simply forgotten who you are."

"I don't understand." Regina's voice wavered with impatience.

"In this school, you will come to know yourself as Divine." Giovanna spoke with authority and great urgency. "Plato believed that our souls dwelt in heaven before descending into our bodies. Those who have come to Earth have been veiled with forgetfulness. The chief task of the soul is to reclaim its divinity. It is a constant striving that keeps us in what Plato called a divine frenzy until our souls fly back to heaven on the wings of moral conduct and wisdom."

Regina was transfixed, unable to respond, while her parents observed Giovanna with reverent curiosity.

"Do you want to drown in forgetfulness, or wake up to a whole new way of being on a whole new Earth? Are we not living in what is now being called the Renaissance, the time of rebirth?"

"I . . ." the girl began to weep. "Yes, I want to remember."

Giovanna gently embraced her. "Together we will stir up a divine frenzy, then!"

Upon leaving, the Strozzi thanked Giovanna profusely for helping their daughter, who now appeared magically re-energized, as though lit up by a thousand candles from within. Uplifted by Regina's enrollment at the academy, Giovanna devoted the rest of the day to domestic obligations—recording expenditures over the past month and ordering new linens, candles, and medicinal tinctures.

She also drew up a list of comestibles that her family would need for the week:

1) Salted codfish
2) Fresh peppers
3) Fresh tomatoes
4) Mushrooms
5) Olive oil
6) Goat cheese
7) Five loaves of bread
8) Three bottles of red wine.

A mild obsession, her lists kept her organized. There were many scattered throughout the pantry, separate notes for separate tasks. It gave her satisfaction to throw the notes away as she completed each task. She preferred to oversee the household operations herself, while entrusting Francesca with the execution.

By nightfall, Lorenzo still had not returned home, which caused Giovanna concern. She paced nervously back and forth in the reception room, occasionally glancing through the shaded arched windows to the street outside, hoping he would soon appear. It was not like him to be so late, two hours to be exact. He had told Giovanna he needed some time alone after work and was going to the Tornabuoni Chapel at Santa Maria Novella church—where his father was encrypted—to clear his mind and pray for his company's good fortune. Giovanna wondered if he had gone to visit Medici at his palazzo.

But she could not ignore the stirrings in her heart that told her otherwise. She had to go out and look for him. After peeking into her private chamber, where Giovannino was sound asleep in Francesca's arms, she put on her long black wool dress coat, which looked more like a robe, and hurried toward the church in the semi-darkness with a burning torch to light her way. There was a cutting chill in the air, and the trees had begun to shed their colorful leaves, announcing the approach of winter. Giovanna had been looking forward to the coming months, when they would move into their country residence further south along the coast in Sorrento. Yet even this prospect did not cheer her. All that was important now was finding Lorenzo.

She passed by Piazza della Signoria, where just days ago the charismatic Dominican monk Girolamo Savonarola had gathered artworks, sumptuous furnishings, books, and other objects he considered decadent trappings of Medician culture and burned them in a huge bonfire. All of Florence was stirred up by this "Bonfire of the Vanities." Against Lorenzo's warnings, Giovanna had slipped out to view the dramatic event, losing herself in the crowd so as not to attract attention. Despite her virtuous nature, she did not support Savonarola or any extreme action that bred destruction. Pieces of charred rubble now lay scattered about the square, filling Giovanna with the same deep sorrow she had felt while watching the massive fire rage.

Suddenly, a loud scream disrupted the relative calm of the city quarter. Giovanna picked up her pace, her heart pounding heavily. As she turned the corner, she noticed two male figures scrambling behind Santa Maria Novella church in the distance, then fleeing in opposite directions. But it was too dark to discern who they were. Panic gripped Giovanna. As she drew nearer, to her great horror, she saw a man lying on the cobblestones in a pool of blood. It was Lorenzo! She dropped to her knees beside him, weeping uncontrollably. He was already gone, having succumbed to three stab wounds in the back. His fears had apparently been justified. Giovanna's perfect world came crashing down in an instant.

"Father! Help!" God help me!" She cried out and fell over Lorenzo's body, whimpering. A small crowd bearing torches gathered around her, but the parish priest was nowhere to be seen.

"The Lord Be with you. Christ Be with you!" One of the townswomen tried unsuccessfully to comfort Giovanna, who could not pull herself away from her beloved.

Chapter Twelve

Lena awoke late the next morning to a wide column of purple light extending along the length of her bed and over her body. How strange. What was that? She recalled the vivid images of Giovanna that had flashed through her mind the night before. Giovanna had been surrounded by that very light. Lena could not remember how long she lay awake or when she had fallen asleep. Maybe she really was dreaming this time. She felt a sudden, piercing sensation in her back, as though someone were stabbing her, and was instantly overcome with grief. Was she feeling Giovanna's grief upon finding her husband murdered? Was she herself in danger? It was all so unnerving. Thoughts of Steinert racing through the darkness with his mysterious companion put her on edge again. Then there was the Baron and his suspicious price list of Ghirlandaio paintings. Perhaps Steinert or the Baron had sent that threatening letter to her in New York. She did not trust either of them.

And where was Henri? She hadn't heard from him since the unsettling night at the Ambassador's reception. Was he still in Geneva? She called and left a message that she needed to speak as soon as possible. The news of Jud and his new girlfriend made her feel even more isolated. She missed him more each day and wished she had never left him. It was difficult to concentrate on her work. There was another email from Max, this time asking her to write an art review. She knew it would distract her from the Ghirlandaio story, which had become overwhelming. She wished she had not come to Paris at all. Max was too trusting of her. What on earth had made her think she could solve this crime? Jud was right; she had been too headstrong and naïve when she accepted the assignment.

At her desk, she began writing Max an email:

I'm coming back to New York. I've made a big mistake.

She felt ashamed as she read the words, and instantly deleted the email. She must stop doubting herself once and for all. She would forever regret running away from such a challenge. She must prevail in her investigation of the stolen *Portrait of Giovanna Tornabuoni*, no matter what the outcome. Having won this battle with herself, she made a list of what to do next:

1) Call the Baron.
2) Call Madame de Trouville.
3) Call Interpol.
4) Visit old master paintings galleries.

She knew the list was not really necessary, as her mind itself was like an impressive filing system, and she rarely forgot work-related details. Nevertheless, her lists made her feel more efficient. Struck with a thought, she searched through her suitcases for the CD Jud had given her months ago. It had instructions on how to meditate and included soothing music that sounded like waves crashing on a beach. For about an hour, she listened to it and practiced meditating for the first time. She tried to calm her mind and focus only on her breath in the present moment, but thoughts of Jud and Henri kept interfering.

Later, she called the Baron for the third time. Blondine finally answered.

"Blondine, please, it's Lena. We met at the Ambassador's reception. How is the Baron?"

"Ducky needs rest and cannot accept calls!" She slammed down the phone.

Despite her frustration with the stubborn young woman, she was desperate to know about the price list she had found in the Baron's jacket, so Lena knew she would prevail. She promptly placed calls to Madame de Trouville and Marv Steinert's contact at Interpol. Unable to reach either of them, she left messages requesting a return call.

The next day after lunch, Lena set out for the art galleries to question more dealers about the stolen painting. Walking purposefully along Rue de Seine, she couldn't resist stopping by Henri's gallery. Was he back in town? Among the treasures inside were a large glass curio of Wiener Werkstätte ceramic bowls in geometric shapes, the elegant desk by Émile-Jacques Ruhlmann that Henri had won at auction, and several pedestals displaying exquisite Art Nouveau vases. Italian, Spanish, French, and Dutch old master paintings hung on the walls, creating an unusual contrast of centuries. Lena's pulse raced, and she held her breath. At the rear of the gallery, slightly hidden by a large lacquer screen, was Henri having an intimate conversation with a tall, blonde woman. Lena strained for a closer look. What a surprise. It was the former owner of the Ghirlandaio painting, Madame de Trouville, whom she had seen at the auction and who had agreed on the phone to be interviewed. Henri looked equally surprised upon seeing Lena and rushed over to greet her, simultaneously trying to shepherd the disgruntled heiress out the door.

"I was just about to call you!"

Stung by Henri's flippant attitude, she ignored him and promptly introduced herself to Madame de Trouville, who sized her up with an air of superiority. Lena did the same. The heiress was striking, though not exactly beautiful, and had a steely, commanding presence. Her hair was pulled back in a large French knot, emphasizing her prominent cheek bones and piercing violet eyes. Lena guessed her to be in her early forties. She cut a sleek profile in her form-fitting black pencil skirt and jacket.

"I hope you're still available for the interview," Lena said in a professional tone.

"I've already agreed, haven't I?" Madame de Trouville replied curtly, sending Henri a sour glance.

Lena was not about to be intimidated. "Can we set a specific date, then?"

"I told you I'd be out of town for a while." She avoided Lena's eyes, as Henri helped her with her fur coat. "I'm leaving for London again tomorrow."

"Yes, but my deadline is closing in. I'll be speaking to an art crimes officer at Interpol soon. It would be a shame not to have your perspective in the story."

"All right, all right, you are quite pushy, mademoiselle!" The heiress reluctantly produced a business card from her purse and gave it to Lena. "I'll be back in eight days. You can stop by my apartment, although I don't understand why we can't do this over the phone."

"In person is always better."

"Then you'll have to keep it short. I'm very busy."

"Thank you." Lena forced a smile, silently pleased with her victory. Madame slid on her leather gloves, nodded at Henri, and marched out of the gallery.

"Au revoir, Geneviève," Henri called after her, turning his attention to Lena. "You look sad today." He scooped her in his arms. "I've never seen you like this."

"C'mon, Henri, don't play games with me." Lena angrily pried herself loose. "Where have you been? I haven't heard from you in days. And given what happened at the fundraiser, I would have thought . . ."

"I had to make a quick trip to London after Geneva for an important client. Almost lost a huge sale. Sorry I didn't call." He reached out to her with a conciliatory smile. "By the way, you look gorgeous today. How about I take you to dinner tonight at Maxim's?"

"No thanks, Henri, I'm busy," she snapped and walked out.

Lena made her way to a number of other Left Bank galleries with renewed determination in search of more clues to the Ghirlandaio painting's shadowy past. Henri would have to wait. She did not confine her interviews to old master paintings experts, however, for she had learned from experience to investigate even the most unlikely sources, which sometimes proved to be unexpectedly helpful. It was not her nature to follow the beaten path. After several hours, drained and discouraged at not having made much progress, she found herself at the last gallery on her list—Découvertes, which specialized in more recent artworks. To Lena's great surprise, the congenial gallery director, Mssr. Renault, happened to know an American friend of the collector Jonathan Fisher Gilbert, to whom the Baron said he'd sold Giovanna's portrait. Henri had failed to get Gilbert's contact information for her, nor had she been able to find it online. The gallery director called Gilbert's friend on the spot and retrieved his phone number and address in the Loire Valley. The friend, who admitted to having minimal contact with the reclusive collector in recent years, further confirmed that his château was located on the outskirts of Blois, an old medieval town on the banks of the Loire River.

Lena took this as a positive sign that she was right not to back out of the assignment. Her keen intuition had served her once again. She could not thank the art dealer enough and promised to write a review on his next exhibition of contemporary art. Buoyed by another victory, she took a long, brisk walk along the Seine to collect her thoughts and enjoy the sunset. She passed by the beautiful Musée d'Orsay, its superb collection of nineteenth- and twentieth-century art housed in a renovated Beaux-Arts train station, and the white-pillared Assemblée Nationale, with the words Liberté, Égalité, Fraternité carved on its frieze. Nearby, on the bricked-up side of an old building was a large mural depicting

Botticelli's *Birth of Venus*—the same painting she had seen in her recent vision of Giovanna and Renaissance Florence. She had studied it in an art history class years ago. What a startling coincidence. Her heart pounded, and her mind felt fuzzy, as though she were losing track of where and who she was. Just across the river was the Quai New York. She struggled to recall her life there, her apartment, her office, her friends. But everything was blurry. She could not even name the streets in her neighborhood. She felt a surge of panic. What was she supposed to forget, and what was she supposed to remember?

As darkness fell and the city lit up, she lingered for a while on the Pont Royal, trying to regain her bearings. Gazing across the river to the Right Bank, where a tourist boat cast its spotlights on the Louvre, she wondered what her journey to the Loire Valley held in store for her and knew only that she had to act quickly. She called Jonathan Fisher Gilbert to set up an appointment.

Unfortunately, no one answered, so she left a brief but urgent message. She began to shiver in the wintry gusts sweeping off the river and dashed to the nearest métro. Lena decided to get off at Boulevard du Montparnasse for a quick meal and a glass of wine at one of the lively cafés. Preferring time to herself, she didn't care that she was not at Maxim's with Henri.

Strolling along the boulevard in search of a cozy spot, she stopped in her tracks at the corner near La Rotonde. Henri and another man were leaving the café together. Catching a glimpse of them through throngs of pedestrians, she thought about what Steinert had told her, how he had seen Henri and the friend who had framed him at this very café. Though she had dismissed the comment, a wave of anxiety now shot through her. She abruptly switched course and rushed back down the steps into the claustrophobic tunnels of the Montparnasse métro station.

The following morning, Lena awoke from a restless sleep to

a loud knock on the door. She slipped on her robe and peered through the peep hole.

"What are you doing here, Henri?!" She greeted him suspiciously.

"Chérie, please accept my apology again for not calling sooner," he pleaded, edging into her apartment. He looked especially handsome with his long wool overcoat and briefcase, his hair still partially wet from showering. "Like I said, I was busy with some business emergencies. I've missed you."

Lena did not have the strength to throw him out. She glanced at herself in the mirror above the sofa. She looked pale and worn out. Her eyes were still heavy with sleep, her dark curls flattened against her head.

"What was I supposed to think? The shooting at the Ambassador's place and then you disappear!"

"Steinert feared for his life and begged me to drive home with him that night."

She sat down at the table, dropping her head into her hands with an impatient sigh. "You two are far from friends. I don't get it, Henri."

"Listen . . ." He lowered his voice as if someone else were listening in. "Steinert said he thinks the Baron knows something about the Ghirlandaio."

"Old news, I figured that out myself." Lena felt increasingly protective of her story and was careful not to reveal too much at this point, not even to Henri. "And what about Madame de Trouville? You never told me you knew her. You were aware I was trying to interview her."

Henri pulled up a chair beside her. "Oh, Geneviève. What a headache, so temperamental! She's upset that I haven't been able to find a painting she wanted. I didn't want that to interfere with your work."

Lena shot him a puzzled look. "And there's something else I'd like to know," she said sternly. "Steinert said you and the guy who set him up meet at La Rotonde café. I saw you there with someone last night!"

"I'm beginning to wonder whose side you're on," Henri complained, wounded. "You know I love you." He gently massaged her shoulders.

"*Love* me, Henri, really?"

"Of course, you *are* my lover," he said defensively. "How about we get together soon, someplace special."

Lena sighed with resignation. "Okay, okay. Call me." She paused to reconsider. Why had she given in so easily? She was lonely for one thing, and she needed a friend. Henri was sexy and available. Pure and simple.

He lit up with an ebullient smile and hugged her. "See you soon!"

Lena shook her head as she closed the door behind him. She spent the rest of the day working on the art review for Max. The extra assignment, which had initially felt like such a burden, was now a welcome relief from the unsettling murkiness that continued to plague the Ghirlandaio story. She berated herself for not being further along by now. After several days had passed without word from Gilbert, she grew desperate and made arrangements to go to the Loire Valley anyway. It would not be the first time that she had shown up on someone's doorstep unannounced.

As the train pulled out of the Gare d'Austerlitz station, she felt so alone, exhausted, and confused. She could not relax. Her old life felt far away, and the train was claustrophobic, packed to the brim with strangers. Wishing for support and a familiar voice, she took out her cell phone and called Hannah.

"Thank goodness you're there. I miss you so much."

"Me, too. Everything okay?"

"Not exactly." Lena drew a deep breath. "Nothing makes sense anymore. There is so much on the line. This Giovanna, she's under my skin. I still see and feel so much about her. Then there's Henri, sexy as hell but so evasive. And I miss Jud, too," she confessed. "Maybe I was wrong about us."

Hannah's voice was comforting as usual. "Just stay focused on your mission. You're always good at that. I know everything will work out."

"Right, I'm not going to let all this get the best of me." Lena perked up a bit. "It would be great to have a drink with you now in SoHo. What's going on?"

"Wish you were here, too. I've been working around the clock, and we're already into a New Year. Nothing much new."

"Okay, call you later. I'm on a train now. Love you."

"Love you, too. Bye."

Lena sank back into her seat, consoled by Hannah's words, and began reading Bill Bradley's book, *Many Lives, Many Miracles*, which continued to intrigue her, despite her skepticism. She underlined a passage that Bradley had written about one of his patients:

> Under hypnotic regression, Jennifer was able to describe her life as Queen Isabella of Spain in great detail—important events, her generosity and good works, even thoughts and feelings. She felt disempowered in her current lifetime, and her reconnection with Isabella helped her to regain faith in herself and her accomplishments.

Was this what she was doing with Giovanna? If so, how might Giovanna help her? It sounded farfetched, and yet she felt undeniably connected to her. After a few minutes, Lena looked up in search of the car with the toilet. A husky, dark-haired man with a pockmarked face in the row opposite was watching her. Frightened, she recognized him as the same man she had seen at the library and then with Steinert that night in front of Notre Dame. Their eyes met, and he suddenly approached her.

"You must stop now, or you will be sorry!" he whispered brusquely.

Lena grabbed her purse and overnight bag and raced through the cars to escape him, finding a seat near the conductor's car. His words reminded her of the letter she had received in New York. Trembling, she believed she was, indeed, in danger. Remembering Jud's CD, she tried meditating, but it was an effort to concentrate on anything until the train stopped at the provincial station in Blois, which looked more like a corner store, still decorated with Christmas lights. Two taxis sat waiting for a fare. Lena quickly slipped into one and gave the driver Gilbert's address, anxiously looking around for the mysterious man from the train. He was nowhere in sight. She remained on edge as they drove through barren vineyards and fields dusted with new-fallen snow and along narrow, cobblestone streets weaving through the town's medieval center, where half-timbered houses leaned precariously against one another. Gilbert's château was about six miles outside of Blois, a center of power during the Renaissance.

When the taxi pulled up at Gilbert's, Lena asked the driver to wait until she confirmed someone was at home. The château's imposing façade, constructed in the Romanesque, Gothic, and Renaissance styles, created the illusion of three separate castles. On one side, there was a grand staircase that zigzagged up five floors, while on the other side a group of wrought-iron porch furniture sat atop the castle's only tower. Fatigued and agitated, Lena knocked furiously on the door. She waited several minutes until an old woman wearing a long white apron poked her head out.

"I'm here for Mr. Gilbert," Lena said, relieved. "I'm a journalist from *Express* in New York." She flashed her business card and turned to wave at the taxi driver. "Can you please come back for me when it gets dark?" she shouted in French. He nodded and drove off.

"He's not here." The old woman was petit and willowy with kind hazel eyes. "Please go away, please, miss."

Lena pushed the door in further. "But I must speak with him today."

"No one's home!"

"You don't seem to understand," Lena pleaded. The uncertainty in the woman's voice led Lena to believe she was lying. She noticed, too, that her hands were trembling. Lena forced her way inside the door as the old woman retreated helplessly into the vestibule.

"I'll just wait here until Mr. Gilbert returns. I have the whole day." Lena smiled pleasantly. Beyond the vestibule, three massive rooms radiated in a semicircle around a spiral staircase padded with a cerulean carpet. Aubusson tapestries depicting bucolic scenes hung from the stone walls. Lena could see from where she was standing that aside from a few old, throne-like armchairs, the rooms were empty. The vast castle made her feel very small, completely irrelevant, on the verge of disappearing without a trace.

"He's upstairs sleeping, miss." The woman finally broke down, nervously wiping her hands in her apron, her eyes averted to the floor. "But I have orders no one is to disturb him."

"I see." Lena was encouraged by this stroke of luck. "Who's orders?"

"Please, miss. He's not well." The old woman began to cry and shake her head from side to side.

"Listen, madame . . ." Lena reached out and gently touched her arm.

"Marie, if you please." She wiped a tear from her cheek with an old lace handkerchief.

"Okay, Marie. I need to know about the painting, the *Portrait of Giovanna Tornabuoni* that's now in the Louvre. Mr. Gilbert once owned it. Perhaps I could go upstairs to see him."

"There used to be many paintings, miss."

Lena hastily scribbled some notes on her steno pad with her Montblanc pen and turned on a small tape recorder for backup.

Marie explained she was Gilbert's housekeeper and had moved

here ten years ago from Germany, where she had learned to speak English.

"Miss Ines never liked me getting in the way," she continued. "So she took care of monsieur, and I took care of the château. Miss Ines, she's the nurse."

"And the paintings?" Lena spoke calmly and slowly so as not to agitate the old woman.

"I'm sorry to be crying, miss, but I'm sad for monsieur. You see . . ." Marie showed Lena to a chair in front of a large fireplace. "He's sick and alone. He did good in the oil business . . . and when he moved here from that big state . . . Texas . . . his family didn't bother with him, except for his nephew. And now . . . he's in a permanent sleep. "

"What do you mean, Marie? Is he in a coma? That's what you call a permanent sleep!"

"I believe that is the word in English."

"And he's now in your care?"

"Yes, a doctor comes from Paris to check on him and feed him through a tube. His nephew pays my wages."

"But I don't understand." Lena surveyed the empty rooms, trying to contain her exasperation with the old woman. "What happened to all his things? He's one of the most important collectors in the world."

"Miss Ines and Mr. Mark had a fight months ago." Marie lifted an iron poker and began turning over the logs in the fireplace. "Mr. Mark, he's monsieur's nephew. I could hear them from the kitchen. But it wasn't my place to get involved."

"And this fight?"

"They took out all the art and antiques, leaving just a few things, as you can see." She swept her arm in an arc. "Mr. Mark loaded up the trucks. Said he was going to donate his uncle's stuff to some museum in Texas. That's when Monsieur Gilbert went into the coma and Miss Giovanna, as you call her, went missing."

Marie pointed to an empty wall imprinted with dusty outlines indicating where several paintings had once hung. "Over there, that's where the painting used to be."

Lena's eyes grew wide as she fumbled to insert a new tape into her recorder. "And what about the nurse, this Ines—she must have a last name—where is she now?"

"Ines Avidon. She has not been back since then."

Lena nervously paced the room. Finally, she felt she was on the verge of an important discovery, the moment she had been waiting for. "And who took Giovanna, Marie?"

"When I heard them arguing, Miss Ines said monsieur had already made up a will. I was peeking through the kitchen door and saw her show Mr. Mark a piece of paper." Marie paused as Lena took notes. She took a deep breath, as if hesitant to betray a confidence, and continued in a wavering voice.

"Miss Ines said monsieur had given some of his paintings to her grandfather, a good friend. Since her grandfather just died, she said those paintings were hers." She closed her eyes and pursed her cracked lips together.

"Oh, no! Do you think Ines Avidon kept the Giovanna portrait?" Lena lifted another notebook out of her purse without shifting her eyes away from Marie, who had suddenly become the most import-ant person in the world to her. She focused on the keys dangling from a rope around her neck. They shone like promises that would unlock room after room of information.

"Yes, I believe that was one of the paintings she took. You see, she was closer to monsieur than anyone else. Especially since the last two years when he hardly got any visitors."

"And you didn't think there was something suspicious about all this, Marie? Why didn't you report the missing paintings?"

"That's none of my business," she snapped. "And I got calls threatening me to stay quiet. A man's voice I didn't recognize." She began trembling and weeping again. "I was afraid, don't you see!"

Lena tried to calm her, clutching her hand in support. "Don't worry, I'll find that woman. You'll be all right." She paused as a thought entered her mind. "Can I go up to see Gilbert now?"

"Miss," she wiped her eyes, "I don't think that is a good idea. I'm not supposed to . . ."

"I won't do anything to jeopardize you, Marie."

The old woman, by now visibly worn out by this unexpected visit, shrugged and reluctantly proceeded up the winding staircase. Lena followed closely behind. Rows of books hugged Gilbert's room like wallpaper, many of the volumes with elaborate gilt bindings. His furnishings were spare—a blue velvet Empire settee and a Biedermeier chest of drawers, atop which lay a hand-mirror, a hairbrush, and various toiletry articles. Gilbert himself was lying on a tall mahogany bed against the far wall, his bearded chin resting on his chest. Long, thin black hair grazed his shoulders. His bony frame was visible through the sheets. His face was pale and square, with fleshy lips and a protruding brow. The late afternoon light filtered through three small windows along one wall, falling in stripes across Gilbert's bed. His room was otherwise dreary and laced with a musty odor of leather and vellum. Arranged on the bookshelves were several display boxes of butterflies with phosphorescent royal blue and orange wings.

Marie lovingly stroked Gilbert's hair. "Something has changed," she turned to Lena, alarmed.

She lowered her head to Gilbert's chest and touched his wrist with her fingers. "Mon Dieu, mon Dieu! He's gone!" She stood, paralyzed, clenching her fists, then let out a shrill wail and broke down.

Stunned and frightened, Lena embraced her. Something was terribly amiss, and she swiftly calculated her next steps, not quite knowing how to react.

"Now, I know, for sure," Marie mourned.

"What do you mean?"

"It's all her fault. It was horrible what she did to monsieur." Marie slumped down on the bed beside Gilbert and began shaking her head back and forth. "I saw it with my own two eyes, but I couldn't tell anyone, not even his nephew. I was . . . too afraid."

"Listen, Marie," Lena reassured her. "You can tell me. You don't have anything to worry about. I'll protect you."

"But I don't even know you," she protested. "Why should I trust you?"

"I'm a journalist. I'll make sure the truth gets out about what happened."

She hesitated, scrutinizing Lena intently, then continued. "For the past six months, Miss Ines kept monsieur locked in his room night and day. She said he was too weak to move, but I never believed her." Marie rubbed her hands furiously on her apron as if hoping to wipe away the horror. "He was already sick in the lungs. That's why she came here to take care of him. But something wasn't right. I could feel it!"

"And then . . ." Lena urged, pausing to turn over the tape in her recorder, then taking notes almost as rapidly as her heart was beating.

"It wasn't my place to interfere," Marie whimpered. "Just like a prisoner he was. Before he went into the coma, sometimes I thought I heard him crying for help."

Lena walked across the room and gazed out one of the small windows at the leafless poplars lining the road that unfurled like a snow carpet from Gilbert's château. There were no cars. Her anxiety mounted. Here she was, far from Paris, with a dead man. And no one knew her whereabouts.

"He was looking so thin," Marie continued, dabbing her tears with her handkerchief. "And he hardly seemed to recognize me anymore. But I didn't understand. I was making his meals every day. And Miss Ines was taking them up to him."

"And then what?" Lena was growing impatient.

"That horrible woman starved him to death—either ate the food herself or got rid of it!" Marie cried, as if realizing the magnitude of the tragedy. "She always returned with an empty tray. Mon Dieu!"

"But what happened when Ines Avidon left? Did you take the food up to him?"

"By then, he was already in the coma. I took the food up anyway in case he might wake up." She drew a deep breath and fell silent.

Lena anxiously paced back and forth in front of Gilbert's bed. Clearly, Ines Avidon was somehow tied to the stolen Ghirlandaio.

"He must have gone for days without food, poor monsieur, while she kept him locked in here. When I'd go to check on him—and it wasn't too often because I was afraid of Miss Ines—he never said a word, just sat up in bed, staring out the window with this big blue blanket wrapped around him. He was not right."

Lena began to feel lightheaded. Her curls were damp with perspiration. She had the overwhelming feeling that her whole future hinged on this incident. It was imperative that she remain discerning and do all she could to protect the story. Her story. One misstep and everything for which she had worked so hard would slip through her fingers. Her mind raced. What if Avidon and the Baron were in on this together? Who was the frightening man on the train? What if *Advance* got the scoop before she did? She was not about to let that happen.

"Mon Dieu, I've been going on for so long, miss. I feel sick to my stomach." Marie's voice diminished to a near whisper.

"Listen, Marie," Lena urged, "you must call an ambulance. I have to go now. Will you be all right?"

"Yes, miss, yes." Marie broke into tears again. "That is the thing to do. I will call Mr. Mark, too."

"Don't worry. I'll get to the bottom of all this." Lena embraced Marie again and rushed back downstairs with renewed determination.

"Wait!" Marie scrambled after her. "There's something I want to give you. I'll be right back."

Marie opened a door off the kitchen and climbed down another flight of stairs to the basement, flashlight in hand. Lena stood at the doorway, peering into the dark, musty abyss, waiting impatiently for what seemed like a long time.

"Here it is!" At last, Marie reappeared, struggling to catch her breath. She presented Lena with a large hexagonal box constructed with many layers of hard wood, so that it appeared almost accordion-like. A floral design was carved on top.

"What is this, Marie?"

"I don't know. monsieur found it a while back at the flea market. A junk dealer told him it was very old and had a mysterious treasure inside. But it could not be opened until the appropriate time." Her voice was still weak with grief. "Monsieur felt it was very powerful, so he kept it in a special place downstairs, out of sight."

"But there's no lid or any other apparent way to open it." Lena turned the unusual box around in her hands, regarding it curiously. It was carved with the same image she had seen on a car decal in Paris on her way home from the market. The overlapping circles formed numerous small interlinked flowers. She also remembered seeing the image in her last vision of Giovanna. But what did it mean?

"The man told monsieur there was a secret way to open it." Marie scratched her head, searching for an explanation. "I think it's about something you do with your hands, the way you move it around. I'm not sure, but I wanted to give you this to thank you for being here at this terrible time . . ." A look of terror eclipsed her face. "Oh no, I must call the ambulance!"

"Thank you very much, Marie. I'll keep it safe." Lena was intrigued by what the treasure might be.

"One more thing," Marie hesitated. "Monsieur said that if someone tried to break or smash the box to get the treasure inside, then bad things would happen to them. It has to be opened the right way!" She shook her head adamantly.

"Yes, I understand." Lena was anxious to leave. "Take care of yourself."

It was just about nightfall. The taxi would soon be returning. Lena turned off her tape recorder, gathered her coat and overnight bag, and waited, shivering, outside the front door. Within minutes, the taxi pulled up, and she sped off.

Exhausted, Lena could think only about the empty feeling in her stomach and how she hadn't eaten since early this morning. The events of the afternoon replayed in her head with a surreal, unsettling immediacy. As she had suspected, it was too late to take the train back to Paris, so she asked the driver to take her to a small inn at the town's center, where she had made a reservation. She ate grilled tuna and a fresh salad at the adjacent café, staring at Marie's strange box on the chair beside her, lost in her thoughts.

Passing through snowy wheat fields on the train back to Paris the following morning, Lena was still shaken by Gilbert's death and unsure of what to do next. Where on earth could Ines Avidon be and how would she find her? So much new information turned up the pressure. There was little time to waste. A French family with an impatient young boy had settled into the seats across the aisle from her, agitating her further. Suddenly, her cell phone rang. It was Steinert.

"Can you meet me Saturday night at the bateau mouche landing under Pont Neuf?" He spoke with a strained urgency.

"What's going on, Marv?"

"I have some information that could be useful to you. But I can't get into it now."

"Why under the bridge?"

"I don't want anyone to see us together. Let's make it seven thirty. See you then!" He hung up.

Though physically and emotionally spent, Lena tingled at the prospect of solving the crime. She dialed Hannah's number and left a message.

"I'm getting closer, Hannah! Talk to you soon."

She called the Baron, suspecting he might know Ines Avidon. Frustrated to have reached his answering machine again, she asked him to call her as soon as possible. Then she checked her messages, watching all the green-shuttered, stone houses speed by through the train window in a silvery mist. Henri had called to invite her to dinner for her birthday at Le Train Bleu. Oddly, the restaurant was located at the Gare d'Austerlitz, where she would soon be arriving. Did he know about her visit to Gilbert's château? He had remembered her birthday, though, and she was cheered at the prospect of seeing him again, for she desperately craved companionship. She accepted Henri's invitation in a text message. Scrolling through her emails, she was surprised to see a brief businesslike note from Jud. She had almost given up on hearing from him.

> Lena, I wanted you to know that I've found another apartment
> and will be moving out of our place next week. I'm seeing
> someone now. Doesn't feel right to stay here. I'll clean up
> before I leave. Good luck with your story. J.

Her heart sank. Though she was not surprised, it was hard to accept the finality of it all. She wiped her tears, regretting her decision to leave him. How she needed his friendship and support now. Even though she had Henri she felt so alone.

Lena grew restless again, grinding her teeth and crinkling her forehead. There were so many unanswered questions. What were Ines Avidon's motives? Why steal the Ghirlandaio when there were paintings by better-known old masters in Gilbert's collection? The top collector's article she had read stated that he owned works by Rembrandt, Raphael, and Goya, among others. Maybe Giovanna's portrait really did hold a special power. But what? If only she could rest. In an effort to tame her raging thoughts, she began counting the barren trees, passing in and out of the window frame, and then the streetlights—one, two, three, one, two—gradually falling into a trancelike state.

Chapter Thirteen

The climb was long and arduous, and Giovanna felt her strength waning. She counted each step with single-minded intensity, eager to reach the cave where she had spent so many rapturous moments. She had often retreated here in the mountains, on the outskirts of Florence near Fiesole, when she needed to rest and gain clarity or simply be in silence with her own soul. She had buried her beloved Lorenzo just days ago, and her heart still weighed heavy with grief.

Memories of his funeral at their palazzo consumed her. His limp, cold body and translucent skin. The dais upon which his body was carried by four of their dear friends. The hole in the wall of their bedroom through which his body was passed to the outside, as tradition dictated. And then the rebricking of that same wall. It was all too much to bear. Equally disturbing was that his murderer was still at large. Tearfully, she rubbed her distended, low-hanging belly. Given her condition, her doctor never would have approved this trek up the mountain. She had had to sneak out of town, commandeering the horse and carriage herself.

But it was the Feast of the Pentecost today, and it was her custom each year to observe this holy day in the cave, which was, for her, a place of refuge and consolation, meditation and rejuvenation. Giovanna had a special fondness for the Pentecost, as it celebrated the descent of the Holy Spirit to the apostles and, by extension, to all believers in the Christian mysteries. Because Mary Magdalene was her patron saint, she paid particular tribute on this day to her, the apostle to the apostles, as she was called. It was believed that Magdalene, also known as Magdalena and Mary of Magdala after the Galilean town of her birth, had traveled to Europe to preach Jesus's message of unconditional love and forgiveness after his crucifixion. Giovanna had read about her life in a manuscript from Medici's extensive collection of rare documents. He was always in search of lost secrets from the ancient world and had often allowed her access to his findings.

Still in mourning, she wore a long black tunic with an emerald sash, which swung to and fro as she walked. She repeated the words "Thy will be done" until she finally reached the mouth of the massive limestone cave burrowing into the mountainside. Stopping briefly to catch her breath, she admired the beautiful view of the patchwork Tuscan hills and farmland. It was not altogether dark inside the cave, as just enough daylight poured in through several small fissures so that Giovanna could see. Nevertheless, she had packed in the sack she had strapped to her back two large candles, along with a pear, a slice of goat's cheese, and a quarter loaf of bread. It was so comforting and familiar to be back here, like entering the womb of the earth, a highly charged repository of the divine feminine energies. Of course, she had never spoken of her exalted experiences in the cave to anyone, for she feared being misunderstood. And she knew that to try to define the ineffable was to diminish its power.

Magdalene supposedly took refuge in a cave in southern France, praying and preaching to the locals, before continuing her journey through Europe, according to Medici's manuscript. Giovanna felt as though she had known her intimately and had spent time with her in that very cave, singing and praying with a small group of women who had surrendered completely to their direct mystical connection with the Divine. She had read that such a group likely existed called the Order of Magdala. When

Giovanna visited this particular cave, she typically found herself alone, which is exactly what she preferred.

She made a small fire with some branches she had gathered. At the rear of the cave was a beautiful, large marble statue of Magdalene that Medici had asked his friend Verrocchio to carve for Giovanna on her wedding day. The sculptor's assistants had hauled the statue up the mountain on Giovanna's request. One of the candles she had left behind at her last visit had remained untouched, along with the now dried pink roses she had left as an offering. She lit the candle in the fire, along with her other two candles, then placed the trio around the statue. With that, she took a stick and carefully began sketching in the dirt a large circle containing multiple, evenly-spaced overlapping circles in a flower-like pattern with a hexagonal symmetry. The Flower of Life.

She had seen the same design depicted in artworks of the past. Plato had believed it contained the sacred geometrical building blocks of the universe. She viewed it as a symbol of the infinite connection between all life forms, holding within itself a kind of mystical record of all that is. "Step out of the circle of time and into the circle of love," she heard a voice reminding her. She had often spoken these words to Lorenzo. They were written by the great thirteenth-century Persian poet and mystic Jalāl ad-Dīn Muhammad Rūmī, whose poems she had read in Medici's library. Stepping inside the Vesica Piscis, the space where two circles overlapped, she began to weep softly and inconsolably. She soon fell to her knees, bowing down in prayer. Her tears gushed in a torrent of grief and anger at Lorenzo's murder. She had never felt so lost and alone and far away, as though she were deep down in a tunnel inside the earth from which there appeared to be no exit. All she could do was ask for mercy.

Then, suddenly and surprisingly, a feeling of unbridled joy infused her heart, expanding it beyond what she had ever felt possible, beyond even her love for Lorenzo. It was as if a fire were burning inside her, melting away any last resistance to her complete, unwavering embodiment of unconditional love. She felt that she had perhaps for the first time merged with the essence of Magdalene herself—as the divine feminine counterpart and mystical equal of Jesus—not just with a remote idea of her. The ancient texts said she was the first apostle to witness Jesus's resurrection into a light body.

As Giovanna well knew, Magdalene was an exemplary teacher and practitioner of the unity consciousness that Jesus himself had embodied, a state of being founded on the need to integrate within oneself the dualities of spirit and matter, light and shadow, masculine and feminine, and the urgent call to embrace one's own divinity. Giovanna gazed upon the statue of the saint illuminated by the candle flames. Her emotions gradually subsided as she tapped into the multidimensional aspects of herself and the knowledge that she existed as everything everywhere. How in the midst of so much pain was she able to access such bliss?

Suddenly, one of the candles stopped burning, and then another, as though someone had just blown out the flames. A chill shot up her spine. "Lorenzo! Lorenzo, is that you!" she called out. She heard his words, as in a whisper, "I'm always here for you." Giovanna had never really believed in the finality of death. Now, she knew without question that it was simply an illusion. We do, indeed, live forever. "I love you, Lorenzo." Her words echoed throughout the cave. "You were right about everything," she thought she heard him reply with his characteristic humor.

She smiled gratefully and began toning for some time the sounds of her soul, accessing what felt like a long buried memory. The sweet, high-pitched sounds were like an angelic light language hinting of ecstasy and eternal splendor. Following this offering to Magdalene, she chanted, "Sophia Christou, Sophia

Christou, Sophia Christou . . ." which connected her with the Christ Consciousness. She repeated the prayer out loud until she lost track of time and space and slipped into a prolonged transcendent communion with Spirit through her own higher self, accessing, finally, the peace that passes all understanding. Her ceremony completed, she bowed in gratitude to Magdalene's likeness, blew out the last candle, and extinguished the fire she had built. Just as she was about to leave the cave, a beam of rose-colored light suddenly appeared before her. It was so beautiful and otherworldly. She was enraptured. Once outside, she knelt beside a mountain stream to splash water on her face and hair. It was a baptism of sorts, as though she had, indeed, been reborn on this day through her communion with Magdalene, showing that she, too, had direct access to cosmic wisdom.

As she walked back down the mountain, she felt lighter and more peaceful and present. She decided she must try to find Lorenzo's murderer herself, not to seek vengeance but to forgive him. She recalled Plato's words, having shared them so many times with the students and prisoners she taught: "Wherefore let us exhort all men to piety in all things, that we may avoid evil and obtain The Good, taking Love for our leader and commander." By now ravenously hungry, she nibbled on some of the pear and cheese she had packed, aware of the slight movements within her belly. She so wished for a daughter this time; there would be much to teach her.

Chapter Fourteen

On her way back home from the train station, Lena felt a sudden, sharp pain in her abdomen, accompanied by waves of nausea. Could she be pregnant? That was unlikely; she had been so careful with Henri. Perhaps she was identifying with Giovanna again, experiencing *her* pregnancy. She abruptly got off the métro at the Saint-Michel station and headed to Notre Dame Cathedral. It was late morning, and the church was less crowded than usual. She instinctively walked to the right and down the wide aisle past several small alcoves bearing life-size sculptures of the Virgin Mary, St. Joseph, St. Paul, and other saints. Tucked into a corner was a marble statue of Mary Magdalene, her hands crossed at her heart. Lena stood gazing at her, recalling her last vision of Giovanna and trying to make a connection. After some time, she fell to her knees and began weeping softly. She was surprised by this outburst, as it was not her nature to engage in public displays of any sort. She felt her heart expanding with love and joy, and began to understand Giovanna's connection with the saint. But why all this now, and what did it mean? Why did Giovanna continue to haunt her? It was as if she were inhabiting two bodies at once.

She was getting distracted from her assignment again. A shiver shot up her back. Ines Avidon, Jonathan Fisher Gilbert's murderer, was still at large. She must find her! Lena hurried out of the church, possessed by her mission. Back in her neighborhood, she passed by the vendors' tables on Rue Daguerre, piled high with fruits and cheeses, and edged her way through the stampede of locals carrying baguettes and sacks of food. She was glad to be home, far away from Gilbert's château and the chilling discovery she had made there. Her concierge, a buxom, middle-aged woman, greeted her with a cheery "Bonjour."

"Votre paquet, mademoiselle." She walked into the utility closet and returned with a large white box. "Alors." She smiled.

"Merci." Lena opened the box instantly. It was a dozen beautiful pink roses. The attached note read: "Je t'adore, Henri."

He was obviously trying to charm her again. Even so, she was touched by his thoughtfulness. Jud had stopped buying her flowers years ago. Henri had presented her with a pink rose when they first met at the auction. And she had seen pink roses around Giovanna. Lena rushed up the spiraling staircase to her apartment, arranged the roses in a vase, and placed the strange wooden box that Marie had given her under the bed. Then she immediately began searching for Ines Avidon in the phone book. The effort was fruitless, for such a woman surely would not list her number. Lena spread a big map of France across her bed and called directory assistance in all the major cities, again without success. Frantically, she searched online for information about Avidon, but to no avail. It was as if she didn't exist. Then she typed in the name Giovanna Tornabuoni like she had several times before. But, again, she did not uncover any new information about her. Lena sat immobilized at her desk, eyes closed, doubting herself again.

The following evening, she put on an elegant black dress and her new emerald scarf and left to meet Henri for dinner. On her way, she noticed through the window of a café near the Denfert-Rocherau métro a young woman staring forlornly into her espresso cup. The woman looked up. It was Blondine, wrapped in a purple patent-leather raincoat. Lena walked in to say, hello.

"What a pleasure to see you again, Blondine." She extended her hand, heartened by this unexpected meeting.

"Lena, right?" Blondine swept her hair away from her face.

"Yes." She did not wish to waste time. "Do you know when I can reach the Baron?"

"Actually, he's at an auction now." Blondine turned her cigarette in the ashtray. Her English was excellent. She spoke tentatively, her eyes fixed on the passing traffic outside. Her face was plainer than Lena had remembered it, yet still possessed of a warm glow.

"How is he recovering, anyway?"

"Not well."

"Great coat by the way."

"Sonia Rykiel." Blondine blushed. "My absolute favorite designer. Anyway, to be honest, I've been very worried about Ducky lately. He's so obsessed with that painting, saying he never should have sold it, that he's going to paint his own!"

"I need to know about the photo of Giovanna Tornabuoni." Lena pulled up a chair, eager to make full use of this opportunity. "I found it in the Baron's jacket at the ambassador's party, along with a price list of Ghirlandaio paintings."

"Ducky's an amateur painter. He says he'll make it look just like the one in the Louvre. Well, that's why he had the stupid photo. He carries it with him everywhere."

Bewildered, Lena scribbled in her notebook.

"And just yesterday, he said he had received a message from Ghirlandaio himself. Can you even believe it?!"

"Really?" Lena raised her eyebrows and continued writing.

"But why on earth am I telling you all this? Wait . . . is that a real Montblanc?" Blondine paused to inspect Lena's pen. "I mean, he'd absolutely kill me if he knew! I'm so worried about him. He won't rest. I told him he needs his rest." Her eyes filled with tears. Lena motioned to the waiter to bring another cup of espresso for Blondine.

"Oh, no, I can't." She dabbed the mascara on her cheek with a napkin. "I'll be late for my aerobics class."

"What's with that painting anyway?" Lena did not discount the possibility that the Baron knew about Gilbert's murder.

"He says he can't bear not being able to look at her every day, and that Ghirlandaio told him how to paint another one. He needs help!"

"The Baron must be under a lot of stress now," Lena said, wishing to comfort her. "He certainly gave everyone a scare at the ambassador's party when he pulled a gun on Marv Steinert. Surprising they weren't both arrested."

"Yeah, thank God for your boyfriend. That's the first time I ever saw Ducky lose it like that in public. You're right, he's definitely stressed out." Blondine leaned over the table and whispered, "And he's beginning to frighten me."

"Then, maybe you should leave him."

"You think so?" Blondine contemplated this suggestion, twisting her torso from side to side and extending her arms above her head. "Just stretching," she sighed.

"It's possible he's sick. And if you think you're in danger . . ."

"You know, you're right." She slung her hair back and regarded Lena appreciatively, as if awakened by the wisdom of an older sister. "Hey, maybe we can get together again for coffee or something."

"Sure. Give me a call." Lena laid one of her business cards on the table.

"And don't forget," Blondine called after her. "Sonia Rykiel. Boulevard Saint-Germain!"

Lena turned and made a cutting gesture at her neck, reminding Blondine of her advice.

Lena arrived at Le Train Bleu, the exquisite Bell-Époque restaurant at the Gare d'Austerliz, tense and unsure of how the evening would unfold with Henri. He was reading a newspaper in one of the old leather club chairs in the bar area. His face brightened instantly upon seeing her.

"So the mystery woman is back!" He took her in his arms and kissed her hard. "I've missed you."

"Have you?"

"Well, Happy Birthday! I'm getting tired of all this traveling. I'd rather spend time with you."

Lena smiled affectionately. "Thank you for the beautiful roses." She retrieved a small wrapped gift box from her purse and handed it to him. "This was supposed to be your Christmas gift."

Henri opened the box and pulled out a handsome pair of black leather gloves with an embossed Gucci insignia. "Thank you, chérie!" He tried them on. "They fit perfectly."

The hostess led them through blue velvet curtains to the dining room, with its tall brass coat racks, large leather booths, and a glass-domed ceiling decorated with scenes from cities along the rail route from Paris to the Côte d'Azur, hinting of the many well-off, turn-of-the-century travelers who had passed through here.

"Shall we have two Kir Royales to celebrate?" Henri slid into the booth beside Lena and called over the waiter.

"You know I love champagne." Though she was happy to see Henri again, she was still preoccupied with her disturbing visit to Gilbert's. News of his death had surely reached his nephew by now, not to mention the local media. A sharp chill coursed through her body.

"How is your assignment going?"

The waiter appeared with their drinks and menus. Lena squirmed; his name-tag said Lorenzo.

"So where are you from, Lorenzo?" she asked incredulously, nervously tapping her spoon on the table.

"Florence."

Lena's spoon fell to the floor. The waiter smiled, picked it up, and excused himself. Trembling slightly, Lena felt as though her every move was being monitored by an omniscient, invisible presence.

"Henri, there's something I need to know," she said with trepidation. "You seem distracted. What is it?"

"I went to see Gilbert. He was in a coma." She gulped her cocktail. "I met the housekeeper, but his nurse, Ines Avidon, was gone. Do you know anything about her?"

She was not about to reveal anything more for fear of jeopardizing her story. Even thinking about the empty château made her uptight. For a moment, she wished she had never boarded that train.

"I knew you'd find him. Good work! Too bad he's not much help to you in that state. Not surprised. I heard a while ago he wasn't well. As for the nurse, don't know her."

Not what she wanted to hear. She hoped desperately that Steinert might be of some help, as she would be meeting him soon. Lorenzo arrived to take their orders. She decided on grilled lobster, while Henri ordered roast duckling and a bottle of rosé to take them through dinner.

Henri spoke animatedly about his recent sales and auction victories. But Lena could not concentrate and had little to say. His voice trailed off into the clamor of conversation and the Ravel sonata being played by a man at the piano in the corner. Black-suited waiters rushed from table to table, wheeling glass carts of the most extraordinary confections. The sweet scent from a towering flower arrangement reminded Lena of a funeral. Nauseated, she could barely finish her meal.

"You do get around, my friend!" A tall, lean man approached their table and shook hands with Henri. He spoke in a crisp British accent.

Henri laughed, surprised. "Maurice, Lena. Lena, Maurice, my attorney and a part-time art dealer himself."

"Good to meet you." Lena offered a weak smile. She was startled to recognize him as the man she had seen with Henri leaving La Rotonde café in Montparnasse. He had a chalky pallor and long sideburns. His movements were stiff and mechanical, his expression distant.

"The honor is mine. I've heard a lot about you." Maurice kissed her hand. "I was waiting at the bar for a colleague and saw the two of you. So I thought I'd say, hello."

"What kind of law do you practice, Maurice?" she inquired.

"You name it, estates, contracts, divorce . . ." Maurice scanned the dining room, impatiently shaking his head. "He's always late!"

"Have you made up your mind about the lacquer screen?" Henri pressured him.

"I told you, Lemien, the price is too high, even for a Dunand!"

Henri rolled his eyes. "Certain things demand certain prices. The rarer it is, the more you pay for it." He sidled in closer to Lena, wrapping his arm around her. "And I don't just mean objects."

Maurice glared at his friend. As with Henri, it was clear he did not enjoy being challenged.

"What do you say, Lena?" Henri turned to her expectantly.

"He doesn't have to buy your screen if he doesn't want to." She bit into an asparagus spear.

Henri fell silent, as a smile of gratitude flickered across his friend's face.

"Maurice," said Lena, "I'm sure you're aware of the alleged stolen Ghirlandaio now hanging at the Louvre?" She was eager to change the subject. Perhaps there was a reason he had shown up just now.

"Of course."

"Could we meet for coffee at your convenience? I have some legal questions about the painting that you might be able to help me with."

"Well, why not. Here's my card." Maurice glanced across the room, where his friend had just been seated. "Gotta run, you two, see you soon!" He shook Lena's hand goodbye, ignoring Henri.

"He can be so rigid," Henri huffed, finishing the last of the roast duckling. "But he'll come around and buy that screen, just wait."

With that, he excused himself and walked over to the slight, gray-haired man at the piano. Before long, Henri took the man's seat and began playing "Happy Birthday" to Lena with joyful abandon, motioning to the other diners to sing along. Lena blushed. His serenade ended with a loud burst of applause.

"I didn't know you played the piano!" Lena said, when he returned to the table. To her delight, the waiter delivered a chocolate whipped cream cake with two sparklers for candles.

"There are some things you don't know about me, chérie." He lifted his wine glass. "To you!"

She kissed him, then suddenly turned serious. "About Maurice . . . He's the guy I saw you with leaving La Rotonde café the other night, isn't he?

"Oh, not that again! For once and for all, he did not frame Steinert!" Henri stroked her arm. "Is that why you challenged me earlier in front of him?"

"I was just reminding you that you can't have everything you want."

"And you don't think you can?"

Lena could not deny that he was right. She playfully stared him down.

"Guess we're made for each other," he whispered in her ear. They fell into a passionate embrace.

One night later, Lena walked hurriedly to the Pont Neuf for her appointment with Marv Steinert. She climbed down the stairway to the Seine, along which several bateaux mouches were docked. A few tourists boarded one of the boats for the last ride of the night. There had been a break in the weather, and it was milder than usual. She spotted Steinert through the mist leaning against the underside of the bridge and clutching a walking stick. He waved the stick when he saw her and rushed over to help her onto the boat.

"It means a lot to me that you've come," he said under his breath. They found a seat at the rear of the boat.

"You're hard to keep track of, you know. I have so many things to talk to you about." Lena gathered her cape at her neck.

"I apologize for this unusual request, but I'm afraid to be seen on the street." Steinert abruptly swirled his head around to check out the passengers, then leaned in closer to Lena. "I believe I'm in danger."

She grew nervous. The large spotlights on the boat lit up the Louvre and cast a golden hue on the plane trees leaning over the water.

"Thanks to her." Steinert pointed his walking stick toward the museum. Lena thought of the *Portrait of Giovanna Tornabuoni* hanging there in the darkness.

"That night at the ambassador's, I was so surprised to see you. And then, when you almost got shot . . ." She lowered her voice. "So it's the Baron von Heisendorf again, isn't it?"

"It's not just the money I owe him. That's not why he pulled the gun on me." Steinert had on a leather-rimmed beret that made him look years younger, boyish even. Despite the arrogance with which he had first greeted her in New York, she sensed from him an unequivocal trust in her. It was possible that he considered her his only ally.

"I don't understand," Lena said uneasily. "What else could he want from you?" She walked over to the railing and looked down at the glistening dark river.

"He thinks I have something to do with that dreadful painting, that I broke into his house and replaced the Ghirlandaio with a fake after I sold it to him." Steinert joined her at the railing, trailing his walking stick in the water. His eyes darted about with their usual watchfulness.

"After you realized it was worth much more," Lena ruminated. "And, of course, Henri advised him that the painting really was a fake. So he quickly passed it off to Jonathan Fisher Gilbert." A wave of panic suddenly consumed her. She felt as though she were going to faint and grabbed onto the railing.

"The Baron's raving mad." Steinert hesitated, noticing the sudden change in her expression. "Excuse me, but you don't look well."

"I'm fine." Lena quickly regained her composure. "Oddly, I just heard from his girlfriend that he's painting his own version of the Ghirlandaio."

"So you can see for yourself. He's out of his mind!" He let out a loud guffaw, attracting a few unpleasant stares. "Look, I don't want to scare you, my dear, but you must be very careful. Von Heisendorf is dangerous. I have my sources. He has many connections in the art world. And there is at least one person who doesn't want this story to break."

"So you think it's really the Baron who's behind all this?"

"I wouldn't doubt it. He may have stolen the painting from Gilbert after he sold it to him, the very thing he accused me of doing."

Lena's head was throbbing. "That sounds like a big stretch." She eyed Steinert with suspicion, pressing her hands against her temples. "And what about you, Marv? What about that smuggling allegation? Oh, and I saw you with some guy outside Notre Dame one night. I think he's following me. I still don't know who to trust!" Her thoughts drifted back to the man on the train, though she couldn't be certain he was Steinert's companion.

"For Christ's sake, I told you to stop listening to that rat Lemien!" He looked around again. "And the guy you mentioned happens to be a trustworthy friend of mine!"

Worried and confused, Lena ignored his insult to Henri. "Then perhaps the Baron knows Ines Avidon." She thought out loud, feeling even more overwhelmed now by the plausible turns her story could take. She wanted desperately to believe Steinert but was unwilling to give into him completely.

"Who the hell is she?"

"Gilbert's nurse." Images of the chilly château, Gilbert propped up in his bed, and Marie wringing her hands made her stomach churn. She leaned over the railing, afraid she was going to vomit.

"Hey, are you okay?" Steinert clutched her arm and pulled her back around.

The boat turned underneath the Pont Alexander III to complete its journey along the other side of the river. Lena watched the Eiffel Tower grow smaller in the distance, its lights flickering through the thickening mist.

"It's just the assignment . . . so many loose ends. It's stressing me out."

Jonathan Fisher Gilbert's murder, allegedly by his nurse, Ines Avidon. The Baron and Steinert's violent argument at the Ambassador's party. The Baron's suspicious price list of Ghirlandaio paintings. Henri's accusation that Steinert smuggled a Sorolla out of Mexico. Steinert's mistrust of Henri and his friend Maurice Blackson, who he says set him up. The Baron's and Madame de Trouville's elusiveness. The shady man on the train who warned her to stop her investigation, the same man she believed she had seen with Steinert that night at Notre Dame. Her head was spinning trying to make sense of it all.

"Lena," Steinert called her back to attention.

"Sorry. All I know is that I have to find Avidon."

"And how do you know about her?"

"When I went to Gilbert's château, his housekeeper told me that Avidon left with some paintings that he supposedly had willed to her grandfather, and the Ghirlandaio was one of them. Gilbert was so sick he had lapsed into a coma. So, of course, he was no help." Lena still didn't trust him enough to reveal everything.

"You're sure she said that?" Steinert fixated on the big clock on the façade of the Musée d'Orsay.

"Yes, of course!" Lena reflected for a moment. "I need to ask you . . . I saw Henri at La Rotonde café with Maurice Blackson. Is he the one you believe framed you?"

"That's the man. But I think you should concentrate your efforts on the Baron now. And, if you like, I can make some inquiries for you about this Avidon woman."

"I would appreciate that, Marv. What are your plans?" She hoped he'd be staying in Paris for a while in case she needed him.

The twin towers of Notre Dame came into view on the left as they whirred past the tip of the Île de la Cité. Lena wished someone would turn off the tinny audiotape describing all the sights in four different languages, which only made her headache worse.

"To continue doing what I do best—buying and selling old master paintings. I'm not going to let some madman get the best of me!"

"So you really wanted to see me because you were worried about me?" She warmed to his presence.

"You could say that." He looked away sheepishly. "And there's one other thing. If you could pass along anything you learn about the Baron, for my own protection, of course."

"Anything, yes."

The glow from the street lanterns along the quai highlighted the creases on his face and the raised veins in his hands. Steinert studied her with the same intense curiosity with which he had examined Giovanna Tornabuoni through his magnifying glass at the Louvre.

"You're shivering." He draped his coat over her shoulders as they turned a bend upstream. "Let's not be afraid." Lena's mistrust seemed to melt into the mist.

Over the next few days, Lena completed another art review for Max, distracted by Steinert's warning and fearful for her safety. For clarity, she also made a list of suspects behind the stolen Ghirlandaio, in order of their involvement.

1) Marv Steinert—New York old master paintings dealer and collector and former owner of the painting who sold it to Baron Eric von Heisendorf. Accused by French art dealer Henri Lemien of smuggling a Sorolla out of Mexico. Motive: Greed

2) Baron Eric von Heisendorf—German art collector and former owner of the painting who sold it to American collector Jonathan Fisher Gilbert. Violent, erratic behavior. Motive: Greed

3) Ines Avidon—nurse and alleged murderer of Jonathan Fisher Gilbert who claimed that Gilbert willed the painting to her grandfather. Still missing. Motive: Greed

4) Anonymous Florence Art Dealer—Sold the painting to Madame Geneviève de Trouville. Motive: Greed

5) Madame Geneviève de Trouville—French heiress who recently sold the painting at Sotheby's for $48 million. Motive: Greed

6) Claude Weintraub—Louvre curator indicted for buying the alleged stolen painting at the Sotheby's auction. Motive: Greed

7) Shady Man on the Train—Also likely seen at the library and with Steinert at Notre Dame. Warned me to stop the investigation. Motive: Greed.

She read the list and, hesitating, added two other names.

8) Maurice Blackson—French attorney who Steinert believes framed him with smuggling charges. Motive: Greed

9) Henri Lemien—French art dealer and collector and friend of Blackson. Motive: Greed.

She knew from her previous investigative reports that no piece of information could be taken for granted. When she finally reached the Baron after numerous phone calls, he suggested they meet in the Parc Monceau on the Right Bank, where he and Blondine usually took their afternoon walk. Later that day, Lena walked briskly along the winding paths of the park, hopeful for another break in her story. She was momentarily uplifted by all the children running about, screaming and laughing joyfully. Senior citizens ambled along with their dogs or sat talking garrulously on the green benches. On one of the benches, near the artificial Roman ruins at the park's center, sat the Baron and Blondine, surrounded by a crescent-shaped colonnade.

"Beautiful day," Lena greeted them graciously.

"Absolutely." Blondine lifted her rhinestone-studded sunglasses to acknowledge Lena. She shrugged as if to resign herself to her relationship with the Baron, despite Lena's earlier advice.

The Baron did not respond, his eyes fixed in the distance.

Blondine nudged him. "Now, Ducky, don't be so rude. You agreed to this appointment."

"Yes, yes, I was just thinking . . ." He nodded at Lena.

Lena sat down on the bench beside the Baron. He had changed since she saw him at the ambassador's party. His eyes looked dazed and glassy. His beard was straggly and overgrown. He sat hunched over, tearing off pieces of a baguette and tossing them to a swarm of pigeons at his feet. Lena noticed he no longer had the use of his left arm, which hung limp at his side. She looked to Blondine for an explanation.

"Stroke," Blondine said.

"Is that why he blacked out at the party that night?" Lena said.

Blondine nodded.

Lena turned to him. "I was hoping you could help me, Baron."

Adjusting his monocle, he regarded her with a bewildered expression, then focused again on the birds. Lena remembered the gun he had pulled at the Ambassador's party and wondered, with some anxiety, if he was carrying one now.

"When he needs a break from his painting, we come here," Blondine explained. "Why don't we get up now, Ducky, and take a little walk. You need your exercise." She helped pull the Baron to his feet.

"Now, Baron, I wonder if you know of a Miss Ines Avidon," Lena inquired, walking alongside him. "She's Jonathan Fisher Gilbert's nurse."

"I don't believe so." He smiled gallantly at a group of young women. "Are you sure?"

"Ducky answered your question," Blondine scolded.

"All right, then, have your heard anything about Gilbert recently?"

"As I said before, I haven't spoken to him in years. Besides, we came here to relax!" He began breathing heavily.

"Yes, we did, now just sit down here." Blondine guided the Baron across the path to another bench shaded by an old birch. He began pacing back and forth, rhythmically stroking his beard.

"Now, what's wrong?" Blondine scowled at Lena, as if blaming her for the Baron's restlessness.

"I must get home! I have come up with a way to paint the lips. Then I will have it completely."

"He's talking about that painting," Blondine said, adding under her breath, "it's absolutely wearing me out. I told him it looked finished to me, but he hasn't put down his brush for even a day." She sighed and fell back onto the bench.

"You mean his version of Giovanna Tornabuoni."

"Naturally."

"Is that why you pulled the gun on Steinert at the Ambassador's party, Baron, because it had something to do with the Ghirlandaio?"

The Baron continued to pace under the birch, sweeping his hands back and forth as if painting an invisible canvas.

"That bastard owes me money from two years ago! Should've shot him right on the spot." He stopped to catch his breath. "And he took my Giovanna away. Left me with a fake. He's the fool you should be badgering!"

Just then, the Baron caught sight of a girl skipping rope a few yards away. "Incroyable! Look at that chin, just like Giovanna's!"

"See, didn't I tell you?" Blondine whined. "You might think it's funny but it's not."

"I don't think it's funny." Lena dropped her notebook back into her purse, frustrated at her lack of progress with the Baron. She began to believe Steinert's accusations, yet the only proof would be to find Avidon herself.

"Have a pleasant afternoon," Blondine said. "Oh, in case you're interested, we got a call from another magazine, *Advance*, I think it was. Well, whatever." She started after the Baron, her wafer-thin body swaying from side to side in the wind. "He's absolutely out of his mind," she mumbled to herself.

Disturbed that *Advance* was making progress, Lena drew a deep breath and envisioned herself again plucking pears from a tree, one by one, taking what she wanted. An exclusive front-page story, a book. But what if Steinert was wrong? What if she couldn't find Ines Avidon? What if Gilbert's nephew was talking to *Advance*? She angrily kicked the gravel with her boot, then hurried back out of the park, reassuring herself that the possibility of any of these things coming to pass was remote simply because she wished them to be so.

Chapter Fifteen

By week's end, Lena found herself in the salon of Madame de Trouville's eighteenth-century townhouse on Île Saint-Louis; it was the opportunity she had long awaited. The French heiress, who had only months ago sold the *Portrait of Giovanna Tornabuoni* at Sotheby's London, surveyed Lena with an aristocratic self-consciousness, her chin held high, her features precise and proportioned. Her blondish hair was pulled back tightly in a knot, the way it was when Lena had last seen her. Lena emanated an air of confidence, dressed smartly in black leather pants and a vest.

"Are you aware that you have lipstick on your teeth?" Madame de Trouville pointed out.

"Excuse me." Embarrassed, Lena blotted her lips with a tissue.

"I see New York is not up to speed with fashion," said Madame de Trouville condescendingly.

Lena was not about to be bullied by this formidable woman. "So about the stolen Ghirlandaio."

"Oh, rubbish! That painting was never stolen from anyone. The press likes to fabricate good stories, as you well know."

Lena steeled herself for what she knew was going to be a difficult interview.

"Come." Madame de Trouville motioned to Lena, her numerous gold bracelets clinking. Her long, yellow chiffon dress grazed the parquet floors as she showed off her sumptuous collection of art and antiques. Each of five rooms was decorated in a specific historical style, with commodes, armchairs, tables, bureaus, and pier mirrors arranged like polished trophies from a hunt. There were paintings, too. An *Annunciation* scene by Mantegna and a portrait of a halberdier by Pontormo hung on either side of a long window opening out from the salon onto a balcony overlooking the Quai d'Orléans.

"You obviously have exquisite taste." Lena seated herself in a white-painted Louis XVI armchair near the window. "Thank you for taking the time to talk to me."

Madame forced a smile and sunk into a silk damask confidante, while her young maid appeared with a silver tray containing a Limoges tea service and a plate of macaroons.

"Giovanna Tornabuoni must have looked just perfect here," Lena continued, thanking the maid. "Why did you sell her? You obviously don't need the money."

"She made me nervous," Madame de Trouville said with a dismissive wave of her hand.

"I don't understand." Lena was gracious but firm.

"Did you know she died in childbirth?" She shuddered briefly and bit off the corner of a macaroon.

"Yes, but why should that make you nervous?"

"I'm superstitious."

Lena noticed a set of small cameos of the British Royal Family on a console table. "You have a fondness for the British, I see."

"I go to the London auctions. The bloody Royals are always bidding on the exact thing I want. I keep their photographs here to prepare me for the competition." Her perfume infused the room with a cloying lilac scent that made Lena queasy.

"I know you sold the Ghirlandaio to the Louvre at one of those auctions," Lena said. "That was quite a coup."

"In my opinion, the picture is cursed."

"And you bought the painting from . . . I'm just guessing here, but could it have been a certain Ines Avidon?" Lena sipped her tea slowly.

"Ines, who? No. No. No," she said, exasperated. "I bought it from the Florence dealer Stefano Testa. He's apparently gone missing, according to the Italian press."

Satisfied with her admission, Lena diligently took notes. "That was not initially reported. Do you have any idea where he might be?"

"God only knows! If you're such a good journalist, find out for yourself." She checked her watch. "Wait just a minute." Madame de Trouville dialed a number on her cell phone. "There's something on the block in London right now that I simply must have." She placed her bids calmly, then slammed down the phone.

"A Charles Rennie Mackintosh desk." She turned to Lena. "I want it for my twentieth-century room."

"Excuse me, madame," Lena blurted, disgusted with the heiress's rudeness. "But an innocent man at the Louvre faces a prison sentence because of your 'cursed' painting, and one of its former owners is now . . ." She stopped, angry with herself for having almost mentioned Gilbert's murder.

"What?"

"Out of his mind!" Lena swiftly referred to the Baron. Struggling to maintain her cool, she checked her watch. The seconds were dashing by. She had less than three weeks to finish her investigation and write the story. Her head felt like it was in a vice.

"I don't believe I owe you any explanation." Madame de Trouville casually finished her tea, while smoothing out a wrinkle in her dress. "You'd think you were on some sort of divine mission, in search of the bloody Holy Grail. All this aggravation over a sickly looking Florentine who I was glad to get rid of!"

"Yes, for forty-eight million dollars!" Lena was growing weary of this laborious tête-à-tête. She wished the assignment were already over and the damned painting destroyed, that she would never again have to speak to the Madame de Trouvilles of the world, much less quote them.

"I'm afraid we're out of time." The implacable heiress sauntered to the door. "I'm already late for the auction at Drouot."

Lena closed her notebook. She had had enough. On her way out, she gazed out the window, suddenly distracted by something she saw in the distance. A young woman walking toward her on the bridge strangely resembled Giovanna, with her high, sloping forehead and pallid complexion, the blonde ringlets at her ears. And she was wearing a long-sleeved gown. Lena rushed over to the window to get a closer look, but the girl was already gone. Feeling weak and lightheaded, she placed her hand on an antique commode to steady herself. She could not believe what she saw lying there—a pair of men's black gloves that looked exactly like the pair she had just given Henri as a Christmas gift. They had the same Gucci insignia.

For a moment, she was unable to move. She felt sick to her stomach and abruptly excused herself. "Goodbye, then."

Madame de Trouville observed her with a puzzled expression. "Au revoir," she said.

Once outside, Lena raced to the spot on the Pont Saint-Louis where she had seen the young woman walking. She had never felt so lost or confused. What to do next? She soon found herself inside Notre Dame Cathedral, temporarily calmed by its all-encompassing silence. Closing her eyes, she whispered softly, "Hail Mary, full of grace, have mercy on me," repeating the prayer over and over again.

It was not like her to seek refuge in a church, let alone pray. Why was she here again? She left and made her way to the other side of the river, saying, "Lord have mercy," with each step, something she had never done before. Then her cell phone rang, disrupting her meditation.

"Lena, where are you?" Steinert was nearly breathless. "I have more information about the painting. Can you meet me at the Pompidou Center? I'm here now looking at the art."

"Yes, of course. I'm not far from you. I'll be there right away!"

"Meet me out front in the courtyard. We won't be seen in the crowd. I'll be waiting for you." His voice trailed off.

Lena raced back across the Pont Saint-Louis, looking up at Madame de Trouville's balcony as she passed. She followed a narrow street winding behind the cheap department stores along Rue de Rivoli. From a distance, she saw a crowd gathering in front of the Centre Pompidou, where jugglers and jesters often performed. Shrieks rang out, and sirens blared. She wedged through to the center to see what had happened. Steinert was lying, arms spread, on the concrete, blood spilling from his ears! Dazed, Lena knelt down beside him, cradling his head in her hands.

"Who could have done this?!" Deeply frightened, she questioned an Interpol cop who was trying to keep the crowd at bay.

"Don't know yet, mademoiselle. A shot rang out from over there." He pointed toward the Café Beaubourg. "Looks like he was murdered."

"I just spoke to him. Poor Steinert. Poor old Steinert." She wiped away tears, shaken to the core.

She began applying CPR in a desperate attempt to revive him. But it was too late. He had already stopped breathing. The ambulance arrived as she knelt in shock on the blood-stained concrete. Suddenly, she noticed someone approaching her through the crowd. It was the shadowy man she had seen on the train. She shuddered and bolted from the scene.

That night, still haunted by Steinert's death, she lay awake in bed wondering if the Baron was involved in the murder, or even the man who had approached her again tonight. Fearful she was being followed, she checked that her door was locked, then rushed over to the window to make sure no one was outside in the courtyard. Why was Steinert killed? What had he so desperately wanted to tell her? Perhaps he had held the key to her entire investigation. It was likely that he had truly been an ally. She envisioned him now in Angelina's café, where they had gone together after viewing Giovanna's portrait at the Louvre, and again heard the pain in his voice as he spoke of his daughter. She saw him, too, on the bateau mouche, trailing his walking stick in the water, his eyes sad and glassy in the spotlight. The phone rang, and she jumped.

"Lena, what's going on over there?!" Max bellowed. "We are struggling to stay afloat here. Time is of the essence. You have two weeks left!"

"I know, Max, I know." Lena tensed up.

"How's it going?"

"Things are reaching a critical turning point."

"Are you in some kind of danger?"

"No, everything's fine." If she told him about Steinert or shared her fear, he might take her off the assignment. "I have two top suspects. The collector Baron Eric von Heisendorf and a woman, Ines Avidon, accused of murdering a former owner of the painting. I'm trying to track her down."

"Two weeks, Lena."

"I've had some setbacks, Max. And I need to go to Florence to finish my investigation."

There was a brief silence. "We better not be scooped on this one!"

"I'll be in touch soon."

"Be careful!"

She searched through the business cards in her purse and dialed Maurice Blackson's number, hoping he might be able to meet her for coffee like he had agreed.

"Don't have time this week. Booked solid." Maurice's response was flat, like a pre-recorded message.

"But I just have a few . . ." He hung up before Lena could finish her sentence. She resented being put off by both his and Madame de Trouville's implied superiority.

She tried calling Henri, who was out of town again on appraisals. "Steinert's been murdered," she said curtly in her message. "Let me know if you hear anything." She was still disturbed to have seen his gloves at Madame de Trouville's, though it could mean nothing. The heiress was one of his client's, after all. Then again, what if he was cheating on her? But she had no time now for lovers' quarrels. Just as she finished booking her travel arrangements to Florence, Hannah called.

"How's everything, Lena?" Hannah said.

"It's so good to hear your voice. How are you?"

"Fine. You sound upset."

"Oh, Hannah. It feels like everything's crashing down all at once!" Lena's voice wavered.

"In your last message, you said you were getting closer and seemed excited. Are you okay?"

"I'm all right, just tired. Please don't worry." She didn't want to frighten Hannah with the news about the murders. "But it couldn't hurt to send some prayers my way."

"Now, I really *am* worried."

"I'm on my way to Florence in two days. This should all be over soon."

"Call if you need me."

"Thanks. I heard Jud's moving out of our apartment. I shouldn't be surprised, but still . . ."

"I'm sorry."

"I have something to ask you, Hannah."

"Sure."

"Can we promise to be with each other at the end, whoever goes first?"

"Leeennnaaaaaa. You're scaring me."

"Sorry, I was just thinking . . ."

"Yes, yes, yes. I'll be there with you, my friend."

"Me, too." Lena blinked back tears. "Talk soon."

Lena took out the CD Jud had given her and tried meditating again. After a while, she was able to quiet her mind a bit. What a relief. Her eyes settled on the Renaissance chalice on her bookshelf that she had purchased at the antiques shop in New York. She poured some Chianti into it and drank slowly and ceremoniously. It felt like something she had done many times before.

The next day, as Lena dragged her suitcase out from under her bed, she saw the antique box Marie had given her. She had not had time to focus on it. She picked it up and tried opening it in different ways but was unsuccessful. How old was the box? Where was it made and by whom? The longer she couldn't open it, the more anxious and curious she became. On a whim, she took the box to the famous flea market at the Porte de Clingnancourt, hoping to find an antiques expert who could answer her questions.

She meandered through the massive market's labyrinthine alleyways inspecting the kaleidoscopic spread of objects in the vendors' small booths. Old clocks, silver tea services, period furniture, paintings and sculptures, ceramics, architectural fragments, Chinese cloisonné vases, Indian miniatures, Art Deco candlesticks, brass incense burners, Moroccan lanterns, didgeridoos, Amazonian seed bracelets, vintage postcards, matchboxes and clothing, and all manner of junk. Yet she found nothing like the box she was carrying and no one with whom she felt like chatting. After a few hours, Lena began to tire of the visual overload and sat down on a bench to rest. An older gentleman in a long wool overcoat was sifting through a pile of doorknobs at a booth nearby. Noticing her, he smiled. He had piercing, deep-set eyes, a closely shaven head and moustache, and bronze-toned skin. His presence was one of quiet, though unmistakable, power. Lena smiled back politely.

"Never know what you'll find here," he said in English, walking over to her.

"It's my first time." Lena introduced herself, happy for conversation.

"Thomas. Mind if I sit down?" He shook her hand respectfully. Lena noticed a small Star of David tattoo on his wrist.

"Please."

"As if I really need another doorknob!" he laughed with slight embarrassment.

"You're a collector?"

"In a way. I have a thing for doors—knobs, panels, knockers, you name it. Really, I'm a curator of rare books and manuscripts at the Louvre."

"How interesting." Lena perked up. "I wonder if you might be able to tell me something about this?" She reached into a shopping bag and lifted out her box. "It's not a book, but you obviously know your history."

Thomas put on his eyeglasses and studied the box for some time, then handed it back to Lena with a look of surprise and expectancy. "In my homeland . . . Israel . . . we say shalom."

"That means peace, I believe." Lena was perplexed.

"Deep peace," he corrected her.

"I don't know what you mean."

"The carved pattern on the box is a very ancient, sacred symbol." He held her eyes in a long, knowing gaze. "It's called the Flower of Life, and within that flower are other symbols with many layers of esoteric meaning that hold the wisdom of the universe."

Lena was intrigued by this new information, remembering how she had seen the symbol before in a car decal and then in one of her visions of Giovanna. "But how old is the box? Where does it come from?"

"Somewhere in the Mediterranean—Turkey, Italy, the Middle East—I'm not sure." Thomas reflected for a moment. "It's probably over four hundred years old and could be worth quite a bit."

Given the many valuable artworks and antiques in Gilbert's

collection, Lena was not surprised. The housekeeper Marie obviously had known nothing about the box. Otherwise, why would she not have kept it for herself?

"There's one other thing, if you don't mind . . ." He spoke slowly and cautiously, as though weighing what to reveal and not wanting to intrude.

"Please tell me." Lena's eyes widened.

"This does not come from my scholarly perspective, but from my mystical studies and my own extrasensory abilities, if you will." He paused to monitor her expression.

"You're a psychic, too?"

"Not exactly. I don't know where you found this," he continued. "But the sacred symbol and the shape, with six sides, represent six different initiations for you."

"What kind of initiations? Why me?"

"I can't tell you what they are," Thomas said kindly. "They are a gift for you to discover. The center represents another one, so that makes seven. Seven initiations total."

He observed her intently, as though he could see inside of her. "You have already passed one of the initiations. The others will come quickly and unexpectedly, and you will come to regard them as key turning points in your evolution . . . should you pass them. You are already working on the second one."

Lena felt uneasy. "How do you know all this?"

"I just know." Thomas looked up to his right and nodded, appearing to have received more information from an unknown source. "Please be patient and gentle with yourself. You must always look inside and not outside for answers. Proceed with caution. The initiations will take the form of specific actions and will be defined in that way. Think of them as a series of verbs or commands. Remember you are always at choice. And should you choose inappropriately, well, I don't want to get into that now."

She squirmed at this particular point. His pronouncements were beginning to feel invasive, and she wasn't sure she believed him. "I appreciate your interest in me, Thomas, but this is a bit bizarre to me. Besides," she added with an undercurrent of anger, "I didn't ask for your advice."

"I understand your hesitation. But I've been guided to tell you this."

"By who?"

"Some higher beings who shall remain nameless." He smiled, lowering his head, as if in reverence. "Relying solely on our five senses is one of the reasons we are disconnected from the light of Source, Spirit, the Creator, call it what you will. We create barriers to the light with our anger, fears, doubts, judgments, worries . . . This is an illusion." He sighed wearily. "We don't believe we are infinite beings of immeasurable power meant to 'have it all,' as we say today. It's true that nothing is as it seems."

"No, it certainly isn't." Lena considered how her own incessant doubts and judgments—whether about Madame de Trouville, the Baron, Jud, herself, whatever—constantly derailed her and made her vision fuzzy. Then she thought of Florence and the enormous pressure of her assignment. The flea market bustle subsided as dusk fell and the vendors began packing up their wares.

"What you think is your work is not your true work." A gentle smile flickered across Thomas's face. He emanated an aura of peace and contentment that Lena had rarely encountered. "Your real investigation has been, up until now, hidden from you. It will gradually make itself known."

Lena was stunned by his accuracy about her investigation. She had not revealed anything about herself. "I'm a journalist, and I do happen to be investigating something. My future depends on its success." She looked down at the box sitting on her lap, the intricate carved floral design in the beautifully grained walnut.

"Indeed, it does, but not in the way that you think." Thomas removed a small sheet of paper from his wallet and drew two interlocking circles on it. "Do you know what this is?"

"Not exactly."

"The Vesica Piscis, another sacred symbol. It's embedded in the flower pattern carved on your box. Pay attention to this. It holds the key to so many of your questions."

The conversation was becoming more and more cryptic, making Lena uncomfortable. And she was eager to get home and rest before her flight tomorrow. "I really should be going now."

"I'm sorry to have kept you so long," Thomas said.

"I enjoyed talking with you." Lena searched for the Vesica Piscis in the carving on the box.

"One last thing," she said, reconsidering and presenting the box to him. "I wondered if you could please try to open this for me. I can't seem to do it myself."

"It's not for me to open." He studied the box carefully again. "There's something for you to find. What a gift!" It was as though he had glimpsed the treasure inside the box.

"C'mon, Thomas, what did you see?" Lena was impressed.

"I can't tell you. You'll know soon enough."

Now, she was even more intrigued. She regarded him with a puzzled yet hopeful look as she stood up to leave. "Why are you so obsessed with doors anyway?"

"Remember the sixties group The Doors," he laughed. "Jim Morrison is buried here in Père Lachaise cemetery. In one of his songs, he says, 'There are those things that are known and those things that are unknown, and in between them are the doors.' The poet William Blake wrote about cleansing our 'doors of perception' so that everything would appear as it really is, infinite."

"You are a most mysterious man," Lena said warmly. "Thank you, Thomas, for everything."

Chapter Sixteen

Lena's pulse quickened with a mix of anticipation and apprehension as her taxi pulled up to a grand old hotel on Via dei Neri in Florence, just steps away from the Palazzo Vecchio and the Uffizi Gallery. Fortunately, as a member of the press, she had been able to arrange a significantly discounted room at the recently renovated fifteenth-century Renaissance palace encompassing an entire block. Transfixed by the hotel's imposing classical façade, iron-barred windows, and massive bronze-studded doors, she recalled her conversation with Thomas last night. The seven initiations. Her "real investigation." The mysterious treasure inside the box. Wondering what it all meant, she drifted into a reverie.

Giovanna's carriage came to a screeching halt in front of her palazzo. She was glad to be back home. As much as she had enjoyed her exalted afternoon in the mountains and cave, she had missed little Giovannino. Her elderly horseman, Pablo, ran to her aid from the stables behind the palazzo, scolding her for taking off by herself without notice. She greeted him affectionately as he tended to the horses. To her surprise, her friend, Domenico Ghirlandaio, had also just arrived, looking rather disheveled in his paint-flecked smock and carrying a large draped canvas. Delighted to see her, he helped her out of the carriage, respectfully kissing her hand.

"I'm so sorry for your loss." His voice was filled with emotion. "I loved Lorenzo, too. It greatly saddened me that I was ill and missed his funeral."

"I know I can always count on your friendship, dear Domenico," Giovanna said.

"I've come to deliver your portrait. We finished it ahead of schedule. I hope it's to your liking, my dear."

But Giovanna's ever-present smile was gone, her expression vacant. Her sparkling eyes had dimmed considerably since they were last together. "Thank you," she said softly, folding her hands at her heart. They solemnly proceeded together through the palazzo's heavy, bronze-studded doors.

A young porter wearing an artist's beret unexpectedly helped Lena out of the taxi, jolting her back to the present. He smiled angelically as he lifted her hand to kiss it. Struck by this intimate gesture, Lena dropped her suitcase on the sidewalk and stared at him, then turned her attention again to the hotel, the Duomo towering in the distance, and the nearby Piazza della Signoria—the city's main square—feeling an eerie déjà vu.

"It's all so . . . so familiar," she exclaimed, bewildered.

Just then, a stout archbishop passed by in a long, billowy red robe with a large gold crucifix dangling from his neck. He regarded them with mild curiosity. Lena found herself bowing slightly, an unusual gesture, considering her typically irreverent streak.

"I hear that a lot," the porter laughed. He was short and balding and barrel-chested with strong, muscular arms and an amiable, rosy glow. Lena took instantly to his upbeat demeanor.

"I really mean it," she said, in an effort to distinguish herself from the casual tourist. Being in Florence for the first time felt like a homecoming of sorts, as though she had returned to pick up where she left off, not knowing why.

"Some say we are living in another Renaissance, a time of great change, newness, and rebirth," he said whimsically, carrying her suitcase into the hotel. "What do you think?"

"Perhaps." Lena reflected for a moment.

She considered how the many upheavals of these times—the fragile economy, the degraded environment, natural disasters, corporate greed, political corruption, religious fanaticism, and other signs of a dissolving world order—felt more like a death. But beneath all that she did sense something else was going on, something of great magnitude that was impossible to define, as though the entire planet was being observed under a microscope in a monumental experiment upon whose success the far reaches of the universe depended. Being so far away from her own day-to-day existence, she suddenly felt very small and unimportant. Just thinking about all the streets and buildings and neighborhoods extending across the Earth, all the people rushing to and from here and there, the packages being delivered, the food being served, the vehicles moving about, made her head spin. And her worries and concerns began to feel inconsequential, absurd even, in the midst of such unimaginable activity. And all to what end?

The porter happily accepted her generous tip, lifting his beret in gratitude, then hurried off as Lena surveyed the regal hotel lobby, her hands folded in a prayer-like gesture at her heart. It was as familiar as the sights outside. The soaring frescoed ceilings and classical moldings. The black-and-white checkered marble floors, old tapestries, and paintings and statues of religious and mythological figures. The dark, ornately carved furniture and arched, blue-tinted windows cast a dreary pall over the interior, which despite its opulence felt sad and heavy to Lena, as though weighed down by a lingering tragic memory. She sat down in one of the armchairs, lifted Bill Bradley's book out of her purse, and began reading it again with urgency, pausing to highlight a passage:

When clients connected with their past lives, they often experienced what I call an inter-dimensional bleed-through whereby present events, sights, and sensations overlap with those of a former lifetime, causing these individuals to feel like they are slipping through time—both a jarring and exhilarating sensation.

Was this happening to her now? One thing was certain. She felt her entire progress depended upon her ability to speak the truth and act on it. A chill swept through her body, momentarily immobilizing her, and again she tumbled back through time.

Chapter Seventeen

Giovanna finally left her home for the first time in days. She could no longer allow herself to be consumed with grief and despair over her husband's murder a fortnight ago. It was time she ended her self-imposed isolation and took charge. She had cried enough tears, said enough prayers. Her friends had been generous and comforting in their outpouring of sympathy, though her own family had not paid her even one visit. Granted her mother was bedridden with disease and did not even recognize her when she last visited. But her brothers could have at least shown their respects. Thanks to Ghirlandaio, all practical matters concerning her husband's business and estate had been settled. With her husband's family stipends and her own inheritance combined, she would have more than enough income to take care of her children and employ her domestic help, and for that she was grateful.

Clad in her long black mourning dress and coat, a veil covering her opalescent face, she briskly made her way to the afternoon market at Piazza della Signoria, not far from her palazzo. The low-hanging bulge in her belly had grown larger and heavier, announcing the imminent arrival of her new child. The joy that would have normally accompanied her state was sadly missing, having been eclipsed by her tragic loss. Even so, her husband's absence was like a raging fire inside her, propelling her forward with renewed strength and determination. At the piazza, amidst the market clamor, she stopped to talk with the townspeople, one by one, inquiring whether they knew anything about her husband's murder. She bowed with gratitude to each person she engaged, prepared to offer a handsome reward in gold. After several hours, exhausted and frustrated, she rested for a while at a fountain, fingering her glass prayer beads slowly and methodically to still her mind and calm her heart. She knew that her mind, when it wandered, could accomplish very little.

With each passing day she felt less and less a part of the swirling activity around her. Paradoxically, the terrible suffering brought on by Lorenzo's sudden death had taken her even deeper inside herself so that she had little need for external indulgences, comforts, and distractions. Observing the passing parade, she recalled Jesus's words, in the mystical gospel that Medici had given her: "Be one of those who pass by." She interpreted this to mean that she must release her attachment to the fleeting things of this world, which are an illusion, because they cannot bring the joy or fulfillment that her eternal direct connection to Spirit provides. As she reflected on this truth, a priest came running up to her from the crowd.

"I heard you were out today seeking news about your husband," he said, catching his breath. He was slight of stature with a long, thin face and tired, sagging eyes. "I don't know how to tell you this . . ." His voice quivered.

"What is it father?" Giovanna pressed.

"I will never forgive myself." Tears filled his eyes. "I accepted gold from your brother."

"But I don't understand, please, which brother do you speak of?" She was filled with dread.

"Now I, too, fear for my life," he whimpered. "But I could not go on like this. You had to know. Your brother, Salvatore, he's the one. He did it, and I saw him. He paid me to keep quiet. That night behind the church, when you found your husband . . ." He slumped forward, holding his head in his hands.

162

Giovanna was paralyzed with disbelief. "Are you saying that Salvatore killed my husband?!"

"Yes, my lady. I am so sorry. Please forgive me, please," he pleaded. "You know our city is in economic turmoil, even as our culture flourishes. Three more branches of the Medici bank have closed. Our patron has let us down. I was afraid I would be left with nothing." He sighed with remorse. "I deserve the whippings of Savonarola."

"You yourself, father, did not commit the crime." She spoke calmly and without affect, as though someone else had stepped into her body and was directing her responses. "You did well to tell me. Your conscience has triumphed. I forgive you for accepting the payment. The rest is between you and God."

"Thank you," he whispered. "Thank you. You are a being of peace seeded by the Father in the lineage of Christo. Such has been said of you, and now I am certain. Many, many blessings to you." With that, he gathered his robes and walked off, mournfully reciting prayers to himself.

Giovanna repeated the shocking words: "Salvatore killed Lorenzo." Her heart raced, and she suddenly began choking and heaving. Now what? It was too much to bear. She sat for some time, staring vacantly into the distance. Then a sharp pain shot through her abdomen. It was not the usual kicking sensation she had often felt. She went back to her prayer beads and tried to calm her heart, while gently stroking her belly, as if to reassure her unborn child that all would be well.

Finally, she rose to her feet, bearing the full weight of her devastation, and wandered forlornly through the piazza. With a spontaneous side glance, she caught sight of her brother, Salvatore, purchasing bread from one of the vendors. She held her breath, stunned by this crossing of paths. Should she act now? She knew without a doubt that her entire future and the future of her child hinged upon this moment, that she had been granted a mere instant to choose her fate and determine her spiritual progress. Overcome with an almost superhuman resolve, she approached her brother and tapped him on the shoulder from behind. Salvatore turned to find her staring him down with the full force of her fury. The blood drained from his face, and his hands began trembling, as he abruptly started to flee.

"Wait!" Giovanna shouted, turning several heads. "There is nowhere to run, Salvatore!" A group of townspeople circled them.

"You don't know what you're talking about!" he lashed out.

"You have violated your sacred contract, brother." She was consumed with grief at what she was about to do, in front of everyone.

"Leave me alone. You forfeited your rights as my sister when you married into the Medici household." He looked weakened and depleted. His clothes were soiled, and his breath smelled of alcohol. Giovanna beheld him indifferently.

"Why did you murder my beloved Lorenzo? Why, Salvatore, why?! What harm did he cause you?" She struggled to keep from breaking down, as the sun sank on the horizon, casting the formerly light-flecked piazza in shadow. It was unthinkable that fate would have dealt her this blow. She could never have imagined as a child, much adored and supported by her parents and showered with every possible privilege, that she would find herself at such an excruciating crossroads.

"How dare you accuse me!" He raised his arms to the sky and bellowed, "Is she not a mad woman?!"

The excited crowd began waving their fists and shouting in agreement, "She is mad! She is mad!"

At that moment, her brother, Stefano, stepped forward, along with several cousins and family servants. He stood defiantly before her, strikingly handsome and self-assured.

"I urge you to recant your accusation, sister," he commanded.

"We are the Albizzi, aligned with the Pazzi, and we are for the people. We will not be humiliated like this in public!"

"Humiliated?!" Giovanna screamed. "Your honor is nothing compared to my husband's life. I demand Salvatore's immediate arrest!" Tapping into reserves of courage that she had not even known she possessed, she steeled herself for an ugly battle and was prepared to fight to the end.

"Recant, or you will be sorry!" Her family shouted in unison.

"I will not betray the truth!"

"Then we have no choice but to send you away," Stefano declared. Gasps were heard from the crowd.

She remained unmoved, standing tall and strong, her hands folded at her heart. "My love for my husband is more important than my own life."

Two family servants, on signal from Salvatore, grabbed her by the arms and carted her away. Giovanna's desperate pleas echoed through the streets unanswered.

Chapter Eighteen

"Signora!" the porter called, walking up to where Lena was seated in the lobby. "Do you still need assistance?" He beheld her curiously.

"No, no thank you." She had lost track again of where she was and how much time had passed. Her heart was pounding, and she felt an ominous foreboding. Giovanna was still reaching out to her through time, but why? It was becoming unbearable to keep seeing and feeling what Giovanna had experienced. She wished the visions would stop and wondered whether she should see a psychiatrist, Bill Bradley perhaps. But she didn't have time now. Her deadline was fast closing in. She had less than two weeks to wrap up her investigation and write the story.

Lena checked into her room and quickly unpacked. Though tired and weary from traveling, she instantly set out to familiarize herself with the city. Wandering through the narrow, winding streets, cramped with hordes of tourists and stalled traffic, she skirted the swerving Vespa scooters. She was on constant alert, as though someone was following her. The ancient buildings and stonework and the breezy, inviting piazzas appeared unreal and insubstantial, more like a stage set that could be dismantled at any moment. The elegantly dressed locals appeared to walk about like actors in a play.

Questioning everything, Lena found her way to the Tornabuoni Chapel inside the stately Santa Maria Novella church, whose classical pink, white, and green marble façade was even more magnificent than in the photographs she had seen. She remembered from her research that Ghirlandaio had depicted Giovanna in a large fresco in the chapel, where members of the Tornabuoni family were entombed. She was taken by its realism and Ghirlandaio's obvious mastery of the human form. There was the slender, ethereal Giovanna in a long gown and mantle standing with a group of women witnessing the biblical meeting between the cousins Elizabeth, who was pregnant with John the Baptist, and Mary, who would soon give birth to Jesus. Giovanna emanated the same grace and dignity as in her much smaller portrait hanging at the Louvre. But this scene, called *The Visitation*, with its near life-size proportions and Florentine cityscape in the background, was even more powerful for Lena, for it seemed to encompass her completely.

An image of Thomas, the mysterious man from the flea market, flashed before her. She thought about the seven initiations he had spoken about, how she had already passed one of them and was working on the second. But what could they be? Typically, she would have dismissed such conjecture, but somewhere deep inside she believed Thomas was onto something and that she must pay attention. She had already risked so much to find herself here at this moment, on the verge of an important discovery. Risk; she turned the word over in her mind. Thomas had said the initiations would be revealed to her as verbs. What did it mean to risk? Somewhere she had read that not taking risks is a lie. Without risking, she pondered, how could we ever know what we're capable of becoming? Tingling with inspiration, she took out her notebook and wrote: "Initiation #1: To Risk." It felt right.

Drawn to the giant golden crucifix hanging above the altar nearby, she impulsively knelt down to pray. To her astonishment, the tiny blue-and-white mosaics on the marble floor were laid out in the pattern of the geometric symbol Thomas had drawn for her. He had called it the Vesica Piscis. Observing the sacred symbol for some time, focusing specifically on the inner oval where the two spheres overlapped, she drifted into a deep peace. Sometime later, she was distracted by a familiar voice.

"I see you are praying, signora."

She looked up to find the young porter from the hotel standing beside her. "Yes, I guess I am." Lena jumped to her feet. "I don't know why. I'm not at all religious."

"I'm not religious either, but I come here to pray a lot," he confided, removing his beret. "It's really more like meditating. I'm sorry to have disturbed you."

"No worries." She paused, not knowing what to call him. "I was just about to leave."

"My name is Massimo."

"Good to see you again, Massimo."

"A pleasure." He regarded her with the same familiar, curious expression as before.

On her way out of the church, Lena stopped suddenly. There was a large bloodstain on the steps. She felt faint and tripped with a frightened shriek. Massimo dashed out to help her up.

"Don't be afraid," he said knowingly. "Fear prevents us from being truly alive."

She thanked him, struck by his pronouncement. When she looked back at the steps, she was stunned to find that the bloodstain was gone.

"All right?" Massimo asked, concerned.

"Yes, yes, I'm okay." Lena felt no need to mention what she had just seen. Could she have been hallucinating? She wasn't sure she was standing on solid ground anymore, which rattled her immensely.

"I have something for you." Massimo pulled out a folded sheet of paper from his pocket and handed it to her. "I was waiting until I saw you again at the hotel. I didn't think it would be appropriate to give it to you in church, but why not?"

Lena began reading out loud what appeared to be a poem, illustrated with beautiful images in the style of a Book of Hours.

"I am the whore and the holy one. I am the wife and the virgin. I am the mother and the daughter." She paused, confused, and glanced at Massimo before continuing. "I am the members of my mother. I am the barren one and many are her sons. I am she whose wedding is great, and I have not taken a husband. I am the midwife and she who does not bear. I am the solace of my labor pains. I am the bride and the bridegroom . . . Why, you who hate me, do you love me, and hate those who love me? You who deny me, confess me, and you who confess me, deny me. You who tell the truth about me, lie about me, and you who have lied about me, tell the truth about me."

She fell silent, unexpectedly moved by the text.

"You can keep it. I have another copy," Massimo offered.

"So many paradoxes." Lena felt as though something of great significance had opened inside her. "What is this?"

"I found the poem in a book in the library and copied it down. It seemed important. It's called "The Thunder, Perfect Mind" and was found in a cave in Egypt in 1945 with some other mystical Christian texts." He pointed to the painted images of long-robed goddesses and flowers in the margins of the document, adding bashfully, "Those are my sketches."

"You're obviously a talented artist and a man of substance. But I'm not sure I understand all this," Lena sighed. "I'm not sure I understand much of anything anymore."

"To me, this text is a celebration of the divine feminine, the hidden, perfect goddess who transcends all things. She exists in every woman. Magdalena was a perfect example." He lit up, humbly awaiting her response.

Lena felt a surge of emotion at the mention of Mary Magdalene and remembered her unusually moving experience with her just recently at Notre Dame Cathedral in Paris.

"That's beautiful, Massimo. Thank you." Her eyes moistened. "But why are you giving this to me?"

"Because you are a flower unfolding."

She did not know how to respond. Perhaps for the first time, she had been shown a glimpse of her true nature. How could a young man be so unbelievably wise?

"I hope to see you again." He placed his beret back on his head and walked off.

Noticing that her notebook was not in her purse, Lena suddenly and anxiously walked back into the chapel. There it was, lying on the altar. She promptly retrieved it and went to view Giovanna again in *The Visitation* fresco. It was not like her to be so forgetful. She wondered whether she was forgetting something else, something of utmost importance. What did Thomas mean when he said her real work had just begun? What could that real work be? Beholding Giovanna among this group of women, she began to see and feel even more about her. Giovanna looked so whole and complete unto herself, radiant with the expectation of her own soon-to-be-born child. She and her husband, Lorenzo, were entombed just steps away from the fresco. Lena stood at their tombs for some time in respectful silence, feeling the deep bond of their love and the tragedy of their eventual separation.

Chapter Nineteen

Giovanna was granted one last wish before she was locked away in the sanitarium inside the Bargello, where her brothers had committed her on grounds of insanity. Even Ghirlandaio had been unable to intervene with this order, for the damning documents had been expediently signed before he learned of her incarceration. There was nowhere for her to turn now, but to her own higher guidance in communion with Spirit, always the one and only constant in her life. Her last wish was to visit the Tornabuoni Chapel, where Lorenzo was lying at rest. Two attendants from the sanitarium—the very same prison guards who had once treated her so kindly on her visits to read to the prisoners—waited outside the chapel for her, while she knelt praying fervently at Lorenzo's marble tomb, knowing that not even death could shatter their eternal soul connection. Undaunted by the other churchgoers filing in and out of the chapel, she repeated out loud in a slow, deliberate rhythm, filled with emotion: "Father, let not Your holy world escape my sight today. There is a real world, which the present holds safe from all past mistakes. All fear is past. Love remains the only present state, whose Source is here forever and ever."

As she prayed, images of her life with Lorenzo flashed before her eyes—their lavish wedding and tender lovemaking, the birth of Giovannino, decorating their beautiful home, carefree Sunday strolls through town, worshipping together at this very chapel, so many enjoyable meals and festive occasions with friends, vacations at their Sorrento estate. When she opened her eyes some time later, one of the sanitarium attendants, a rough, stone-faced man, signaled that it was time to leave. It seemed that the minutes had passed in an instant. She said goodbye to her beloved husband with great sadness, for this would be her last visit to his tomb. She knew deep within her heart that death was an illusion, a doorway to other levels of divine love, and that the body was merely a container for the soul, which lived forever. But it was nevertheless comforting to connect with Lorenzo's earthly remains in this way. In a final tribute to him, she removed her gold wedding ring—a symbol of their eternal love—and placed it inside a crack in his tomb, wiping her tears with her dress sleeve. She felt as though she had taken him within herself, fully merging with him energetically. "I *am* the bride and the bridegroom," she whispered.

She suddenly felt lightheaded. Afraid that she was going to lose her balance, she reached for a column to steady herself, startled by a painful cutting sensation in her arm. She looked down to find that her sleeve was moistening with blood and saw that she had inadvertently brushed against a damaged sharp area of the column. A few marble shards had pierced her skin, and she quickly plucked them out. Wrapping a silk scarf around her arm to stem the flow of blood, she pondered the strange incident. An image of a crown of thorns came to her. She remembered reading in an esoteric text a theory about how Jesus transcended his suffering on the cross by withdrawing his attention from his physical vessel and placing it on his light body, the high-frequency energetic imprint of his very essence that he had worked diligently to cultivate and which extended beyond this dimension to the higher realms. It was the supreme sacrifice of his earthly self to his infinite, immortal connection with the Divine. She knew that she, too, and all others could similarly attain this state, though the church would have considered it a heresy, having suppressed these mystical teachings.

In the wretched state in which she now found herself, she was coming to know something of sacrifice. She noticed the blood stains had quickly dried on her sleeve and that her pain was already greatly diminished. Indeed, she was not a body in space and time. That was what Jesus had taught through his example. Sometimes in bed with Lorenzo, she had lost track of where his body ended and hers began. It had been a brief taste of what she was now experiencing at a deeper level. She intuitively walked back to the altar and stepped into the Vesica Piscis symbol laid out in the stone mosaics. She had often worked with the symbol at her inspired retreats to the cave near Fiesole, where she worshipped and communed with her patron saint, Mary Magdalene. Now, so raw with her own pain and suffering, she felt more prepared to receive the symbol's sacred transmissions. Standing at its center, her mind stilled and serenely present, she felt as though she had entered that state of infinity to which she had always aspired. In this unified state, there was both male and female, spirit and matter, the sensual and the sacred. She was momentarily and completely transported, and even saw herself floating, viewing her immediate surroundings from above.

"Signora!" the attendant called out sharply. "Signora! We must leave."

Giovanna reluctantly pulled herself away from her beloved, as her captors held her by each arm and led her out of the church. She walked with great dignity and self-assurance through the streets on her way to the Bargello.

Chapter Twenty

Upon leaving the chapel, Lena felt very lonely and was grateful to be back among the crowds. She was refreshed by the warm Tuscan sun and the bustle of activity in the streets. She had lunch at a small rustic restaurant on Via degli Strozzi, studying her maps and calendar while she ate. Eleven days hardly seemed like enough time to complete her assignment. All the loose ends were overwhelming. She would have to rely now more than ever on her intuitive guidance, as very little made sense in her investigation—particularly her intense connection to Giovanna. Though she was always her own harshest critic, she could not identify any missteps so far. Even so, she remained on alert and reminded herself to trust no one until they proved themselves trustworthy. Steinert had been her one ally, and now he was gone.

Something did not feel right, as though a shadow was hovering over her, a heaviness she could not seem to shake. She tried not to think about the danger she could be in. Of course, Max had warned her, though had he known the extent of the danger, he likely would not have assigned her the story. From now on, Lena knew she would have to proceed with even greater discernment and clarity. Her thoughts turned to Thomas again and her supposed initiations. He had said she was already working on the second one. Envisioning the box carved with the beautiful Flower of Life pattern, she hastily took out her notebook and, underneath the words "To Risk," scribbled "To Discern." She felt certain that it was her second initiation and reassured herself that nothing would prevent her from writing the truth about Giovanna. Uplifted by this new insight, she paid for lunch and headed back into the sunshine in search of the art dealer Stefano Testa, from whom Madame de Trouville had said she bought the Ghirlandaio.

Lena made her way through snaking traffic toward Via della Condotta, not far from her hotel, where the Primavera Gallery was supposedly located. She passed by artisan shops specializing in stone cutting and stucco and glass work, several leather goods boutiques, and then through a lively open-air market selling everything from slabs of butchered meat to fresh fish, fruits and vegetables, spices, large bolts of fabric, and inexpensive house wares. As she rounded a corner, to her astonishment, five peacocks strutted across her path in single file, their brilliant royal blue and green feathers marked at their tips with colorful "eyes." Along with several other bemused shoppers, she stopped for a moment to admire them. It appeared that the peacocks had escaped from a stalled truck transporting a number of creatures most likely to the local zoo. Lena wondered whether the profusion of feathered "eyes" was a reminder to remain even more watchful as she continued on her mission.

By the time she reached Piazza della Signoria she was tired from the long walk and sat down to rest on the ledge of a beautiful, large fountain. Across the way, at the foot of the Palazzo Vecchio, the imposing town hall anchoring the square, was a dazzling array of towering bronze statues from the Florentine Renaissance. Referring to her guidebook, she identified them one by one. Giambologna's equestrian statue of *Cosimo I*, Cellini's *Perseus*, and a copy of Michelangelo's *David*, among others. She observed with cool detachment the massive, frenetic piazza, bursting with camera-toting tourists. Flocks of pigeons scavenged for crumbs at their feet. A small bronze plaque set into the pavement marked the location of Savonarola's "Bonfire of the Vanities" and his execution pyre. In one of her visions, she had seen Giovanna walk through this very square dressed in black. A shiver shot through her body. She looked around suspiciously, afraid again that she was being watched. She began to feel uneasy, breathless, and promptly crossed the square to continue searching for Testa's gallery.

She walked the entire length of Via Condotta to Piazza San Firenze without success. The Primavera Gallery was nowhere in sight. The address she had found online was obviously outdated—another unforeseen obstacle. She was growing wearier by the minute. Focusing on the daunting, fortress-like Bargello across the street, she held her breath. A woman in a Renaissance dress appeared to be pacing along the exterior of the tower. She looked strangely familiar, like Giovanna. Shaken to the core, Lena fled in the opposite direction until she reached the Ponte Vecchio. She gazed hypnotically at the Arno River from the side of the bridge, exhausted and gasping for air. The faint outline of a man's face suddenly appeared in the water, haunting, like a death mask. Frozen with fear, she was nevertheless captured by the face, which drew her even deeper into a trance-like state.

Chapter Twenty-One

Having passed another restless night in her tower cell, Giovanna awoke shivering in the predawn chill. The single worn blanket was barely enough to keep her warm. As was her habit each morning, she slipped into her black woolen dress and stockings and knelt by her bed to pray with her string of glass beads until the sun rose. The tiny, dim space, with a narrow plank bed, a single shelf, and straw-seated chair and table, was not unlike the oppressive cells of the prisoners she had often visited. Yet she felt even more claustrophobic here. Never would she have imagined herself in similar circumstances.

"Mangia!" She was interrupted from her prayers by the prison guard pushing a tray of food under her door. On it were a slice of bread and cheese, a few olives, and a cup of water.

Giovanna carried the tray over to the table and began to eat, mostly for her unborn child. Though she had fallen into deep despair upon her incarceration weeks ago, particularly because her baby would soon be born in squalor, she gradually began to accept her fate and with each passing day became more and more indifferent to her own perceived suffering. How she wished to see Giovannino. But she had instructed her housekeeper, Francesca, to keep him sheltered from her wretched surroundings. Though Ghirlandaio had promised to do everything in his power to secure her release, she did not hold much hope, for her family was a formidable force, as he himself had acknowledged. She tried to stay as present as possible, detached from future outcomes and past events over which she had no control.

After her scant meal, she meditated for a while and continued to purify herself by visualizing the violet flame of pure divine love consuming her entire being. Then she climbed back into bed and read from one of her favorite books, the *Gospel of Thomas*, containing the mystical sayings of Jesus, which had become her greatest support in these darkest hours. There were other books stacked in the corner, mostly of metaphysical content. Francesca had brought them, along with a leather-bound journal, a quill pen, and several bottles of ink, with which she recorded her thoughts daily.

Her time passed solemnly, silently, and uneventfully, at least as measured by the outside world. But as she turned further inward, her days were anything but uneventful. *"I am enlivened by the growing light within my heart and the laser-like focus of my mind,"* she wrote in her journal as sunlight spilled through the single narrow window of her cell. *"I have entered an ever-expanding, I would almost say, crystalline, state of awareness."*

Then, in a sudden flash of inspiration, she began writing a letter. As if guided by a higher power, she felt an urgency to speak to the women of the future who would be aligned with her consciousness. She sensed they would be entrusted with a great assignment and that she was somehow connected with it. Perhaps someone would one day find her letter, and it would be read by many:

To all my sisters, in body and soul,

Though long in my grave, I still weep. For the blood on my family's hands cannot be erased. It has spilled throughout the ages and courses yet through your veins. According to plan, it is for you, dear women, to remake the dream. Reverse speed ahead; the way is clear. By the time you read this, you'll know what I mean. Remember, what is Real can never be threatened. I am you, and you are me.

Love and Only Love,
Giovanna

Startled by a loud outburst on the street below, Giovanna dropped her pen and rushed to the window to have a look. A crowd had gathered in heated anger, shouting, "Long live Medici! Long live Medici!" She gasped at the sight of a man being held by the shoulders and dangled from a window across the street. He was screaming and pleading desperately for his life. She recognized his large silver belt buckle and severe, tortured face. It was her brother, Salvatore! Her heart sank with anguish. She watched with horror as he was tossed violently to the ground. With blood spurting from his ears and mouth, he was dragged through the streets by the Medici sympathizers to shouts of "Death to the Pazzi! Death to the Pazzi!" They were obviously settling the score for Lorenzo's murder. She had seen such brutality before. Sadly, it was typical of her fellow countrymen to seek revenge this way, and then dispose of the corpse in the Arno River. She broke down, weeping in despair that she herself had been the agent of her brother's demise.

She had already forgiven Salvatore for his crime, and now she would have to forgive his murderers, too. So much was being asked of her. How could everything have turned so dark? Yet she knew it was all nothing more than a raging mad illusion that she herself had created. Yes, she created every last detail! It was as if the anger, hatred, violence, and evil inside her, pious as she was, were being mirrored back to her by these events. No one existed here on the plane of duality without a shadow side, and she realized that she must now embrace and integrate the darkness within herself so she could rise above it. Otherwise, she could continue to resist it and impede her journey toward wholeness. She was finally ready to take full responsibility for writing this script— a terrible nightmare play in which she was an actor—in the same way that everyone else wrote and acted in their own individual productions with all their attendant emotional drama, hatred, and pain.

But why would she have created such insanity? She knew it was because of her guilt for participating in the illusion that we are separate from each other, Spirit, and our own highest selves. She had tried to explain these concepts to Lorenzo on many occasions, but her perception was much clearer now, and it all made more sense. She could only forgive herself and everyone else. And with even greater devotion, she could continue to live up to the ideal she had long ago taken as her divine mission—to be and teach love. How Salvatore had challenged her on this. She remembered reading in one of the mystical texts in Medici's library that "the holiest of all the spots on earth is where an ancient hatred has become a present love." She vowed to continue to work diligently at cleansing and activating the seven main energy centers of her body with special meditations that helped her to vanquish her hidden demons, just as her patron saint Mary Magdalene had done and instructed in her gospel. Like Magdalene, Giovanna deeply desired to craft her own light body, which would allow her to ascend fully into the realms of higher consciousness.

There was a loud knock on the door. The sanitarium attendant announced she had a visitor.

She was uplifted to see Ghirlandaio, who greeted her with tenderness and urgency.

"My dear Giovanna, I am sure you have heard all the commotion outside."

"I saw what happened to my poor brother." A knife-like pain pierced her chest, and her eyes filled with tears again.

Ghirlandaio was taken aback. "But why should you mourn the murderer of your husband?"

"Was his life any less valuable?" Giovanna gently countered.

The painter glared at her in bewilderment, as was often the case when she challenged his perspective. "I have some good news. I have been working with Medici to get you out of here. As you know, we must proceed cautiously, as his life is also in danger."

"Oh, Domenico, you are an angel!" She embraced him, noticing how tired he looked.

"I am confident we will succeed." He squeezed her hand to reassure her.

"I can see in your face that you have been working too hard. You need some rest."

"You are quite right," he sighed. "My workshop has grown, and I am training new painters to keep up with the commissions. But that is of little import compared to your wellbeing." He nodded at her large, inflated belly.

"The prison doctor said my child is due any day now." She spoke without affect, drained of the joyful expectancy any other young mother would have felt. Her thoughts drifted to little Giovannino and her sorrow at having been so cruelly separated from him.

Ghirlandaio, a parent himself, was visibly moved by her suffering. "You do not deserve the indignity of giving birth in this hell hole, my Giovanna. You are a woman of noble lineage."

"Dear Domenico, when you define me, you negate me."

He paused, confused, then continued with resolute firmness. "In any case, we hope to have you released as soon as possible."

"I know I can count on you. But if you should fail, I will not think any less of you. I have made peace with my days here. Do not despair for me." She projected an aura of peace and tranquility that defied reasoning.

Just then, the attendant opened the door to escort Ghirlandaio away. "I will be back soon," he declared, kissing Giovanna's hand with reverence.

Chapter Twenty-Two

Lena walked unsteadily back to her hotel, trembling and questioning her sanity. Whose face had she seen in the Arno River? Was it Giovanna's brother, Salvatore, whom she had just witnessed being murdered in her last vision? And was that Giovanna's ghost pacing the Bargello tower earlier? She did not know where to turn. Rushing into the lobby, frazzled, she dialed a phone number, at first missing the appropriate keys.

"Jud, I need to talk you!" She left a panicked message. "I never should've taken this assignment! I miss you."

She instantly regretted the impulsive call. But someone other than her concierge in Paris should know her whereabouts. Not wishing to worry Hannah with a phone call, she sent her a brief text message with the hotel phone number and address. Then she noticed that she had missed a call from Henri. He wanted to meet her the following evening at Caffè Rivoire on Piazza della Signoria to enjoy the first night of Carnevale. What was he doing here? She could not remember telling him that she would be in Florence. She sent a text accepting the invitation. It would surely be a relief to see someone familiar, but Henri would have some explaining to do again.

Momentarily uplifted by this turn of events, Lena asked the hotel concierge for directions to the Primavera Gallery. He thumbed quickly through an art directory and wrote down an address that was different from the one she had found online. Apparently, the gallery had recently moved. Then she remembered something important.

She ripped out a page from her notebook on which she had jotted down the words painted in the background of Giovanna's portrait.

"Do you know someone who can translate this for me?" she asked the concierge.

He squinted, trying to make out the letters.

"It's Latin," Lena said impatiently.

"Why, yes, I will send it to someone I know at the Uffizi Gallery, signora." He smiled, happy to be of assistance.

She thanked him and left the hotel with renewed enthusiasm, blocking from her mind the events that had so disturbed her earlier. When she arrived at the Primavera Gallery on a side street near the Uffizi, she was surprised and disappointed to hear that Stefano Testa had recently sold his business. The new owner had no information on his whereabouts. Had Madame de Trouville known about his status when she'd interviewed her? Was it possible that she was protecting him? Lena jotted a few notes and left the gallery more discouraged than ever. Testa was her last remaining lead. She still didn't have a story, just a lot of conjecture and suspicions. It felt like she was walking blindfolded in circles through a labyrinth with no exit. The only thing left to do was to track down Testa. Perhaps he was also connected to Ines Avidon, who had thus far remained elusive. Now, Lena would have to question more art dealers in Florence.

It was almost dark when she stopped at a nearby caffè. Having little appetite, she ordered only a small salad and a cup of tea, noticing she had developed a slight chill. It was typical of her to wear herself ragged and ignore basic needs when she got wrapped up in her work. Jud had often pointed that out to her. Jud. Why had she called him? She thought she had let him go for good, especially after hearing about his new girlfriend. And why was Henri in Florence? All she wanted was to sleep and forget about Giovanna, the haunting visions, her looming deadline, Jud and Henri, to forget about everything.

Lena awoke after noon the following day, angry at having slept so late. She checked her phone messages. No word from Jud, only a voicemail from Hannah:

"Lena, I got your text message with the Florence address. Are you safe? I'm worried about you. Please let me know!"

Lena called her back and left a message:

"I'm okay, Hannah. Don't worry. I'll call if I need you."

On the concierge's recommendation, she set out for the local flea market in search of a costume for the Carnevale. She welcomed the distraction. The flea market, with its narrow, winding alleyways and numerous cramped vendors' stalls, reminded her of the Porte de Clingnancourt market in Paris. She stopped to have a look at one of the stalls displaying antique and vintage clothing from the Middle Ages through the mid-twentieth century. Sorting through a rack of Renaissance dresses, she found a floor-length, boat-neck gown with colorful patterned sleeves and a sheer embroidered cambric mantle much like the one Giovanna wore in her portrait. Why not go to the Carnevale as Giovanna? She was pleased with the idea and didn't care what Henri would think. The vendor, a perky, cat-eyed woman, led her behind a white curtain into a makeshift dressing room with a long mirror. The dress fit perfectly.

"Here, signora, try this," the vendor suggested in broken English. She slid through the curtain a black satin eye mask attached to a small stick. "It's our tradition to wear masks at Carnevale. Most are much more elaborate."

Lena held the mask up to her eyes. The costume suited her. She felt lighter, as though a dark cloud had lifted. The article had extracted such a toll. Why not enjoy herself for a brief time, she reasoned, silly as it seemed? She paid for the items, dropped her mask and clothes in her purse, wrapped her cape around her new outfit, and set off for Piazza della Signoria, anxious about her meeting with Henri. Along the way, she was greeted with smiles and a few compliments from curious pedestrians and other costumed revelers. It was early March, when Florence and other Italian towns came alive with Carnevale parades and festivals celebrating both the arrival of spring and the final days before Ash Wednesday and the solemn restrictions of Lent. Tonight was the beginning of the weeklong festivities.

Walking slowly and steadily with the same grace and dignity that Giovanna might have displayed, Lena tried to imagine how the city appeared in Giovanna's day. Merging more fully with her essence, Lena's haunting vision yesterday of Giovanna pacing the tower, though still unsettling, now seemed less threatening. She felt a bright, new confidence rising within her and everything she set her eyes upon appeared bathed with light. While she pondered these strange new sensations, a little girl, no more than four or five years old, ran up to her sobbing, and grabbed hold of her hand. Lena bent down to comfort her, trying to communicate. The child kept repeating, "Mamma, Mamma!" She was obviously lost.

Lena led her by the hand in earnest search of her mother. Within minutes, she spotted a distraught Italian woman screaming out her daughter's name from a street corner. Lena rushed over to reunite the two. She was warmed by the mother's tearful expression of relief as the child ran ebulliently into her arms. How refreshing to have been of service in this small way, momentarily dropping her own worries and concerns, expecting nothing in return.

Passing by a disheveled old woman begging on a curbside, Lena spontaneously helped her to her feet and guided her to the nearest caffè, leaving her with thirty dollars for a meal. She would never forget the woman's grateful smile and the surge of joy in her own heart, which began to feel so newly expanded. Further down along Via della Ninna, she was startled by a barrage of loud shouts in Italian and southern-accented English. An American tourist was arguing with a shopkeeper outside a jewelry store. Though it was not her nature to intervene in situations concerning others, Lena walked over to the two men to see what the commotion was about. They were arguing over a defective gold necklace that the tourist had bought for his wife and wanted to return.

"Can I see the necklace?" Lena inquired.

The perplexed shopkeeper showed it to her. Lena inspected it carefully. One of the chain links was malformed. She tried it on, glancing at her reflection in the shop window.

"I think it's beautiful. Is this for your wife?" she turned to the tourist, a pudgy, middle-aged man with thick-rimmed glasses.

"Why, yes. Yes, it is," he replied, eyeing her with suspicion.

"I'm sure she'll love it. That tiny flaw is barely noticeable."

"Bellissima!" the shopkeeper said, admiring the necklace on Lena.

The tourist stood scratching his head and contemplating his options. "Okay, okay. I'll take it."

The men parted peacefully, thanking Lena for resolving the dispute. Empowered and supremely present, she approached Caffè Rivoire on the piazza. Henri was sitting at a table by the window. By now, it was dusk, and festive torches had been lit around the square. Her heart fluttered with an unwelcome anxiety.

"Ah, there you are!" He stood up to greet her, inspecting her costume with bemused curiosity. Lena?"

"I decided to have some fun and dress up as Giovanna." She forced a smile, half-resisting Henri's embrace.

"I thought you'd be happier to see me, chérie." He was dapper as usual, in his well-tailored business suit and crisp white shirt. "I wanted to surprise you."

"That you most definitely did." She stared him down, taking a seat beside him. "You haven't called, Henri. How did you know I was in Florence?"

"I stopped by your apartment the other day," he said. "The concierge told me. She was collecting your mail."

"How clever."

"I've already ordered for us. I knew you'd be on time." He leaned over to kiss her neck.

Lena ignored him, turning her attention to the colorful floats and huge paper puppets parading around the square in the tradition of Renaissance carnivals. There were effigies of current politicians and historical figures like Julius Caesar, Cleopatra, and even Lorenzo de' Medici. The locals were out in full force, dressed as courtesans, clerics, jesters, dragons, ballerinas, and other whimsical characters, gathering in small groups or wandering about arm in arm. There was a Grand Inquisitor wielding a torch and a Mona Lisa with her head poking through a frame, among other elaborate costumes. Drums, tambourines, and flutes resounded amid all the revelry. It was quite a spectacle, yet Lena felt oddly removed from it.

"All right. All right! I'm sorry I haven't been in touch." Henri caressed her hand. "I know how busy you are. I didn't want to disturb you. And I've been traveling like crazy."

"I left you a message that Steinert was shot and killed. No response, nothing from you. I found that strange."

"Look, I'm sorry, but the old man had it coming to him. The Baron's been after him for a long time." His eyebrows arched in expectancy. "It was the Baron, wasn't it?"

"Maybe, maybe not." Lena recalled the Baron's obsession with the Ghirlandaio. "The Baron has been acting very strange lately. Like a borderline lunatic. He's even painting his own version of Giovanna."

"You're full of good news tonight." The sarcasm in Henri's voice annoyed her. She wondered why she even agreed to see him again.

"I don't suppose you know anything more about Steinert?"

"I've told you everything I know. I can't write your story for you."

"How am I going to make sense of this mess?!" She buried her head in her arms.

"Don't worry yourself sick. It's just one article."

"I've had very little support. You're always out of town, Henri, which doesn't make things any easier." Recalling her recent disturbing vision—or was it a hallucination?—of Giovanna, she began to feel tense and fatigued.

There's something I want to tell you," she continued, weighing her words. "Just yesterday, I saw a woman who looked like Giovanna pacing the Bargello tower. It scared me. I saw a woman in Paris, too, on Île Saint-Louis, who looked just like her. I wonder if someone is playing around with me, trying to set me up." In need of reassurance, she eagerly awaited his response.

But Henri appeared preoccupied, as though he had drifted off somewhere far from their present encounter. He studied her with a puzzled look. "Your imagination is going to get you in trouble, chérie."

Her resolve strengthened despite her reservations. "There's no turning back now, Henri. I'll do whatever it takes to get this story!"

The waiter delivered plates of fried calamari and linguini in red clam sauce, along with a bottle of Pinot Grigio. Lena was hungry and happy for the food. They broke some fresh bread and dined silently for a while, watching the fanfare on the piazza. Two young men wearing chasubles with huge crosses dangling from their necks entered the caffè. They stopped before Lena and Henri, made the sign-of-the-cross, and mumbled something in Italian. Lena lifted her mask to her face and thanked them for the benediction.

"It's chilly in here." Henri rubbed his hands together. "They should turn on the heat." He anxiously scanned the caffè, as if he were expecting someone.

"Oh, and there's one other thing I forgot to mention," Lena hesitated. "The gloves . . . I saw your gloves at Madame de Trouville's." She felt her anger rising and bristled at the thought of the impudent heiress.

"So what? She's a client."

"Really? Is that all?" Lena was not in the mood for his usual nonchalance.

"Don't be ridiculous. We have a professional relationship, period."
He regarded her wistfully. "You're the one for me. There's no one else."

"Nice try, Henri, but I don't believe you." The bell sounded in the
clock tower across the square. Her pulse quickened at the sight of
two ravens swooping down against the darkening sky.

"I came all this way, and for what?" Henri looked away, visibly
offended, folding and unfolding his napkin in tiny triangles. "In
fact," he abruptly pushed the table away, "I don't have to listen to
this!" He stood staring at her, his eyes dark and forbidding, then
stormed out of the caffè.

"*You* don't have to listen to this?" Lena shouted. She set out after
him, ready to tell him how she really felt.

The crowd in the square had increased considerably since she
arrived, and she pushed through the swell of costumed bodies.
Her mantle fluttered about, nearly transparent in the moonlight.
The scene was like a still from a Fellini film. The Cleopatra she
had seen earlier, in her flowing white toga, was being carried on a
rattan stretcher by two handsome slave boys and fanning herself
with a peacock feather. A jester in a green-and-yellow jumpsuit did
several back flips in front of her, while a man dressed as a Greek
warrior approached her for a light for his cigarette. Surprisingly, he
reminded her of Jud, with his sandy hair and refined features. How
far away her old life seemed now. And she half-wished to have it
back. She found her way to a church at the edge of the piazza and
sat down on the marble steps. Henri was nowhere in sight.

After a few minutes, she resumed her search, despondent and
exhausted. As she turned a corner, she noticed a shadowy figure
trailing close behind. She recognized him in the glow from a street-
light. He was the same man she had seen in Paris with Steinert and
then on the train, when he had warned her to stop her investigation. Her heart raced as she dashed through the streets without
looking back.

When she arrived at her hotel, she was breathless. At least for now, she had escaped her pursuer. She glanced cautiously through the window to make sure he was gone. There were only a few straggling merrymakers and a stray dog. A momentary relief, though she could not help but feel she was in grave danger. Indeed, she had been warned—by Steinert, the Baron, Henri, and even Jud, before she left New York. In her usual stubbornness, she had chosen to ignore them. She checked her cell phone. No word from Henri. Massimo spotted her from the porter's desk.

"Signora, you look troubled," he said politely.

"Oh, Massimo," she said, relieved. "I was looking for my friend. I lost him at the Carnevale tonight. He's French, average height, dark brown hair and wearing a nice suit. His name is Henri Lemien."

"Don't worry, signora, I will look for him."

"You are so kind, Massimo. How can I thank you?" She smiled tentatively.

"Please, try to relax and get some sleep," he urged. "I'll make some calls to the tourist hotels where the French usually stay. I'll let you know."

Back in her room, Lena took off her costume, packed it away carefully, and collapsed on the bed. She slept restlessly, shaking every now and then, as though she were having a bad nightmare. Halfway through the night, she awoke abruptly with intense stomach pains, groaning and rocking back and forth.

Alone in her cell, Giovanna screamed in agony, her legs open wide. It was early morning when the contractions began. The doctor was not scheduled for another visit until tomorrow, and the thick stone walls were impervious to her screams. She felt the baby trying to come out, and she tried to push as hard as she could. The pain was unbearable. "Lorenzo!" she called out. "Lorenzo, I need you!"

Chapter Twenty-Three

Lying in bed in a hazy half-slumber, Lena struggled to understand why she had experienced such extreme stomach pains overnight. Was it food poisoning from the calamari and clams? Then she remembered that Henri was still missing, and her anxiety returned. There was a loud knock. She jumped out of bed, slipped on her robe, and peered through the peephole in the door; was it Henri? To her astonishment, it was Jud! She was momentarily immobilized and could not speak. After a few more knocks, she opened the door. He cautiously stepped inside, beholding her silently for some time.

"Jud!" He appeared different to her than when she last saw him in New York. There was stubble on his chin and the beginnings of a moustache. His eyes were tired and distant. He looked rougher, less refined, as though he had just returned from a wilderness outing.

"Your message." His tone was edgy. "You sounded so stressed. I was worried about you. So I called Hannah, and she gave me your address here."

"I see." Touched by his concern, she did not know how to respond.

"Look, Lena," he said, shaking his head with resignation. "No matter what happened between us, I'll always love you. I can't help it. I even feel responsible for you in some way. I thought you might need me. That's all I can say. So here I am." He stared at her indifferently, waiting for a response.

"It's the last thing I expected, Jud." Lena took a deep breath and sat down at the edge of the bed, nervously swinging her leg back and forth. "But it's good to see you . . . really, it is." She smiled, comforted by his presence, then grew somber.

"I have to say, you don't look well." He paused to study her, visibly surprised by how much she, too, had apparently changed. "So pale and frazzled. I've never seen you this way."

"You have a girlfriend now. Why would you care about me?"

"I just told you why! Maybe this wasn't a good idea, after all. Hannah wanted to come, but I insisted, thinking you might be in real danger. She's very worried about you, as you can imagine." He stood tall and defiant, his arms folded at his chest. "*Are* you in danger?"

Lena wanted to throw her arms around him, but she couldn't. She instinctively held out her hand, palm down, as if waiting for him to kiss it.

"What?" He was taken aback by this strange gesture.

Lena's initial joy at seeing him faded to confusion. "I thought it was over between us, Jud," she said abruptly. "I can't deal with this now. I really can't."

Jud's sudden appearance combined with her unnerving connection to Giovanna, who was so familiar yet so frightening, was all too much for her.

"I don't get you, Lena. I'll never get you." He walked over to look out the window at the street below, as if to ground himself in the mundane sights and sounds of daily life.

Lena began pacing the room in a daze, her hands clasped at her heart, reciting the words to a prayer. "There is a real world, which the present holds safe from all past mistakes. All fear is past . . ."

At a loss, Jud helped her back to the bed. "Lena, are you okay? You know I'm always here for you."

"This Giovanna, she's somehow taken hold of me, gone deep inside." Lena stared blankly into the distance. "I'm afraid . . . like I'm losing my mind or something."

Jud grasped her hand, wanting to protect her. "Lena, it's not like you!"

She searched for a rational explanation. "Could this be a big joke, Jud? Did someone drug me?" she hesitated, trying to compose herself. "Do you know anything about past lives?"

He gazed at her with disbelief, put off by her odd behavior, her cool detachment. "That's ridiculous. What good is the past when you can't see what's right here in front of you, in the present?!"

Crestfallen, Lena fell silent. Not even Jud could help her. She felt so lonely and disconnected and didn't know how much longer she could stand this torment.

"I'm worn out trying to get through to you, Lena," Jud continued, defeated. "I'm done. Sorry I came." He turned to leave.

"Please, Jud . . ." Lena started. Her heart sank as the door slammed behind him.

It was the same old pattern. She challenged him by speaking her truth, and he didn't understand, which only made her feel worse. She wished she hadn't called him, that he had never shown up, so gallantly and unexpectedly. All for what? She didn't need anyone, never did. She could take care of herself!

Just then, someone knocked on her door again. "Signora, sorry to disturb you."

Lena could see through the peephole that it was the concierge and immediately cracked open the door.

"The answer to your request. From the Uffizi curator." He handed her an envelope. "Excuse me," he said sheepishly, obviously embarrassed to find her in her robe.

"Thank you, sir, for taking the trouble."

She opened the envelope and read: "If thou, O Art, couldst represent also character and virtue there would be no more beautiful picture on earth." It was the Latin inscription on Giovanna's portrait that she had sent to be translated. The curator had noted it was from an epigram by the ancient Latin poet Martial. She pondered the words, filling with sadness as she connected again with Giovanna. Suddenly and inexplicably, she began choking and gasping. Suffocating, she rushed to open the window. She observed with detachment the chaotic bustle of the streets. Her mind was fuzzy, and she was unsteady on her feet. The stressful, grinding activity of the past weeks had caught up with her. She had never felt so fatigued. Her limbs were like dead weights, and her body wanted only to rest.

The next day, though still emotionally and physically spent, Lena resumed her work with determination, trying to forget about Henri's disappearance, Jud, and her confusing emotions. She had located several old master paintings dealers online and planned to interview them about the missing Stefano Testa. But first, she needed to find more information about the real Giovanna. Hurrying to the town hall in search of old records, she checked her cell phone again.

No messages. Was Jud still in town, or had he already flown home? Regretting her rude behavior, she called his cell. No answer. On automatic pilot, having surrendered to what she could only call a higher guiding force, Lena was at the mercy of something relentlessly pushing her forward. However uncertain and unsettling the path ahead, she could not back off. She had to continue taking action, trusting that everything was in perfect order. Something had shifted inside her. She was no longer in complete control. That was hard to admit. Perhaps it was one of the initiations Thomas had told her about.

She stopped in the middle of the street, took out her notebook and wrote down "To Trust," just below the words "To Risk" and "To Discern." How difficult it had been for her, all these years, to trust. She had always been so alone, without parents or family for support. And in the orphanage, she had had to fend for herself, forever on the lookout for another child wanting to steal her meal portion, her pencils and schoolbooks, her favorite dress among the few she owned, or the attention of Sister Ruth, scant as it was to begin with. She had always felt she never had enough. How often she had pushed and worked and tried so hard to get what she wanted. What a struggle. But did it have to be that way? She was tired of struggling. She had spent so much time regretting the past and worrying about the future that she realized she had rarely been present in the moment, in the here and now, where everything felt okay, even good, because there was nowhere else to go.

Satisfied with her revelation, she proceeded down the street, cheered by the thought that she was being guided and protected and provided for, whatever the external circumstances. It certainly was a test, an initiation, and she found comfort in knowing that if she hadn't already mastered it completely, she was well on her way, at least as far as this assignment was concerned. What a relief to know that no matter how many metaphorical cliffs she jumped off there would always be a safety net beneath her or, as she preferred to imagine, a pair of arms to hold her. She felt liberated. The ancient, proud city appeared even more beautiful to her now in the glittering sunlight, as if reborn anew.

At the imposing, old-world town hall Lena asked for directions to the records room and anxiously proceeded down a flight of stairs. She presented her press card to the buxom attendant, who led her to a shelf of musty file folders. Lena pulled out a file marked GIOVANNA TORNABUONI. In it were the young Florentine's birth notice and marriage certificate, a beautifully illustrated page from a prayer book, and a crinkled, faded piece of parchment on which was penned a letter signed by Giovanna herself. Lena's eyes widened. What a thrilling discovery. "Please, signora," she asked the attendant, who was standing watchfully nearby, "would you translate?" The woman read out loud in a hushed, solemn voice as Lena hastily took notes, intrigued by Giovanna's words:

To all my sisters, in body and soul,

Though long in my grave, I still weep. For the blood on my family's hands cannot be erased. It has spilled throughout the ages and courses yet through your veins . . .

As Lena finished copying down the letter, she began to feel claustrophobic. Struggling to breathe, she thanked the attendant and abruptly rushed back outside for some fresh air. She walked a few blocks, pondering Giovanna's letter. Just ahead, the Bargello loomed ominously. Lena slowed her steps, and her heart began pounding. The woman who looked like Giovanna was pacing the tower again in her long flowing dress. Only this time, she turned toward Lena, as if beckoning her. Suddenly, from out of nowhere, a red Fiat raced right at her. Terrified, she turned a corner and ran as fast as she could to avoid it. But the car picked up speed and swerved to follow her. She was clearly a target. The car was moving so fast she could not see clearly who was behind the wheel. Her adrenaline pumping, she dashed inside a caffè to hide. She called Max on her cell phone.

"I can't go on . . ." she began. Spotting the red Fiat again, she abruptly hung up.

But, after all she'd been through, she couldn't stop now. Mustering all her strength and determination, she left the caffè and cautiously followed the car, careful to keep a low profile. Fortunately, with the continual starting and stopping of the traffic, she was able to follow it for some time until she finally lost sight of it near Santa Maria Novella church across town. Exhausted and distraught, she collapsed on the church steps. While trying to call Max again, she saw the Fiat parked down the street and froze with fear. There were sounds coming from inside the church—muffled voices. The door was slightly ajar, so she edged inside. It took her eyes a while to adjust in the darkness.

Flames from rows of candles revealed three figures huddled near the altar. Lena held her breath. There were Henri, the mysterious man from the train, and the woman she had seen earlier dressed as Cleopatra, costumed in a billowy white tunic with gold serpent bracelets and a large amethyst scarab around her neck. They were engaged in a heated conversation. Otherwise, the church was eerily empty. It was all she could do to stay steady on her feet. Crouching behind one of the rear pews, hidden from view, she turned on her small tape recorder and strained to listen.

Henri, who was holding Cleopatra's hand, leaned over to kiss her. Lena angled for a better look at the woman. It was Madame de Trouville! She felt faint. As she suspected, the two were lovers.

"I told you to stop worrying so much, Ines," Henri consoled her. "Everything's under control."

Ines?! Lena was sick with dread. The thick, cloying scent of frankincense permeating the church made her gag. Ines Avidon, Gilbert's treacherous nurse, who had starved him to death and made off with the Ghirlandaio! She and madame were apparently the same woman. So many deceptions and betrayals. How could she have been so naïve?!

"What do you mean, she escaped?!" Henri thundered, turning to their burly accomplice. "You used to work for Interpol, for Christsake! You had a very simple assignment. Run her over, and make it seem like an accident!"

Lena could not believe what she was hearing! She caught a glimpse of the man, illuminated by the burning candles on the altar. His face was leathery and pockmarked, and there was a vacant, soulless look in his eyes, just like she had remembered him from that day on the train.

Perhaps he had been trying to protect her, already having received his assignment, when he had warned her not to continue with hers. The shocking revelation was just beginning to sink in. They were going to kill her. *Kill her.* In a split second, everything came crashing down. She was terrified, crushed. Her relationship with Henri had been a sham. All part of a plot to get rid of her. Her natural first instinct was to run—as far away from the church as possible. *Now.* But she couldn't move. How could she leave now that she finally had the story, the real story?

"But . . ." the hired hand protested.

"Just finish the job!" Henri demanded with callous indifference.

Lena despised Henri. She had never before felt such loathing for anyone, except perhaps for herself. It was as though she had been dumped head-first into a swamp, filthy deep with mud, and it was only a matter of seconds before she would suffocate.

"You son-of-a-bitch!" shouted the hired hand, as he stomped out through a side door.

"It didn't help that he knew Steinert," Henri said, disgusted. "The old man was protecting her."

"Just because he tipped me off about her investigation, and I had him send that threat letter to her in New York, didn't mean we had to use him again!" Avidon challenged him. "We should have gone with the same guy we hired to kill Steinert."

"Too late, Ines."

Avidon took out her compact and began wiping off her Cleopatra make-up. "I don't see why I had to come here, Henri. Another one of your silly ideas, just like that interview with her, in my own home yet. But you insisted. And like an idiot, I agreed!"

Lena's heart ached with grief for Steinert. These people were cold, diabolical criminals. And she had been sleeping with one of them. Lightheaded, she gripped the side of the pew. It was too painful to listen further. But where could she go? She would not be safe anywhere, as long as her death warrant was still out. Mechanically, she dissociated herself from the situation, becoming, in effect, a detached observer of her own imminent demise. It was like she had left her body and was now floating above it. She had once read that at times of extreme trauma and distress, parts of one's soul splinter off in an automatic self-preservation response. Was this happening to her now?

Henri knelt at the altar and bowed his head. "You know, sometimes I wonder if this was all worth it," he said, his voice cracking with remorse. "I mean, these are innocent people. Steinert, what did he know? And Lena . . ."

"He was getting too close to her, you said so yourself!" Avidon cut him off. "An important dealer like that, with all his connections. We couldn't take that chance." She took a candle from the iron stand near the altar and began lighting the other candles with it.

Henri nervously combed his fingers through his hair. "What are you doing that for?"

"Offerings. I'm lighting one for you and one for me, hoping everything turns out as planned." She proceeded ceremoniously, hesitating before each candle.

Henri walked up behind her and blew out the candles. "I must be out of my mind. This is all so simple for you, isn't it?!" he shouted. "How could I have let this happen? What in hell was I thinking?"

"You really do love her more than you do me," Avidon said with anguish. "I never should have fallen for you to begin with, painting or no painting!"

"Stop that, Ines." Henri embraced her. "You know I'd do anything for you."

Lena closed her eyes, still in shock.

"No, you mean you'd do anything for $21 million. That's what you mean, Henri! And when I stop to think about it, you haven't done all that much."

"I got Maurice to draw up that phony will, didn't I? I'd say he deserved his six million cut. And what about your $21 million?! Just be thankful you're a very wealthy woman because of me, Madame de Trouville." He surveyed her imposing, statuesque figure. "I like the name I chose for you. It fits somehow."

"And you're a very wealthy man."

"Where would you be now, do you suppose, if I hadn't stopped to help you with your luggage at the Blois station two years ago?" He reached out to her.

"I would be just fine." She pulled back.

"Holed up with Gilbert in that dreary château, that's where you'd be!"

Lena listened in shock, her heart racing at the mention of Gilbert.

"If you really loved me, you wouldn't have gone with her." Avidon genuflected and sat down in a pew, where she began reading a prayer book.

"You know why I stayed with her," Henri shot back, following her to the pew. "To steer her off track, that's why. I'm so sick of explaining things to you." He lowered his voice to a loud whisper and pulled the prayer book from her hands.

"And I was just dessert on your business trips."

"Don't talk such nonsense. What more do you want from me?!"

"I want her out of the way," she said with finality. "I'm afraid, Henri. Someone's going to find out about us."

"Done."

Lena remained motionless, as though they were speaking of someone else. The moonlight spilled in through the arched windows along the nave, highlighting a fresco of *The Assumption*. Madame de Trouville appeared less real now than when they had first met. She was more an apparition than a woman, a malevolent, foreboding shadow.

"Ines." Henri squeezed her hand tightly. "I swear I won't let anything happen to you, to us. Tomorrow, we leave for Paris."

Nothing could have prepared Lena for this betrayal. How could she have let it happen? How could she ever have gotten involved with Henri? So what if he was a good lover. Another wave of fear gripped her. She turned off the tape recorder and slipped out of the church as quietly as possible, praying they wouldn't hear her.

On alert for the red Fiat, Lena hailed a taxi. Once back at the hotel, she raced to her room and frantically threw her clothes into her suitcase. After she booked a flight, she settled her expenses in an adrenaline daze. She could not speed fast enough to the airport along streets littered with party debris, cigarette butts, and confetti from the night before. Still shaken while waiting for her flight, Lena called Interpol.

"Monsieur Crespin, Lena Leone here. I know who stole the Ghirlandaio!" Her voice rose with urgency.

"Please slow down, mademoiselle." The Interpol officer spoke in an official tone with a heavy French accent.

"Henri Lemien and Ines Avidon, they're the ones."

"Where are they?"

"On their way to Paris. Can you send some officers to 43 Rue de Fleurus tomorrow at one p.m.? That's Lemien's address. I'll be there."

"No, it's too dangerous, mademoiselle."

"Please, sir. I need to finish my reporting, please! I'll be okay."

There was a brief silence. "Okay, be careful, then! Au revoir."

Lena breathed a sigh of relief. It was hard to believe she finally knew the truth and could begin writing her story, though it would be such an effort to concentrate. She quickly dialed a number on her cell.

"Hi, it's me," she said, when Hannah answered. "I'm okay, it's over, and I'm coming home."

"Great news!" Hannah exclaimed. "Sooner than I thought."

"I have a few more things to do, but I'm telling Max I'm coming back to New York. I finally have the story, and it's going to be big. Max will be thrilled. I almost gave up."

"That's it? That's all you're going to tell me?" Hannah protested.

"Wait, you didn't tell *me* Jud was coming to Florence! I'm sure you know by now it was a short visit. Only made things worse."

"Sorry, Lena, I was so worried about you. I wanted to come myself, but he wouldn't let me. I'm just glad you're okay."

Lena softened. "I know."

"Jud said . . . you weren't yourself." Hannah paused, weighing her words. "He said you were edgy and confused and abrupt with him."

"I was a mess. I don't feel good about it. I was under so much stress."

"Wait, what about that guy, Henri?"

"He knew everything all along, the scum," Lena's voice quivered. "More than that, it was all a setup. He's a murderer, and he used me as a pawn!"

"Oh, no! I was right to be so worried! But you got the story. I knew you would. You must be excited about that, at least."

"I'm not sure how I feel anymore."

Just then, the airline made an announcement: "Boarding, Flight . . ."

"I have to go, Hannah."

"Okay, get home safely! Love you."

"I love you, too."

Lena noticed a text message from Max that she had apparently missed earlier. He was concerned about being scooped and pressured her again to finish the article. She quickly wrote back:

I have all the missing pieces now. Will start writing soon. You won't believe it. Don't worry abt. Advance. I'll explain later.

Back in Paris, Lena reviewed her notes of everything that had happened in Florence and filled in the gaps. The following afternoon, she pulled on her cape and left for Henri's apartment, where she had arranged to meet the Interpol officers. Despite the risk, she left earlier than planned, her tape recorder in her purse. A taxi horn blared as she crossed Boulevard Raspail without regard to the traffic. "You're going to get yourself killed!" the driver yelled in French, leaning out the window.

Lena trembled climbing the spiral staircase to the penthouse. She turned on the tape recorder, leaving her purse slightly open, and knocked forcefully at Henri's door.

"I've been trying to reach you," he greeted her nonchalantly.

"How strange. I've been at my place since I got back from Florence." She marched past him into the apartment. Heading straight for a black lacquer console displaying an expensive Venini glass vase, she picked it up and hurled it across the room, shattering it to pieces.

"Good God!" Henri shrieked, rushing over to the mess. "What are you doing? You're crazy!"

To Lena's surprise, Henri's attorney friend Maurice was seated on the sofa, bent over a marble chessboard.

"Maurice," she acknowledged.

He nodded somberly, avoiding her eyes. He continued to study the chess pieces, lifting one and then another before placing them back in the same position.

She stood still and defiant, struggling to suppress her rage.

"Listen." Henri's tone was conciliatory. "I left because, well, I don't know why I left. The carnival had a strange effect on me. I'm sorry, I wasn't myself." He sat down across from Maurice and pushed one of his pawns along the board. Lena noticed his shirt was wrinkled and soiled.

She watched them with disbelief, impressed by Henri's ability to focus on a silly game, while everything else was falling apart around him.

"I see. You weren't yourself." Lena stretched her arms along the back of a calfskin sofa, swinging one long leg over the other. "Do you think you might get me a drink, Henri?"

He reluctantly rose and headed for the kitchen, then returned, sauntering, with three beers.

"So Maurice." Lena directed her attention to the chess game. "How's everything?"

"Fine," he said, scowling. "Let me give you some advice, buddy." He turned to Henri, while moving a bishop and snatching Henri's queen.

"You should always be on the offensive, anticipating the opponent's move," Lena interjected, "and never, never on the defensive."

"That's right." Maurice was noticeably surprised by her remark.

Lena studied him with deep curiosity. His high, flat forehead and ridiculously long sideburns made him look like he should be wearing a top hat in a Dickens novel. "How much do you suppose it will cost, Maurice, to buy a new house, a new car or two, a boat, maybe, whatever you want?" Lena felt the heat rising in her face.

"What a question!" Henri forced a laugh.

His apartment was in perfect order, as usual. Not one thing out of place, not even a stray magazine or newspaper. Lena could just as easily have been sitting in the Art Deco wing of a museum. Her eyes settled on a beautiful Georg Jensen silver bowl, displayed on a tall marble plinth at the center of the living room.

"What are you getting at?" Maurice demanded.

"C'mon." Lena grew impatient. "You must have some idea of what to do with your six million." She did it. She dropped the bomb. There was a brief silence as she held her breath.

"You don't know what you're talking about!" Henri began pacing the room like an animal in captivity, his eyes full of fear.

"I saw you." Lena rose to her feet, her fists clenched. "I saw you!" she burst out, "in the church . . . you bastard!" She pounded Henri's chest.

"Stop!" Henri grabbed hold of her. "I said stop it!"

"You both disgust me." She leered at Maurice, whose chalky face had turned a shade paler. "I was going to end up just like Steinert and Gilbert, wasn't I? I heard you. Murderers! You and your deranged Cleopatra!"

The two men listened, speechless, as she proceeded to expose their crime.

"Hiring Maurice to draw up that phony will claiming that Ines Avidon owned the Ghirlandaio under her grandfather's legacy. Avidon masquerading as Madame de Trouville. Brilliant. You were sleeping with *her* all along!" Numb by now to the danger she was in, Lena reveled in her power, in Henri's helplessness.

"Where is she, goddammit?!" Henri bellowed, looking at his watch. "Late, as usual. I told her we needed to leave, *now*." He mumbled a few words to Maurice.

"Well, chérie, I'm sure your editor would be proud of you." Henri wrapped his arm around her with a false smile. "But we'd like to offer you an even greater reward."

"Don't touch me." She pushed him away. "And stop calling me 'chérie.' What a joke!"

"How does a two-million-dollar cut sound?" Maurice pulled a checkbook out of his blazer, wrote out a check, and held it out to her.

"You're pathetic, Maurice." Lena tore the check to pieces. "I'll be sure to write about this, too, and how you faked Gilbert's will."

She continued at a breathless pace. "And Stefano Testa, the Florence dealer who supposedly sold the painting to your friend, Madame de Trouville, he was another pawn. He never had anything to do with you."

"I think you should leave now, or you'll be sorry," Henri threatened.

"My head is splitting." She scrutinized Henri intently. He was actually shorter than she had first realized, and his hands and feet were huge, such unattractive features on a man of his size. His lips were so thick, and his eyes so close together, that it was hard to believe she had been attracted to him at all, that she had slept with him, despite his overwhelming first impression.

"If you print the story, no one will believe you anyway." Sweating profusely, Henri wiped his forehead with a handkerchief.

"He's right," Maurice warned. "Who are you going to quote? The Baron, that old fool? What does he know? Steinert's gone, poor fellow. And Gilbert, even if he were alive, he wouldn't have a clue." He nodded at Henri, as if to signal that the time was right.

"I know what I know, and I'll write what I've seen and heard for myself," Lena said with reckless boldness.

"Well then, your article should read just like fiction." Henri laughed.

"You can't stop me." She reached for the telephone, hoping desperately that the Interpol cops would soon show up. "Why don't you explain everything to the police."

"What in hell do you think you're doing?!" Maurice yanked the phone away from her, leaving thumbprints on her arms.

Lena didn't have the strength to resist. She tried not to show how terrified she was.

"Do that and you're dead," he growled, twisting her arms behind her back. "And if you run that story, you're dead, too. Either way you don't have a choice."

"Ouuuuuch! You're hurting me," Lena cried.

Henri watched, expressionless, making no effort to move. At that moment, the door swung open, and Ines Avidon appeared, wearing sunglasses and a white scarf around her head and wheeling a suitcase. She ran to Henri and fell into his arms.

"I can't do this," she complained, weeping. "I just can't do it!"

Henri shook her, "What's going on?"

"He's calling again, and now I think he's following me. I can't take it anymore. They're going to find out, Henri. I'm sorry I ever met you!"

"Who, that guy from Interpol? I told you, Ines, just forget about him." Henri removed her sunglasses, revealing her swollen, red eyes. "C'mon, we're leaving now!"

"What's *she* doing here," Avidon turned toward Lena, stunned.

"She was just about to leave." Henri gathered Lena's cape and motioned her to the door.

"Miss Avidon," Lena said, unleashing her fire again. "Your instincts are accurate!"

"What do you know? You're just a hack reporter!" She shot Henri an angry look, demanding an explanation.

"She heard us in the church in Florence. She knows."

"I knew it. I knew someone would find out!" Avidon pulled a gun from her purse and aimed it at Lena.

"Ines!" Henri shouted.

There was a loud shuffling sound in the hallway. Suddenly, the two Interpol officers charged in, guns in hand.

A wave of relief washed over Lena, and her body went limp. "What's done is done," she muttered.

"No matter what you think, I really did care about you," Henri whimpered as he and his friends were being handcuffed. Avidon was passed out on a chair, while Maurice remained silent, his head hung low.

"It wasn't supposed to be this way, not this way at all." Lena brushed away a tear and started for the door, hesitating at the entrance to Henri's gallery, where the seventeenth-century vanity paintings, with their pearls, mirrors, and skulls, hung one on top of another. There were more now than she had remembered, some stacked against the wall without frames. She turned off the tape recorder in her purse and hurried out and down the staircase.

The bell from Saint-Sulpice church broke the cool evening air. Crossing through the Luxembourg Gardens on her way home, she tried to make sense of everything that had happened—the murders, deceit, and greed. Her immense fear melted into rage. Henri had used her and tossed her away. How could he have been so cruel? Her cell phone rang, calling her back to attention. It was Max, with impeccable timing, as usual.

"Lena, to say that I'm displeased is an understatement." His tone was belligerent. "In fact, I'm damn angry right now!"

"What's wrong, Max?!" Lena's stomach tightened with anxiety.

"I hate to tell you this, but your story has been scooped!"

She froze in her tracks. "I don't understand. That can't be! No, I don't believe it!"

"It wasn't *Advance*, like I had thought. *Libération*, the French newspaper, broke the story today on a tip that came in from Interpol yesterday."

"But how do you know?!"

"I called them myself," he barked. "All this for nothing. What a waste."

Lena was speechless.

"Get back to New York, Lena. I don't know how much longer we'll even have a magazine." He hung up before she could respond.

Devastated, she stopped at a kiosk to read the headlines: "$48 Million Art Theft Solved." No, not this! It was too much to bear. Even worse, it was her doing. After all, she had notified Interpol, and they had leaked the news. Sick to her stomach, she walked the streets for several hours in a daze, oblivious to the activity around her. How could she face Max again? Would she even have a job when she got back to New York?

By early evening, she found herself at the Louvre just before closing, standing in front of Giovanna's portrait. She could not say why she needed to see her again. It was as though Giovanna still harbored one last secret. Lena beheld her for some time, trying to connect with her. Why had she shown herself in those haunting apparitions in Florence and earlier on Île Saint-Louis? Why all the unnerving visions? What was she trying to tell her? Beyond Lena's shock at seeing her story scooped by another newspaper, Giovanna herself continued to be a source of agonizing torment.

Standing there before her, Lena felt as if she were seeing through Giovanna's eyes, feeling with her heart. Giovanna was no longer a two-dimensional depiction but a living, breathing being. Lena began to lose track of time and space, an alarming sensation that left her feeling hazy and ungrounded. She felt weak and suddenly collapsed. The dangers and disappointments of the assignment had taken their toll.

"Mademoiselle!" A museum guard came running over, knelt down, and began breathing into her mouth. He promptly revived her and guided her to a bench.

"Merci, monsieur, merci bien." Startled and embarrassed, Lena assured him, half-heartedly, that she was okay.

As she pulled out a tissue from her purse to wipe her face, a business card tumbled out. The name on it was BILL BRADLEY, psychiatrist and author of *Many Lives, Many Miracles*.

Chapter Twenty-Four

Lena waited impatiently for about an hour before Bill Bradley's receptionist showed her into a comfortable room with a window looking out onto the Place de l'Opéra. There was a big leather armchair and a sky-blue upholstered divan, upon which she eagerly took a seat. Two tall, hearty palm plants and several framed embroidered Asian textiles added warmth to the otherwise spare surroundings. Within minutes, Bradley appeared with a broad smile, dressed in sporty khakis, a white shirt, and tennis shoes.

"So nice to see you again, Lena," he said in the gentle, soft-spoken manner she had remembered. "How are you enjoying your stay in the City of Light?"

"Dr. Bradley, I can't believe I'm sitting here."

"Bill, please," he interrupted her, relaxing into the armchair. His casual familiarity put her instantly at ease. "Take your shoes off, lie down, and make yourself comfortable."

"It's just this . . . woman in the painting. Giovanna, she seems so real. And I can't get her out of my thoughts. It's like I can see right into her life, things that happened to her, how she felt. She comes to me a lot . . . in visions or like some kind of ghost. It's so strange and scary."

"I can see you're very agitated," Bradley said.

"Embarrassed, too, to be telling you all this, after grilling you so much at your reading."

"Please, there are no judgments here."

"Let me explain better," Lena collected herself. "I'm on an assignment to write about a stolen famous painting that sold for a huge sum at auction. It's a portrait of a young Florentine woman, Giovanna Tornabuoni, by the Renaissance artist Domenico Ghirlandaio. I don't understand my connection with her, and it's driving me crazy."

"Well, let's see what else you can remember." Bradley smiled compassionately, while guiding her into a hypnotic state. "Relax and close your eyes. Imagine yourself in some kind of vehicle, a plane, a boat, a spaceship, even, and travel back to Florence at the time of the Renaissance. Take your time, and let me know when you've arrived."

He waited patiently until Lena nodded her head, yes. "How did you get there?"

"A hot-air balloon."

Her everyday self knew this sounded absurd, but her journey seemed all too real for her to question it. She was aware of being in this room with Bradley, yet at the same time she was also somewhere else. It was a most unusual feeling, like the dimensions of time were bleeding together again.

"And where are you now?" he asked.

"I'm at a celebration, in a beautiful garden."

"What are you doing there?"

She crinkled her forehead, as if straining to see. "I'm . . . I'm dancing." She felt instantly lighter, joyful even. "Dancing with a man who appears to be my husband. He's tall and dignified. And very good looking," she smiled. "Everyone is clapping and cheering."

"What are you wearing?" Bradley guided her further into the regression, recording on a legal pad everything she was saying. "Look first at your feet."

"I see satin slippers; they're rose colored. And there's a garland around my head, like a laurel wreath or something. My dress is white and chiffon-like, long and billowy. I have on what looks

216

like . . . slashed, or cut open, white gloves." Lena paused to contemplate the scene before her eyes, which was becoming increasingly more vivid.

"Why are you celebrating?"

"It's my . . . wedding," she said, surprised. She shifted slightly on the divan. Her whole body was tingling. And she saw herself glowing with tiny points of light.

"What else do you see?"

"There's a long, what looks like a banquet table draped with a cloth with tiny red circles on it. The table is lavishly decorated with flowers and vines, and platters with fruits, meats, breads, and cakes. There are crystal bowls of pastel-colored nuts—almonds, I think— and wafers with our names impressed on them. Family and friends, we're all singing and laughing and holding little packets of almonds tied with pink ribbons." Surprised by the clarity of her vision, she strained to see more. "There are men playing flutes and women with tambourines. My husband and I, we're drinking from a big silver cup with two handles. It appears that we're being toasted by a powerful gentleman. I am embarrassed by his compliments . . ." Consumed by the cascade of images, she stopped for a moment to catch her breath.

"Excellent," Bradley said. "What about the ceremony itself? Try to go back a bit in time."

"We're standing at an altar in a church." She paused, recognizing something familiar. "It looks like Santa Maria Novella. I'm wearing a white cap. It's embroidered with beads and metallic thread. The priest is blessing us and then, funny, my husband and I appear to be shaking hands. It's like a solemn oath, a contract of faith. Then we exchange rings. My wedding ring is gold, shaped like a crown, with a coat of arms. I see the year 1486."

"You're doing great." He continued to make notations. "And after the wedding celebration?"

"I . . . I see that I have a baby boy, and I'm very happy." Lena smiled, feeling the warmth in her heart.

"Beyond that?"

She skipped forward in time and stiffened with apprehension. The lighthearted joy that she had tapped into instantly gave way to an immense sadness.

"My husband was murdered." Her chest began heaving as she relived the grief. "My brother did it. I am exposing him in public. My family is enraged. Now, I'm in a prison cell, giving birth. I'm so lonely." Lena was silent for some moments.

"Love holds no grievances, knows no boundaries," she repeated, fidgeting nervously as though having a bad dream. She suddenly began to weep.

"Lorenzo! Lorenzo!" Giovanna yelled again, as she continued to push the baby out in waves of great pain. "Love holds no grievances, knows no boundaries. All is forgiven and released."

The prison guard had heard her screams earlier and sent a midwife to assist with the birth. Drenched with sweat and greatly weakened, Giovanna fell silent as the midwife delivered her child.

"It's a girl!" the elderly woman announced excitedly, holding the perfectly formed infant up for her to see.

But Giovanna made no response. Her lips were frozen in a gentle smile, her countenance serene. The midwife saw that she had stopped breathing and anxiously tried to revive her.

"Lord have mercy!" the distraught woman cried. "Help, please! Help!" The prison guard swiftly answered her call.

"I'm so sorry," she said mournfully. "The lady has died." She cradled the newborn close to her chest as the guard ushered her out of the cell.

"Okay," Bradley said gently, acknowledging Lena's discomfort. "It's safe to come back now."

"Come back?" She was disconcerted.

"Yes, travel back in your balloon to this room, where you are lying here and now," he advised. "You can leave Giovanna for now. Take your time, and come back into your body as Lena."

How odd her name sounded. She repeated it to herself. Lena. Her eyes still closed, she did as directed and began to sense the hazy borders of her body and immediate surroundings, which gradually solidified into what she remembered them to be. She opened her eyes, still moist with tears, and turned her head toward Bradley, who was calmly taking notes.

"What time is it?"

"About 11:00 a.m."

"Wow, a whole hour has passed," she said in disbelief. "It felt more like five minutes to me."

"Yes, time can bend and shift like that when we're doing this work."

"What do you think happened?" She instinctively looked down at her hand, half expecting to see a wedding ring.

"That's not for me to say. It's your journey. You did well, Lena. You were able to regress more easily than most."

"This is so bizarre. My head is spinning. I'm confused." She sat up and mechanically put her shoes back on.

"Just check in with yourself. What did you *feel* in that lifetime?" His eyes flickered with compassion.

Lena took time to reflect. "Love. Betrayal. Abandonment. Grief. Forgiveness. But love most of all. Love for all things." She drew a deep breath and smiled peacefully. "But I don't know what to believe. The ring. The year 1486. Is it possible I really was Giovanna in another life?"

"I can't confirm that one way or another. Only you know. It will take some time for you to process all this. Just stay calm, and watch for new insights."

She was surprised to have found Bradley so detached and wished for more commentary. Then again, she respected his professional distance. His ego was in check. He was clearly trying to empower her.

"Remember, I'm always here if you need me," he said warmly.

Lena paid her bill and left his office puzzled, yet deeply moved. It was an unusually bright, sun-drenched day, and the sky was a clear cerulean blue. As she walked leisurely across Rue de Rivoli through the tall iron gates into the Tuileries Gardens, she felt full and expansive. And there was something else. A humility that she had never known had begun to awaken in her. She could see now that she had always been so busy proving herself, achieving and overcoming and trying to succeed, that she had not always been able to stay present and centered in her heart. For it was her own heart, above all else, that Giovanna had so deeply entered. It was her true compass, the source of all her wisdom and compassion, the source of all healing.

Lena sat down on one of the green metal chairs under a huge chestnut tree sprouting its first early spring leaves. She thought about the people she cared about who had caused her great pain. Her parents for abandoning her. Jud for not understanding her. Henri for betraying her. And then all those with whom she did not have a personal connection but who she felt had hurt or violated her in some way. Madame de Trouville and the hired assassin were extreme examples. How useless it was to blame others for her suffering, when she could so easily shift her perception, like Giovanna had done. There was no need to attack or defend, no victims or perpetrators, no good or bad, just lessons that she herself had created for growth and expansion. And if all this was true, then how could she harbor any resentment or anger toward anyone, even when her very life had been threatened. She was stunned to have received so many new insights, catalyzed it seemed by Giovanna, who she now believed was, indeed, her own former self, strange as that sounded. Her deep-seated feelings of abandonment and betrayal must have carried over from that lifetime, if not from many others. And she felt she could now release them. How liberating and healing.

Her heart fluttered as tears began welling up again. She took out her notebook and read over the initiations she had recorded over the past weeks: "To Risk." "To Discern." "To Trust." She believed she had passed another one and wrote down, "To Forgive." What a relief to forgive everyone, even herself, for participating in a drama of her own making. She remembered that Thomas had said the initiations would occur in a specific order, one after another, as she crossed new thresholds of awareness. To Forgive. That was an especially difficult one, but she knew she could not proceed through the remaining initiations unless she passed this one, as had Giovanna. She said silently to herself: "I forgive my parents for abandoning me. I forgive Jud for not understanding me. I forgive Henri for betraying me. I forgive myself." She repeated these affirmations until she felt she had arrived at a place of neutrality and non-judgment. This, she realized, would be an ongoing practice. But for now, she could move forward with a lighter, more peaceful heart.

She picked up a black-and-white pigeon feather lying at her feet. It was a reminder of this new lightness of being. She smiled joyfully as she watched a group of school children laughing and playing tag around a newly budding flower bed. Her despair over what appeared to be her failed assignment had momentarily and magically dissolved. Vivid scenes from her five-year relationship with Jud flashed through her mind. Their first meeting at the Shakespeare Festival in Central Park. Long walks through the city. Lively conversations. Moving in together. Weekends Upstate and on Long Island . . . There were more highs than lows. How fortunate they had been.

Paging through her notebook, she came across the letter written by Giovanna that she had found and copied at the town hall in Florence. She had almost forgotten about it. Reading it again, she wondered what Giovanna had meant . . . "Remember, what is Real can never be threatened. I am you, and you are me."

Suddenly overcome with the urge to go back to Florence, she left the park and rushed back to her apartment. She booked an evening flight, packed a suitcase, and made herself a goat cheese crottin and a big salad. Wishing to toast her progress, she poured what was left of the Chianti into her Renaissance chalice and ate ravenously between sips of wine. Why did she need to go back to Florence? It felt like she had some unfinished business at Santa Maria Novella church. What she was to do there she did not know. But she was buzzing with electricity and needed to talk to someone. She called Hannah.

"Sorry, I know it's late there . . ."

"Hi, how's everything going? When *are* you coming back?"

"In a few days. But I couldn't wait. I have something incredible to tell you."

"What is it? You sound much better than last time."

"I saw a psychiatrist who specializes in past-life regressions. Like hypnosis. He took me back in time. I connected deeply with Giovanna . . ." She hesitated, realizing that what had felt so real to her would most likely seem outlandish to her friend. "Hannah, I really do think I was her, she was me. I know it sounds crazy."

"Is this guy for real? Wow, that's hard to believe, Lena."

"I know, I know. It was for me, too, at first. But I think Dr. Bradley is a gifted healer. Oh, Hannah, I've had so many new feelings and insights. I'll share everything with you soon."

"You know what? I *do* believe you. Who am I to question your experience? You always have my support."

Lena's upbeat mood momentarily faded.

"Hey, are you still there?" said Hannah.

"My story was scooped. French newspaper." Her words fell flat.

"Oh, no! That's horrible! I'm so sorry."

"I was beyond crushed, as you can imagine. But, now, I'm okay.

Much better than I would have thought under the circumstances, surprisingly."

"Thank God."

"By the way, have you spoken to Jud?"

"I called and left a message after he left Florence. But I haven't heard from him."

"You know, Hannah, I see now that I walked away from a wonderful man."

"Maybe you did. Or maybe there's someone else for you." Hannah was typically ambiguous. She was not one to give advice, and though this sometimes frustrated Lena, she respected her for it.

"All I can say is I forgive everything that happened between Jud and me. And I forgive myself."

"That's huge, Lena. I admire that."

"Anyway, I've been beating your ear for weeks. What about you? Have you seen Max yet? I hope so!"

"Such pressure," Hannah laughed. "We just met for coffee a few days ago."

"Excellent! It's only taken him a few months," Lena teased.

"Oops, one of my patients is beeping me. Have to go. Take care of yourself. I can't wait to see you."

"Me, too."

Partially visible under Lena's bed was the mysterious box that Gilbert's housekeeper had given her. She had almost forgotten about it. She picked it up, turned it around, and tried to open it. But again, she was unsuccessful. She ran her hand over the beautiful carved Flower of Life. What could possibly be inside? Thomas had said she would one day be able to open it, after she had passed all seven initiations. If she was doing her work properly, then there were only three left. What were they? She felt Florence held another key and, given her transporting experience with Dr. Bradley, was more certain than ever that Thomas was onto something.

She anxiously shoved the box back under the bed and left to catch her flight to Florence.

The following day, Lena arrived at Santa Maria Novella church at the close of morning Mass. It was March 17—according to the church bulletin, the Feast Day of St. Joseph of Arimathea. She remembered from her world religions class in college that he was the uncle of Jesus, who supposedly traveled forth from the Holy Land with a chalice filled with Jesus's blood from the crucifixion—the legendary Holy Grail, some believed, whose whereabouts have remained a source of speculation. Waiting patiently as the churchgoers filed out, Lena bristled at the sight of the rear pew behind which she had hidden days ago, eavesdropping on her own pre-meditated crucifixion of sorts.

She proceeded into the sumptuous Tornabuoni Chapel, with its exquisite frescoes and the massive dangling gilt crucifix above the altar with the realistic carved and painted Jesus in extremis. There were the engraved marble slabs on the floor to the left, marking the tombs of Giovanna and her husband, Lorenzo, along with other family members. Overcome with emotion, she fell to her knees on Giovanna's tomb, giving thanks for her exemplary life, as well as for the many beautiful revelations that the young Florentine had shown her. Propelled by an inner urgency, Lena then walked over to the altar and compulsively began searching underneath and around it and down along the marble floor, but she found nothing.

Distraught, she returned to Lorenzo's tomb and ran her hand along the surface. Recognizing an obscure crack in the marble, she dug inside it and felt something. She saw it was a gold ring and removed it. She turned it slowly in her hand, examining it closely. A crown-shaped ring with a coat of arms, inscribed with the year 1486. She had seen it in her session with Dr. Bradley and in one of her visions—the wedding ring that Giovanna had hidden centuries ago as a final tribute to her husband and their great love. Lena sat down on the tomb and began weeping with joy and gratitude as she placed the ring on her left ring finger. It was as if a piece of her soul had finally returned to her, as if a sacred inner marriage had occurred, a divine union between the male and female sides of herself. The ring was a symbol of this wholeness.

Giovanna's presence was once again all encompassing, and Lena believed that it was she who was guiding her. For this new knowledge was clearly of a higher order than what Lena had previously been capable of accessing. She felt whole and complete and filled to overflowing with the sweetest, most expansive feeling. A feeling, or rather more a state of being, that she could only call love. It was not a particular love reserved for specific individuals but rather a universal kind of love that, indeed, knew no boundaries, and therefore included everyone and everything.

How could she, Lena, the worldly, hard-driving journalist who had always felt so alone and unworthy to receive, come to such a realization? Why was she granted this gift? A voice, perhaps Giovanna's, whispered: "You are in a state of grace. Do not question. Do not doubt. Do not fear. All feelings of lack and limitation are an illusion." Lena realized that this self-doubt, which she had been carrying all her life, which had undermined her relationships and her own true power, no longer served her. She noticed the Vesica Piscis mosaic embedded in the floor in front of the altar, where she had stood upon first entering the chapel over a week ago. That's when Massimo, the hotel porter, had shown up and given her a copy of the beautiful mystical poem "The Thunder, Perfect Mind." She had memorized a few lines and whispered them now as she stood at the center of the sacred symbol, in the space where the two interlocking circles overlapped, her eyes closed. "I am the mother and the daughter. I am the bride and the bridegroom . . ."

All her energy flooded into her heart center, and in an instant everything became startlingly clear. There was no separation between herself and others—no subject, no object. That's what Giovanna had meant in her letter, when she wrote, "I am you, and you are me." And if this were really true, then how could she, Lena, not always exist in a state of perfect wholeness. There was nothing to do but to be. No more struggling to achieve anything. So this is what love felt like, a place of no opposites, only integration and oneness, which is accessible to us always. "What is Real can never be threatened," Giovanna had written. She had meant that only love is "Real." Lena had never understood love until now, thanks to Giovanna, who was just another aspect of herself. It was her own heart, above all, not her head, that contained and emanated this wisdom.

She pledged to live more fully in her heart, which was a kind of crucible in which her entire being had been transformed, as in an alchemical reaction, where two distinct substances merge to become something new and unique. Pondering this insight, she recalled a high school chemistry paper that she had written about alchemy. What a strange subject for a teenager to have chosen. Perhaps it was the resurfacing of a long-buried fascination with and even ancient mastery of that skill. "The way in and the way out is through the heart," Jud had said to her before she left New York. She was beginning to understand what he meant.

"What is my purpose?" she asked, as though standing before a tribunal judging her progress. She waited earnestly for an answer. Then she heard a voice and wondered if it was Giovanna's.

"Your purpose is to heal yourself and others by holding and seeding light wherever you go. Your purpose is to perform the sacred marriage within. Your purpose is to be and teach love. That is what Magdalena and the Order of Magdala have always done." The Order of Magdala? Did she belong to this order? She thought about her name, Lena. It was part of the word Magdalena. And she had read in what little recorded information existed about Giovanna's life that Mary Magdalene was, indeed, her patron saint. It made sense that Giovanna would be in this lineage. And if that were true of Giovanna, then so would it be of her. Such a concept was almost too much to comprehend, so vast and limitless. Yet neither could she deny the possibility. She felt suddenly bathed in a liquid light, consumed again with joy and also humility. She stepped out of the Vesica Piscis and ceremoniously left the chapel.

Once outside, she sat down on the church steps, where she had formerly stopped to rest, albeit in a much less exalted state while being chased by the red Fiat. She believed she had finally reached and passed through her fifth initiation. Taking out her notebook, she wrote down, "TO LOVE," in capital letters to emphasize its importance. Lena contemplated her initiations and why they had happened in a particular order, as Thomas had predicted.

1) To Risk
2) To Discern
3) To Trust
4) To Forgive
5) TO LOVE

Each one had served as a foundation for the next one, forming a ladder of increasing depth and complexity. How could she learn how to discern if she had not risked? How could she trust without knowing how to discern? How could she forgive without first trusting herself? And how could she truly love if she could not forgive? It was as if her entire being had been disassembled and put back together again.

She remembered once again that today was Joseph of Arimathea's Feast Day. What was the Holy Grail, really? Why were all the pilgrims endlessly in search of it? Where was it hidden? Today, Lena believed she had found her own Holy Grail, and it was inside herself, in her own heart. She glanced at her watch, feeling again the elasticity of time. Barely ninety minutes had passed, but it had seemed like an eternity. A taxi pulled up from out of nowhere, as though expecting her. On her way back to the airport, she noticed three bumper stickers, one after another, on three different cars, magically displaying the same message: ALL ONE.

Lena spent her last day in Paris packing and strolling around her favorite parts of the city—the Luxembourg Gardens, elegant Île Saint-Louis, and the Place des Vosges, its massive courtyard surrounded by old red-brick façades. She walked until sundown, all the while reshaping her past, discarding outmoded thoughts and perceptions, hopes and expectations, and making room for new ones. This shedding of her old self was simultaneously disorienting and exhilarating. There was nowhere else to go but the present here and now. Graceful harp music hummed in the Place des Vosges, as a fire-orange sun descended behind a row of mansard rooftops. Mothers coddled their babies. An old man lay sleeping on the grass. A young couple stood kissing under a stone archway. Filled with a deep peace, she knew this moment would stay with her forever.

THE THIRD MUSE
Love

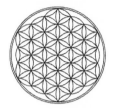

Chapter Twenty-Five

It was raining when Lena arrived in New York. Her heart leaped, as usual, upon entering the city. As the taxi swerved westward through Central Park, she rolled down the window to have a better look at the beautiful cherry blossoms, which had arrived earlier than usual this third week of March. She welcomed the wet, fresh scent of spring. Nothing had changed, she decided, inspecting the park. She was glad for that, as so much had changed inside her. A wave of anxiety gripped her. She was worried about her job again and Max's disappointment in her. Would he fire her? And how would she adjust to a whole new life without Jud? At least, she was excited to see Hannah again. Thank goodness for her. A procession of brightly clothed people marched along the roadside, led by a man carrying a statue of a young woman sitting cross-legged on a cushion, an oval halo rising from her head.

"Who's that?" Lena mused aloud, referring to the statue.

"Prajnaparamita, from Sanskrit, the goddess of transcendental wisdom," said the Indian taxi driver, turning to her and smiling.

"We could all use more of that," Lena joked, watching the buildings rise beyond the park like steel spikes.

New York had a decidedly masculine presence—with its phallic verticality and emphasis on success, power, material wealth—compared to Paris, which felt so soft and elegant and feminine. Each city represented for her the delicate balance that she would have to maintain within herself. A white light broke through the clouds and made everything look phosphorescent. The taxi shot down the West Side Highway, the Hudson River to the right shimmering in all its majesty. If she could just be like the river, she thought, flowing effortlessly through the surrounding chaos.

As they finally skidded to a stop amid the renovated warehouses and cobblestone streets of her Tribeca neighborhood, she grew even more anxious. The ailanthus trees were just beginning to bud. And the familiar sweet scent of coconut and peanut oil from the local Thai restaurant greeted her. Saddened to see that the Korean grocer had closed and that old Mrs. Molino was not at her window perch, Lena settled her fare, jumped out of the taxi, and began climbing the staircase of her building apprehensively, leaving some of her luggage in the vestibule.

When she entered her apartment, it looked different, foreign even, as if she had never lived there. Jud's leather armchair and stereo were gone. She walked through each room. His desk was gone, too, and his clothes from the closet they had shared. Her plants were brown-edged and droopy. She began to weep. She had not expected to be back in New York so soon. She had wanted to stay in Paris as a correspondent for *Express*; at least Max had not ruled out the possibility. Her story was supposed to run in next month's issue. Jud was gone. The feeling of loss was overwhelming. It was like she had jumped off another cliff and was suspended again in a fog, unsure of how or where to land. Her eyes settled on a book lying open on the bookcase. It was an old copy of the poet Rainer Maria Rilke's *Duino Elegies*, one of Jud's favorites. She walked over to find a piece of paper wedged inside:

Dear Lena, this is for whenever you come back, if you come back. I'm sorry it didn't work out for us. We obviously need to move forward now with no regrets. I left the key with Mrs. Molino. I wish you well in all that you do. Jud.

Heavy-hearted, she tore up the note and went back downstairs to bring up the rest of her luggage. Then she called Hannah. Disappointed not to have reached her, she left a message, then threw on a raincoat, without bothering to unpack. For the next hour, Lena wandered aimlessly about the Tribeca streets. It was still drizzling, which only added to her dreary mood. Having been so uplifted by her time in Florence just days ago, she couldn't understand why she felt so different now. It was as if Paris, Henri, Giovanna, Dr. Bradley, Santa Maria Novella church were all nothing more than a dream. She glanced at her hand. The ring she had found in the church was still there on her left ring finger. Exhausted, soaked, and hungry, she stopped for a quick bite to eat at The Odeon diner on West Broadway.

"Cheer up, beautiful," said an elderly gentleman at the table beside her. His eyes were a brilliant blue, his expression indifferent. He was dressed smartly in a flat wool herringbone cap and a tweed blazer.

Lena nodded with a tepid smile. She didn't feel much like conversing, particularly with a stranger.

"Do you live here?" he inquired.

"Yes, I suppose I do."

"Howard," he said, "nice to meet you . . ."

"Lena."

"Sorry, but I couldn't help noticing you." He slowly sipped his coffee. "You have a certain, I don't know, presence, I guess you could say."

"Thank you," she replied, warmed by his compliment. The waitress approached, and she promptly ordered potatoes and fried eggs and a cup of tea.

"And I thought, why would this beautiful young woman have any reason to be sad?" Howard continued.

Lena began to feel annoyed by this intrusion. "Who says I'm

sad?" She caught herself reacting, then returned to her center, something she would not have done in the past.

"You're right, guess that was my projection," he confessed. "I lost my wife a few months ago. Still adjusting. I suppose I see sadness in everyone."

"I understand." Lena identified with his pain. But hadn't Giovanna shown her she was never alone? She was always connected to her own higher self and guidance and did not need anyone to validate her worth. Jud's absence, Max's anger at her, the scooped article, all of it seemed strangely inconsequential now.

"You know, sometimes this city is just downright ugly—the streets, the buildings, the rat race." Howard stared forlornly out the window. "Oh, here I go again."

"Nothing un-beautiful exists outside your own mind," Lena said, surprised by her remark. It had not felt right to use the word ugly.

"I never thought about that." He was visibly taken aback.

"I believe everything that happens to us is our creation." She ate her eggs slowly and appreciatively. "We are not victims of anything 'out there.'"

"Does that mean I created my wife's death? Doesn't make sense. Why would I want to do that?"

"Yes, you chose to have that experience so you could move beyond loss, become more self-reliant and whole in yourself." Lena was aware that she was speaking differently now, as though on a mission to assist this man, to bring him to a greater understanding. It felt like a creative energy was working in and through her, and she saw herself simply as a messenger.

Howard reflected for a moment, nervously tapping his water glass with his spoon. "Well, I don't know. Maybe that's true. Maybe it is."

"It's easier to forgive what happens to you when you take responsibility for it." She continued eating silently, while he settled his bill.

"Thank you, Lena, for your wisdom today," Howard brightened. "I feel better having met you."

"Thank *you*, Howard."

She was grateful to have been of service in this small way. Two coffee cup stains on the table—interlocking circles—reminded her of the Vesica Piscis, the sacred symbol embedded within the Flower of Life design on the mysterious box Marie had given her in Paris. She still had two more initiations left. What were they? She finished her lunch and stepped out into the city again, renewed. She checked her phone messages. No word from Hannah yet. There was an email from Max, though, asking her to contact him when she returned to New York. He was out of town this week but wanted to see her soon. Lena bristled with anxiety, concerned about her future with *Express*.

Crossing the street, she noticed a car parked at the corner with the same bumper sticker she had seen in Florence: ALL ONE. The synchronicity cheered her, and she knew in that moment exactly what she had to do. She would write her article anyway and send it to Max. So what if the French newspaper had already published its own article? That was only a simple, straight news story reporting the basic chain of events behind the scandal. She had been so devastated at being scooped she hadn't even considered another option. She had a personal, inside perspective on the investigation that no other reporter had. And why stop at the article? She dared to imagine a cover story, even a raise.

Back at her apartment, she finally unpacked and placed the Flower of Life box on a bookshelf in her office, where she would have a clear view of it while working. Then, with singular focus, she sat down at her desk—the one place that had perhaps defined her more than anything—and began writing her article.

Over the next several days, she kept a vigil at her apartment, leaving only to buy food or to break in the late afternoon for a cup of tea and a pastry at the café down the street. She also called Hannah again and left another message, concerned that she had not yet heard from her. With her postcard reprint of Ghirlandaio's *Portrait of Giovanna Tornabuoni* propped against her desk lamp for inspiration, Lena wrote feverishly and sporadically, pausing to reflect for long stretches. She reread the epigram by the Latin poet Martial, which the Italian museum curator had translated, and decided to use it in her lead paragraph:

"If thou, O Art, couldst represent also character and virtue, there would be no more beautiful image on earth." These words by the ancient Latin poet Martial appear in the $48 million *Portrait of Giovanna Tornabuoni* (1488) by the Renaissance master Domenico Ghirlandaio. Beauty, character (or truth), virtue (or love)—noble ideals of the Italian Renaissance—are no less apt as guideposts for our own time, a New Renaissance in art and culture, science, society, and spirituality. What I had thought was my real work when I began this assignment—to solve and write about the crime of the stolen *Portrait of Giovanna Tornabuoni*—was later revealed instead to be the catalyst for a series of unexpected, life-altering initiations, which showed me that "the only true aristocracy is that of consciousness," as the British writer D.H. Lawrence once said . . .

Lena smiled at her spontaneous reference to Lawrence, the subject of Jud's new biography. She turned her tape recorder on and off. The sound of Henri and Ines Avidon's voices nauseated her. For a moment, she was back at Santa Maria Novella church, trembling and terrified, as they plotted her murder. Her eyes rested often on the postcard. Giovanna looked so quiescent, radiant, composed. Lena imagined herself sitting at a long table with Henri, Maurice, and Avidon as Giovanna poured golden white light into each of their chalices and spoke of love. So many emotions flooded through her.

She got frustrated trying to remember things like how many paintings Henri had in his collection, how long he had been an art dealer, or exactly when he and Avidon had met. But such details were inconsequential compared to the real story, the story of her personal journey. And that is exactly what she wanted to write about, such a departure from her heavily reported, fact-crunching articles, even though she doubted Max would be interested in such a story. How believable would it be? Was she jeopardizing her reputation, just as she was beginning to make a name for herself? *Express* was, after all, an art magazine. But she didn't care. She was writing this piece for herself more than anyone else, and it would be the first of its kind that she had attempted.

She pondered her initiations. If there really were to be seven, then she could not include the last two in the story not yet knowing what they were. Why not leave the article open-ended, suggesting there was more to come in a postscript? Anything was possible now. She had the power to create whatever she wanted. She had just spoken of this power to Howard at the diner. It seemed one of the main reasons for living was to create, enjoy the fruits of our creations, and then create again. How simple yet how easily we veer off track into dramas of our own making that often bring needless suffering.

When she finally found her voice, she worked incessantly and almost effortlessly, documenting both the truth about the stolen painting and her own experience. She wrote of Giovanna's provenance, of the Louvre's $48 million purchase of the Ghirlandaio at a London auction, and the curator's indictment on suspicion by Interpol that the painting had been stolen. She wrote about the collector Jonathan Fisher Gilbert's formidable nursemaid, Ines Avidon, and her assumed identity as Madame Geneviève de Trouville, of her avarice, cunning, and murderous acts. How she starved

Gilbert to death in his Loire Valley château and took off with his paintings. How she orchestrated the murder of Marvin Steinert, the well-known New York art dealer. She wrote of Avidon's accomplices—her lover, the old master paintings and Art Deco dealer Henri Lemien, and Maurice Blackson, the attorney who executed the fraudulent will claiming that Avidon owned the Ghirlandaio under her grandfather's legacy—and of their ultimate arrest (for which Lena took credit).

She also wrote of Baron Eric von Heisendorf's role as an unwitting pawn, and finally of the importance of the *Portrait of Giovanna Tornabuoni*, one of the finest paintings produced by the Renaissance master Ghirlandaio. At the same time, she was completely transparent, expressing her own involvement in the ordeal—her romance with Henri and her intense connection with Giovanna and all that she had taught her. She even wrote about her past-life regression with Dr. Bill Bradley and finding Giovanna's wedding ring in Florence. In a final dramatic flourish, she included the letter written by Giovanna that she had discovered in Florence. It was challenging to write with such honesty, and she tried not to censor herself, though she knew the story would sound outrageous to many. Would it ever be published?

Early one morning, the phone rang. It was Hannah.

"What a relief to hear from you," Lena said.

"You, too!"

"Where were you?"

"You won't believe it. Max invited me out to his house on Long Island for a few days. I forgot I had turned my cell off." She paused.

"Wow! That's great." Lena froze for a moment, feeling anxious again about her fallout with Max over the article.

"Lena, I know this is a sensitive situation. I don't want your working relationship with Max to affect our friendship. You mean so much to me. I had to take this chance with him. You knew it all along."

"I just want you to be happy. How did it go? You sound so upbeat."

"We had a wonderful time. He's smart and handsome and caring." She stopped short. "So when am I going to see you?!"

"How about Thursday for tea at the Carlyle Hotel? Your day off. I need a New York fix."

"Great, it's a date! Does two o'clock work?"

"Perfect."

Lena hung up feeling even more empowered. She put the finishing touches on her article and emailed it to Max, restless with anticipation. Working to erase any remaining doubt and hesitation, she continued focusing on her goal—the publication of this article. She visualized the cover story, too, and the raise, all the while feeling joy and gratitude at having already received them. Out of habit, she then wrote a to-do list:

1) Call Max
2) Publish article
3) Get cover story
4) Get raise
5) Buy food
6) Call plumber

The following morning she checked her email. Max had not yet contacted her, so she called the magazine and set up an appointment. Fortunately, his secretary, Cecile, said he had an opening later that afternoon.

When Lena arrived at the offices of *Express* on West 57th Street, Cecile, a matronly woman, smothered her with a hug.

"You look like a completely new person!" She shook her head in disbelief. "Everyone looks so much better after they leave this place. I love the ruffled blouse and long skirt, so feminine and Parisian," she said admiringly. "Wait till Max sees you! He's still at his last appointment, should be back soon."

"Just like him to be late," Lena quipped.

The nondescript offices had a lifeless, stagnant feel. She had not missed the confinement of a daily routine. Her old life seemed so small now. She walked down the corridor in search of her office. Another name was on the door—Sara Sax, who was not present at the moment. Everything inside had been rearranged—the desk, computer, file cabinet—as if she'd never worked there. Lena surveyed the scene with detachment, then proceeded to Max's corner suite, which had a gorgeous view of Central Park. As usual, it was cluttered with stacks of magazines and newspapers. There were the two Scandinavian armchairs, the dartboard behind the desk, and the framed series of Ellsworth Kelly prints. Nothing had changed. She paced back and forth across the room, growing more anxious by the minute. She knew she had taken a big risk with the article. How would Max respond? Would he even want her to continue working for *Express*? Suddenly, he appeared with his usual air of gravity, clad in a white shirt and red suspenders.

"Lena," he said formally. "Welcome back."

"Good to see you again, Max." Lena mustered her resolve and sat down.

"You look different somehow." He adjusted his tortoiseshell glasses, inspecting her with bewilderment.

"Funny, Cecile said the same thing. Maybe I am."

She noticed how much he had changed, too. He was not the overworked, worn-out Max she had always known. He had apparently been going to the gym. She noticed how his shirt hugged his chest, how he no longer slouched but stood erect. There was a light in his eyes that wasn't there before. It was as if someone had lifted a heavy weight from his shoulders. All this she attributed to Hannah.

Max pulled a newspaper from one of the stacks and held it out to Lena. On the front page were Ghirlandaio's *Portrait of Giovanna Tornabuoni* and headshots of Henri Lemien, Ines Avidon, Maurice

Blackson, Jonathan Fisher Gilbert, and Marv Steinert. The past months flashed before her like a series of dream images. Was Max trying to intimidate her? She half-missed his doting on her in his clumsily flirtatious way. But she was so tired of trying to please him and everyone else. It was time she started honoring herself. Seeing Giovanna's image again brought her back into her heart.

"I saw the article in Paris," she said. "I went out to find a copy right after I heard the news."

"We had a lot riding on this, as you know. If only you had moved faster." His tone remained professional. He scooped a handful of darts from a desk drawer and began firing them rapidly at the dartboard, his back to Lena.

"How do you think I felt? After all that work and everything I'd been through!" The wrenching anguish of that moment, when she had heard the news, came rushing back. She flinched with regret, then collected herself.

Max continued hurling the darts. "Yes!" he shouted. "Bull's eye!"

Lena was baffled by his odd behavior. She had exposed her soul in an article, and he had not even acknowledged it!

He leaned over his desk, peering at her inscrutably. Lena stared him down.

"Congratulations, Lena!" The corners of his mouth eased into a smile and then a wide grin. "You have just written your best piece ever."

She was startled at first by this unexpected response, then a wave of relief washed over her.

"Thank you, Max."

"Not what I expected from you."

"I hadn't planned on this. It was a surprise to me, too. I guess I found the courage to dig deep for the real story, my story."

"It's so raw and full of feeling, a side of you I've never seen," he continued, paging through the article. "And it's perfect timing."

"What do you mean?"

"We're making some changes in the magazine to attract a wider readership. I want to add some narrative pieces, and yours fits the bill." He reclined in his chair, triumphantly strumming his suspenders. "That said, I must admit the past-life stuff is a bit far-fetched for me. But when you look at all the spiritual books selling now, I'm sure enough people will identify."

"Great. Everyone wins!"

"Believe me, I really had to work on the suits upstairs for this revamp," Max confided. "And that's not all . . ."

"Don't tell me, you're doubling everyone's pay," Lena joked.

"I'm giving you the cover story for the first issue." He smiled with satisfaction. "Besides, the lackluster story in the French press is no competition."

Lena could barely contain her excitement. "That's incredible!" It was exactly what she had imagined.

A sunbeam shone through the window and alighted on the dartboard, drawing her attention to the bull's eye, where the dart was still firmly anchored.

"As for the images, we have that great portrait of Giovanna." He paused, lost in thought. "And we'll try to get some of the Ghirlandaio frescoes in the church."

"I guess the Paris correspondent plan is off," she interjected.

"For now, but who knows what the future holds." Max called through the telephone loudspeaker to Cecile. "Make a note that I want Lena's name on the masthead as features editor. And she's getting a raise, too, yet to be negotiated."

Lena listened, incredulous. The gifts kept flowing. And though Max was delivering them, she realized she had created them for herself. She was teary-eyed. "I'm so grateful."

She was finally ready to receive the abundance she deserved, having never thought herself worthy of it. And she understood there was no limit to what she could create, if only she could keep stepping out of her own way and continue to trust. To Trust, that had been an important initiation. Suddenly, a memory resurfaced, and she saw herself as a young girl telling Sister Ruth at the orphanage that she wanted to be a well-known writer and travel the world. To which Sister had sternly replied, "You can't *always* do what you want to do, dear." And she had most innocently said, "Why not?"

As if reading her mind, Max added, "I'm curious about those last two initiations, Lena. When you know what they are, let's do an afterword or postscript in issue number two. I'm sure the readers will want to know."

Lena smiled ebulliently. Unbelievable! That, too, was exactly what she had foreseen.

"Absolutely."

"Sorry, but I have another appointment." He stuffed a stack of papers into his briefcase and held out his hand in a professional bond of trust. "Oh, and you can have Tom's office now. He's moving on."

"I can't thank you enough, Max."

"Thank *you*," he said, rushing out the door, "for sending me your beautiful friend, Hannah."

"I was waiting for you to bring that up," she teased. "I'm happy to be of assistance. Most dating services charge a fee, you know."

He laughed and waved goodbye.

Buoyed by her new triumphs, Lena headed home by foot—from midtown to the Flatiron District to Union Square and across to the West Village, where she stopped to relax in Washington Square Park. As usual, this magnetic leafy vortex was surging with activity—break dancers with boom boxes, wandering tourists, New York University students, romantic couples, dog walkers, chess players, and the occasional wino. She found a spot in the sunshine on an empty bench and watched the scene with amusement and almost child-like joy. She thought of the Paris parks she had so loved. How rapidly one experience had been exchanged for another, like a stage set. She considered the role she had played— the creator of her own show.

It was as if everything she had ever wanted, all the abundance she could possibly desire, already existed somewhere outside of space and time. And if she wanted to pull it down into the here and now, like she did today in Max's office, all she had to do was switch to a different frequency in her thoughts. Like turning the channel on a radio and tuning into another station. Her achievements had always come with a struggle. Maybe it didn't have to be that way.

Chapter Twenty-Six

Lena waited under a tasseled silk chandelier in the tearoom of the Carlyle Hotel, one of her favorite New York oases. Inspired by the sultan's dining room at Topkapi Palace in Istanbul, it was lavishly decorated with banquettes made of antique kilims, plush red-fringed velvet chairs, small marble-topped tables, and hand-printed wallpaper.

"I missed you soooo much!" Hannah said as she walked up from behind and threw her arms around Lena.

"It's so good to see you again." Lena said.

Hannah looked vibrant in a sexy wrap-around skirt, revealing more of her well-toned figure than usual. And there was a new aura of calm about her.

"You're incredible!" She beheld Lena with admiration. "Max told me what happened!"

Lena grabbed her hand and guided her to a private corner table. "C'mon, there's so much to talk about!"

For the next two hours, they indulged themselves on Assam tea and scones with berries and Devonshire cream as they laughed and shared.

"What a story," Hannah said. "It could be a movie! And what happened to Henri?"

"Arrested, with the other two crooks. Interpol followed me to his apartment." Lena shivered reliving those frightening moments.

"I can't believe you did that!"

"Me neither. I was either obsessed or possessed."

"Who would've guessed?" Hannah threw her arms up. "You had the adventure of a lifetime, and I finally found that elusive someone. All my searching and bad dates. And he was right there in your office all along . . ."

"Yeah, I'm so glad you didn't inseminate yourself with that turkey baster!" Lena joked as they burst into laughter.

"Remember what you told me?" Hannah met her friend's eyes, as she often did, full of generosity and trust. "That I would just know. And that when you know something, you better act on it right away, because chances are you'll never know the same thing in the same way again." Her voice cracked. "I'm so happy."

Lena squeezed her hand. "You deserve the best. Max appears to be a different man!"

Hannah smiled. "So what do you think those last two initiations could be?" In her typical manner, Hannah deflected attention away from herself. "And that box, what could be inside?"

"I have a feeling I'll know very soon."

"So how does it feel to be home?"

"It was so sad to walk into an empty apartment," Lena blurted. "I wish things hadn't gone so badly in Florence. I'd feel better if I could see Jud again and explain my behavior. But I know he wouldn't respond if I called him. Maybe I should just go to his office. What do you think?"

"Only you can answer that, Lena."

Lena grew pensive. "I should never have let him go. I feel like I ruined something special."

Hannah responded only with a supportive smile.

With barely a pause in their conversation, they proceeded arm-in-arm up Madison Avenue. After Hannah headed off, Lena cut across to Fifth Avenue and continued northward along the eastern fringe of Central Park. She walked for a long time until she found herself at the rose garden in the park, where she and Jud had spent many romantic times. The roses were just beginning to bloom in a profusion of colors. Their scent was exquisite, reminding her of Giovanna. Columbia University, where Jud worked, was about ten blocks away on the West Side. She impulsively called his office, debating whether to leave a message, and then hung up. Should she just show up instead?

She picked up her pace with determination and, after walking for quite a while, made her way through the large iron gates and quadrangle to Webster Hall, where she sat down on the steps and waited. Thirty minutes passed and still no sight of Jud. She was acting like a foolish schoolgirl. As she got up to leave, she looked up, and there he was, walking toward her. Her pulse raced. He was wearing jeans, a white shirt, and black blazer and carrying his old, worn leather briefcase. His eyes widened upon seeing Lena. Clearly shocked, he glared at her, waiting for an explanation.

"Jud," Lena reached out to him. "Don't be mad. I just thought . . ."

He shook his head and defiantly walked away.

"Wait!" Lena shouted. She rushed after him.

"I'm sorry about what happened in Florence. I wasn't myself. And I really did appreciate you making that long trip. But things are so much better now and . . ."

"Time to move on, Lena." He gazed at her with indifference, as though they barely knew each other.

Lena's heart sank as she watched him stride back through the quadrangle to who knows where. He was right, she acknowledged. Time to move on. What had she expected? Deflated, she took the subway back downtown, spontaneously got off at 86th Street, and headed eastward through Central Park to the Metropolitan Museum of Art.

She proceeded up the grand staircase of the museum, following the signs to the Egyptian exhibition "Echoes of Immortality: Art and Love in Ancient Egypt." The rooms were crammed with visitors wearing headsets and pontificating in loud whispers. She was attracted to two large granite sculptures of the pharaoh Ramesses II and his wife, Nefertari. They were seated on thrones side by side. Their countenances were imposing and enigmatic, seemingly harboring the hidden wisdom of the ages. The description label read: "Ramesses II, 1303 B.C.–1213 B.C., the greatest pharaoh of the Egyptian Empire, and Queen Nefertari, who believed they were joined in perfect, divine love, which never ceased to exist." Lena studied the statues for some time, feeling their curious power, strength, and solidity. The pharaoh and queen's connection did, indeed, appear to transcend time. Lena's disappointment at her rejected attempt to reunite with Jud came bubbling up again. For a moment, she hurtled back in time, and saw herself dressed in a long white robe ceremoniously lighting a torch in an ancient temple, tending a flame that was meant to burn always. She was alone and melancholy. The vision vanished just as a young woman wearing a headset bumped into her, apologizing.

Nearby, a richly painted chunk of limestone caught her attention. It was a mural fragment from a tomb in the Valley of the Queens depicting the Egyptian gods Isis and Osiris standing on the fertile banks of the Nile River underneath a vaulted starry sky. Lena recalled the legend of how Isis had searched relentlessly to recover pieces of her beloved Osiris, who had been dismembered by his jealous brother, and how she had succeeded in "putting him back together," making him whole again. The placard said, "For the ancient Egyptians, death was a doorway to other planes of being and other levels of divine love, not the end but the beginning. When two souls complete unto themselves united, having balanced their masculine and feminine sides within, they sparked an eternal love that transcended time and space. It was a God/Goddess love that knew no boundaries or separation."

Lena was overcome with emotion. Inspecting the stone fragment more closely, she noticed, to her great surprise, a faintly carved Flower of Life symbol to the right of the two deities. Holding within its sacred geometry the wisdom of the universe, as Thomas had explained, it obviously crossed cultures and timelines. Her thoughts turned to the box. What was inside of it? She still had not succeeded in opening it.

Reigning over their earthly and heavenly kingdoms, the king and queen, god and goddess, reminded Lena again of her own immortality, just as Giovanna had done, and of the eternal love Giovanna believed she shared with her husband. She touched the gold ring on her finger and folded her hands at her heart, feeling the fire of Giovanna's love, which was also her own.

Again, she contemplated her fifth initiation, To Love. It was ongoing and ever-deepening. She left the museum, recharged by the exhibition.

Weeks later, as she sat in her office paging through the *New York Times*, she stopped suddenly, surprised to read that Jud would be giving a lecture on behalf of the Leukemia Foundation. She ripped out the announcement and stuffed it into her purse. That Sunday, she slipped into the main hall of the Universalist Society on Central Park West. There was Jud on stage, speaking passionately to a large group of people. She suspected most of them were either leukemia survivors or loved ones of those, like his sister Lindsey, who had perished from the disease. Lena took a seat at the back, hoping he wouldn't see her.

"True service is about giving and expecting nothing in return," he declared. "It is about sacrificing ourselves to something greater for the benefit of all. And it is ultimately an expression of love, an infinite, universal love that flows through everything . . ."

He projected an air of confidence and certainty, commanding the audience's full attention with an unmistakable presence.

"And in closing, to quote the early twentieth-century Christian philosopher and mystic Pierre Teilhard de Chardin," Jud said, "'Someday after harnessing the winds, the waves, the tides, and gravity, we shall harness the energies of love, and then for a second time in the history of the world, man will have discovered fire.'" He bowed humbly and walked off stage to a loud burst of applause.

Was that the man Lena had known all these years? Perhaps it was the same old Jud, who was simply allowing more of his true essence to show. Deeply moved, she waited backstage until most of the crowd had filed out. She cautiously approached him. Upon seeing her, he took a step back, shaking his head.

"Lena, I thought we agreed to move on," Jud said.

"I just want to talk to you, nothing more." She spoke calmly. "I loved your speech. It's hard to believe it's been so long since Lindsey passed." Lena recalled how deeply Jud had been affected by the loss of his sister. He had often told her how she had been such a comfort to him during that time.

"I don't know what there is to talk about. I saw and heard everything I needed to know in Florence."

"Please, Jud, we've shared so much. Why can't we just be friends? No grudges, no hard feelings."

He made no response.

"I have so much to explain. I owe it to you. A lot happened after you left Florence. I think you'll be surprised." She smiled hopefully.

"Why were you so rude to me in Florence? I dropped everything, flew all the way out there to help you."

"Jud, I was a having a breakdown." Her face clouded over.

"You just don't give up," he sighed. "Look, I need to wrap things up with the people from the Foundation. Why don't we meet across the street in the park afterwards. We can talk there."

She smiled. "Great! How about at that little gazebo overlooking the lake, where we used to go?"

"Okay, but only because I know you won't stop bugging me. I'll be there in about forty-five minutes."

Lena arrived in Central Park to find the gazebo thankfully unoccupied. It was a balmy, sunny day. The wooded pathways were still carpeted with a thin layer of cherry blossoms. She sat anxiously waiting for Jud as two gondolas lazily plied the lake, placid and serene. He showed up tense and preoccupied.

"Here I am," he said tentatively.

Lena beheld him as if for the first time, admiring the sculpted precision of his face, his liquid blue eyes and tall, streamlined physique. At this moment, he appeared more desirable than ever and even more unattainable. She would give anything to have him back.

He stared into the distance.

"Your speech was so moving. You showed such strength and resolve. Not just what you said, but how you said it."

"Thank you."

"You've changed since I last saw you. What happened?" She sidled up closer to him on the bench.

He scratched his head. "Guess I just woke up one morning and wondered, is this all there is? You, know like the old Peggy Lee song."

"There's got to be something more," she affirmed.

"Yeah," he nodded.

"I feel the same way. In Florence, after you left, I received an incredible gift." She held out her hand to show him Giovanna's ring. "I found this in the Tornabuoni Chapel. See the date, 1486. This ring belonged to Giovanna, the woman in the painting."

"Sorry, Lena. This stuff is so crazy." He got up to leave. "I just can't go there."

"Please," she pleaded, pulling him back. "Just listen."

She proceeded to tell him about her life-changing journey, her words racing, her voice crackling with enthusiasm. "The murders, the deception, all the twists and turns, I wasn't sure I could do it.

To think I almost got myself killed! And then my haunting connection with Giovanna just took over . . ."

Jud's indifference faded as he, too, became swept up in her story.

"I know it's hard to believe, but I feel I was Giovanna in a past life," Lena said. "I learned something hugely important from the whole experience."

"And that would be?" Jud's tone was skeptical.

"I've always felt so alone, never trusting anyone, including myself. I see what was holding me back. I was afraid to love and afraid of being abandoned. You probably knew that, and at some level I suppose I did, too. But I had to be pushed to the edge to really look at it and own it."

Jud's eyes brightened. "I did know that."

"Giovanna's greatest gift was being able to love deeply, even though she lost everything." Lena gazed out over the lake, half hoping Giovanna would show herself again, like she did in Florence. "I was always so obsessed by beauty and pursuing the truth that I ignored the most important thing—love, my third muse. Now, I feel like I can finally allow myself to really love and be loved."

Jud leaned forward, his eyes square with hers. "It's far out, Lena. Why should I believe you?"

"I know it's a lot to take in," she acknowledged. "I guess we'd have to spend time together."

He studied her intently. "You know, something about you has changed, too." Just then, his cell phone rang.

"It's Camille," he said, glancing at her number.

Lena's entire body contracted. She had conveniently forgotten about his new girlfriend. She closed her eyes in an effort to wish her away.

He didn't pick up the call. "Sorry," he said, turning his attention back to Lena. "We stopped seeing each other a few weeks ago. She still doesn't get it."

Relieved, Lena took a deep breath. She looked upon him with renewed passion. "I love you, Jud," she blurted.

"Lena, you put me through hell. I don't want to get hurt again. How can I trust you?"

"I'm asking you to try."

His expression softened. "I'd like to be able to. I'm not sure." He instinctively reached out to her and took her hand in his. "I'm still crazy about you."

"Remember when we first met, here in the park all those years ago?" she said wistfully.

"Yes." He pulled her close. "Shakespeare in the Park. *Othello*. We didn't see much of it. We were too busy talking."

"Before I left for Paris, you said, 'The way in and the way out is through the heart.' You were right. I didn't understand that before."

"I know."

"But I do now."

The entire park—the towering apartment buildings fringing Central Park West in the distance, the leafy treetops, the rolling lawn and smooth granite boulders, the lake and the gondolas, everything—seemed to melt away. All that existed for Lena was the expansive, bright light of their combined energy, sealing them off from the world. The past had disappeared and with it all the old ways, the old pain and sorrow, the old paradigm. Nor did the future exist. There was only the joy of the eternal present moment.

"Let's step out of the circle of time and into the circle of love." Lena spontaneously whispered the same words Giovanna had once spoken to her beloved Lorenzo.

"Who said that? I like it."

"Rumi, the thirteenth-century Persian poet."

Jud embraced Lena. "Let's give it a try."

Teary-eyed, she smiled gratefully.

Jud regarded her reverently and lifted her hand to kiss it, pausing to admire her Renaissance ring. "I will always love you, Lena."

He reached into his pocket, pulled out a pear, and offered it to her. "This was supposed to be my lunch. I know you love these. A small token of affection."

"Thank you." Amused, she accepted the pear.

Upon leaving, he asked to see her again that night. Filled to overflowing, Lena decided to stay a while in the gazebo. She didn't know what would happen with Jud, but she was so thankful for a second chance with him. Finally, it all made sense to her. She searched inside her purse for her Montblanc pen and a slip of paper and wrote down, "To Serve." Her sixth initiation. Any kind of service first required a sacrifice of oneself to an all-encompassing Love. She had needed Jud to mirror that to her. It felt so right and satisfying. But there was one last initiation, according to Thomas. She thought for a moment and, suddenly, it came to her: To Evolve. She jotted it down. Of course, there was only endless expansion. Giovanna had known this, having passed through each of the same initiations. Smiling, Lena noticed the word love was embedded within the word evolve. Thrilled with the completion of her "real work," as Thomas had called it, Lena wrote down all of her initiations again in the order in which they had occurred:

1) To Risk
2) To Discern
3) To Trust
4) To Forgive
5) To Love
6) To Serve
7) To Evolve.

But how did she know they were the right ones? What if she had missed something? She quickly banished the thought and focused again on all that she had accomplished. They were the appropriate initiations for *her*, and she was sure Giovanna would agree. She also knew that her "real work" was not really finished, for these initiations would likely be ongoing at higher levels of mastery, and surely there would be others. Then she realized the full meaning of what Giovanna had written in her letter to "all my sisters." Giovanna had somehow known, beyond space and time, that there would be a new Renaissance—a renaissance of the heart, a whole new way of being on a new Earth—with women like her leading the way.

Lena wanted to jump for joy, so she did. She leapt up and pumped her fist in the air. "Yes!" A few passersby turned to look, and she shrugged. As she headed back home, her thoughts turned to the mysterious box in her possession. Hadn't Thomas said that once she passed her initiations, she would know how to open the box? With anxious anticipation, she hastened to the subway.

Once home, she ran up the staircase to her apartment and pulled the box off her bookshelf, passing her hand over the carved Flower of Life on its cover. She turned it around, like she had so many times before, trying to hit upon the exact motions that Thomas had said would open it. After several minutes without success, she grew frustrated and dropped the box on her desk. How could she not complete this one last mission after all she had been through? She drew a deep breath, picked up the box, and tried again. Only this time, she quieted her mind, allowing her hands to move and turn intuitively in a series of gestures. Finally, the lid budged, and she was able to slide it off. She held her breath. She could not remember feeling so excited. Her pulse quickened. She peered into the box, but there was nothing inside. How disappointing. She ran her hands along the inside of the box, feeling something sharp. It was a small piece of paper that had been attached to the bottom and painted over so that it was barely distinguishable from the dark wood. She carefully peeled it off. On the reverse side, written in a beautiful faded and apparently ancient script, was the following saying in both Italian and English:

The seeker should not stop until (s)he finds. When (s) he does find, (s)he will be disturbed. After having been disturbed, (s)he will be astonished. Then (s)he will reign over everything.

Someone obviously had added the letter *S* before the word "he." Below it were the letters GT. Lena could not believe what she was seeing. Were they Giovanna Tornabuoni's initials? Did she write the saying down so many centuries ago? It was all too much to comprehend. Lena reread it several times, feeling in the core of her being its profound depth and import. Without knowing why, she began to weep, until something dawned on her. She retrieved her wallet and pulled out the fortune she kept in it. Stunned, she read it again: "Soon you will reign over everything." The same words. She excitedly turned on her computer and looked up the saying from the box. It was from the *Gospel of Thomas*, one of twelve ancient books found in 1945 in a cave in Egypt and containing the secret mystical teachings of Jesus.

Perhaps Giovanna did put this saying in the Flower of Life box and cleverly added all the *S* letters, as Lena wanted to believe. It sounded farfetched but not impossible given Giovanna's deep connection to Mary Magdalene and Jesus and their sacred partnership. Or perhaps someone else wrote it down and simply acknowledged the source with those initials. Either way, Lena believed she had received yet another remarkable gift. Overjoyed, she clasped her hands at her heart and reread the saying aloud, substituting "she" for "he."

"The seeker should not stop until she finds. When she does find, she will be disturbed. After having been disturbed, she will be astonished. Then she will reign over everything."

THE END

ACKNOWLEDGMENTS

I wish to express my heartfelt gratitude to those who helped bring this novel to fruition. Thank you to book publishing and marketing expert Stella Togo for your wonderful talents and devotion. Editors Marlene Adelstein and Betsy Robinson, you are simply the best. Cover designer Kathi Dunn and layout designer Dorie McClelland, your stellar design skills are much appreciated. To my family and my husband, Mieshiel, I am blessed by your unwavering love and support.

DANA MICUCCI is also the author of *Sojourns of the Soul: One Woman's Journey around the World and into Her Truth*, which won a gold medal in the Nautilus Book Awards; *Artists in Residence: A Guide to the Homes and Studios of Eight 19th-Century Artists in and around Paris*; *Best Bids: The Insider's Guide to Buying at Auction*; and *Collector's Journal*. She has written for many publications, including the *New York Times, Chicago Tribune, International Herald Tribune, Architectural Digest*, and *Town & Country*. She divides her time between New York City and Taos, New Mexico.

Made in the USA
Middletown, DE
11 February 2019